Orewall

By

Nicoline Evans

Author: Nicoline Evans – www.nicolineevans.com

Editor: Kate Watts – www.kateedits.com

Cover Design: Julia Iredale – www.juliairedale.com

A special shout-out to my beta readers and a big thank you to everyone who has offered me support (in all ways, shapes, and sizes) during this entire process.

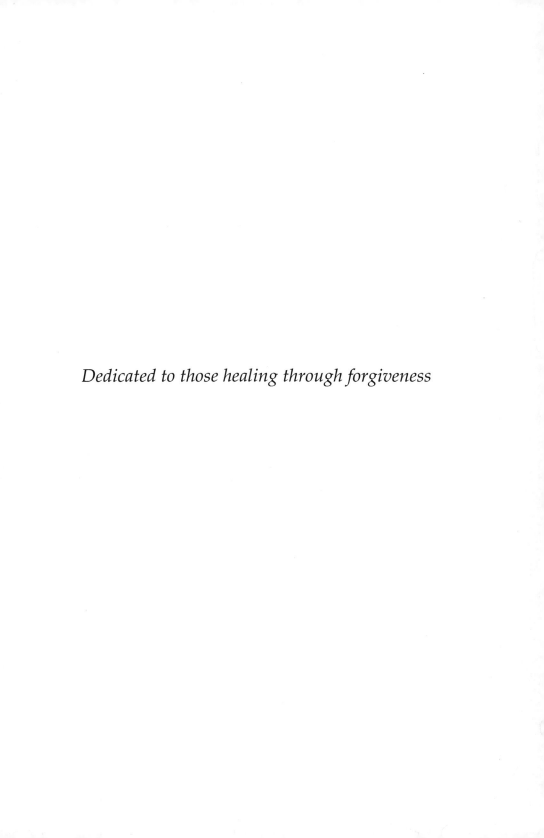

Dedicated to those healing through forgiveness

Planet: Namaté of the Avitus Galaxy
Year: Cycle 2082 around the Nebila Sun

Prologue

Today marked the tenth anniversary of his abandonment. Rhoco Leath examined his hands and noted how much he had grown. His cratered palms had doubled in size since the day his mother left and all the scars were new. Though they were ugly, he wore them with pride. He was the master of his life, his fate, and he had his perseverance to thank for the man he was becoming.

Just as any Boulde child, Rhoco was left at age five to survive or die. His mother prepared him for the moment she'd leave forever, but no amount of preparation could truly prime a child for utter isolation.

The departure hurt less now than it used to. He cried the day his mother left him on the dunes, but never again since. Even when his first home collapsed after wasting three months building it, he swallowed every ounce of grief and frustration. Even when he was forced to live, shelterless, in extreme weather for an entire year, he shed no tears for his misfortune. Even when he realized his fate was doomed to working the Orewall mines, he suppressed the urge to pity himself. Rhoco soldiered on, and as a result, became sturdy and indestructible. His mind was impenetrable, permitting no emotion, no weakness. His durable body could withstand the salted lashings within the mines. Nothing scared him, and nothing caused him pain, because nothing could possibly hurt worse than watching his mother walk away.

To commemorate this day, he sat atop the dune his nook of a home was carved into and watched the black ocean ebb and flow from sunrise to sunset. Only the ocean could soothe his hardened demeanor. The salty wind gusted against his rock-solid skin, forcing him to feel. Though it was minimal, as was the resulting sensation, he relished in the brief moment of sensed touch. As a man with skin made of stone, he didn't experience that often, so he enjoyed feeling whenever it occurred.

"Hey there, little sludge," a voice called from the shoreline. Rhoco looked down to see his neighbor, Cybelle Steen, on her daily jog.

"I'm not little," he replied.

"You'll always seem little to me," she shouted back with a shrug, never slowing her momentum. Another moment, and she was gone as quickly as she arrived.

Rhoco wasn't fully grown, but he was getting there. In five years, he'd be a full-size, heaping Boulde of a man. He wanted to grow to his maximum potential, so he exercised and ate the recommended diet of grains and greens to stay healthy.

The day of melancholic remembrance passed, and he decided to spend his final day off from the mines in the desert. He shoved a spoonful of granola into his mouth before charging out the front door. With heavy steps he trudged over the sandy dunes, leaving the cool, breezy climate for one that was drier and much less kind. The temperature rose ten degrees within the first half hour of his walk, and by the time he reached the village of Teht, he was drenched in sweat. The cloudless sky offered him no shelter from the sun's blazing rays. There was no ocean breeze or shady trees to minimize the squelching heat. He regretted making the trip to this hellish den of a place until he remembered why he had come: Grette.

Like him, she was a Fused from two differing bloodlines, but due to her innate gardening talent, she was among the lucky few chosen by the Royals.

Rhoco searched the sweltering landscape for a sign of her. When he spotted the gardeners' white bonnets, he broke into a brisk jog. Each footstep came with a thud as he ran to her.

Grette was with the other botanists—some chosen Fused, others Purebreds—and all were examining the state of a patch of dead cacti. Rhoco hid behind the largest cactus he could find and observed.

Grette was beautiful, a Fused born of purple tanzanite and marble. Her shiny, lavender hair cascaded to the middle of her back, and her large, periwinkle eyes always sparkled at him with admiration. He mentally beckoned for her to give him that look now, but she was too caught up in her work.

Love in Orewall was frowned upon, and in their case, love was perfectly foolish. Like every first generation Fused, she had a chance to cleanse her line and Rhoco was just a scoundrel getting in her way. He often wondered if he was being selfish, if he was ruining her opportunity for a better life, but then she'd give him that look, as if he put the sun in her sky, and he was reminded that their budding love was mutual.

The gardeners finished their experiment and separated for a break. Grette looked around, gaze bright with hope, for the Boulde she most wished to see. But Rhoco remained hidden, enjoying her anticipation for a moment before showing himself.

Her face brightened at his reveal, but she contained her thrill. They were not supposed to engage. Rhoco was a miner and she was on the fast track to a luxurious life inside Amesyte Valley.

"You came," she said with a smile that barely contained the joy exploding within her chest.

"Of course I did," he replied, able to play it cool, but desperately desiring to hold her. He imagined she'd fit perfectly in his arms.

"There's a dance tonight," she said. "In the village of Kevir."

"Near the valley?"

"Yes, right outside the western range."

"No one told me."

"I just did," she baited him.

"Are you asking me to be your date?" Rhoco grinned.

"Of course not."

"Well, I'm not going if I can't have you by my side."

"Are you asking me to be *your* date?" she teased.

"I suppose I am," he answered, smiling. "Will you?"

"Of course I will," she smirked. She elevated to her toes and planted a kiss on his cheek before departing.

Rhoco remained behind in a heavenly stupor. After a long, drawn-out year of flirting and anticipation, they were *finally* making progress. Grette chose him, despite his status and potential. He had nothing: no chance at a life in Amesyte Valley, nor of a career better than mining, yet she picked him.

But happiness made him nervous. He learned early on that such a feeling was fleeting and the letdown was always more impactful than the buildup, so he tried to stifle his delight. Though he suppressed his elation, it bubbled below the surface, begging to escape and revealing itself in the hop in his step.

Back at the dunes, Rhoco immediately headed to the ocean. He stripped off his trousers and waded through the water until he was waist-deep. Any farther and he'd be risking death. Men made of stone could not swim and he accepted this fact. He splashed the water all over his naked body, cleansing himself of any residual mine dust. The soot stuck everywhere: under his fingernails, behind his ears, up his nose. With diligence, he bathed every speck of dirt off his body.

The sun set with haste and Rhoco was running late. Still, he paused to check his reflection in the water. In the glow of twilight, his pale green eyes reflected back at him as he examined the dark, wet hair clinging to his forehead. He brushed the medium-length strands from his eyes, aware that the desert heat would dry his tresses long before he reached the dance.

The parting light of day revealed that he looked his best. He wasn't much for vanity; if he had his way, he'd always be covered in a layer of mine dust, but today was different. It wasn't about him. It was about Grette, and he wanted the night to be perfect.

Wearing his best pair of trousers, he darted back into the desert. His bare, malachite chest was cleansed and polished so thoroughly, the green flecks hidden in his skin sparkled in the moonlight. This rarely happened, so he smiled, certain Grette would be impressed.

He ran the whole way, snagging random cacti flowers as he went.

When he arrived at Kevir Village, Grette waited for him at the edge of the dance floor. Her back was turned as she watched the other young Bouldes dance, so she did not see him approach.

"Have you seen my date?" he whispered in her ear, moving her long hair away from her face. On the side of her neck was a freshly inked symbol of a crown—a permanent mark indicating she was a chosen Fused. He ignored the tattoo that divided them and continued. "Her name is Grette and she's the most beautiful girl here."

Grette's lavender eyes lit up at the sound of his voice. She spun to face him, gaze gleaming with adoration.

"I thought you might ditch me."

"Never."

He handed her the messy bouquet of desert flowers and she eyed him harshly.

"They are beautiful, but dead. You killed them."

Realizing his mistake, Rhoco felt like a fool.

"I killed them for you?" he attempted, aware that no backpedaling would correct this blunder.

"It's okay, I forgive you." She smiled. "Just don't do it again."

Rhoco nodded, grateful this did not ruin the mood. He wrapped his arm around her and swept her onto the dance floor.

A band of Diabases played their lithophones while the minors mingled. The melody they created was wistful and subtle, and the enchantment of the ringing rocks allured all within earshot. With Grette safe in his embrace, Rhoco felt like he was floating. They twirled to the up-tempo, yet melancholic song. The rhythm kept them moving while the mood deepened their connection. Entranced by the tune and with eyes locked, they spiraled happily, lost and found within each other.

The song was ancient and the arrangement flowed up and down the scale. Rhoco and Grette were young—only fifteen years old in a world where people survived for hundreds—but they felt wise. Their shared connection was a perfect, special bond few experienced, and they understood their luck.

"Will you stay with me forever?" Rhoco asked.

"For as long as my forever allows."

He leaned in to kiss her. The moment their lips touched, the rest of the party disappeared. Only the music remained, thrusting them upward into the whirlwind of the moment. They lingered, spellbound by love.

Though Bouldes could discern extreme temperatures and sturdy impacts, interactions such as another's delicate touch, the feeling of holding something in their arms, or a kiss were difficult to perceive. Rhoco and Grette could not feel the sensation of this kiss, but the tenderness of the act registered in their minds as significant. Finally, Grette ended the moment and smiled up at Rhoco.

"I want to show you something."

She took his hand and pulled him away from the party. They exited the torchlit area and entered the dark desert.

The sound of nocturnal sand critters was louder in the dead of night. They rattled, scuttled, and howled, reminding Rhoco of the perils hidden in the shadows of Orewall.

"Where are you taking me?" he asked.

"You'll see."

She tugged him along without explaining her motives. He was so smitten he did not argue. He'd follow her anywhere, even to the edge of the world, if she so desired.

They reached the exterior wall of Amesyte Valley and after rounding a large basalt rock protruding from the mountainside, their destination came into view: Karxane Village, home to the botanists.

A row of huts decorated with flowers sat in the distance.

"Is this where you live?"

She nodded, smiling, and led him into her hut. Thick, interwoven rose vines formed the walls, and four granite beams in each corner of the house supported the stone slab that served as the ceiling. This was a sturdy home, constructed by the Royals. Colorful blossoms covered the space, peeking through the walls and spreading across the stone ceiling like wildfire. The aroma of gardenia and fresh moss filled her home, a scent so refreshing Rhoco wished to breathe it in forever.

"The Royals built you a good one," he commented, thinking of his alcove, which was nothing more than a muddy hole in a dune.

"I'm fortunate, I know." Confessing her privilege made her uneasy. "I wanted to show you my garden."

She pointed to a far corner of the spacious hut where a thick set of purple and orange flowers grew. Their stems braided together and scaled from the sand to the roof, then spanned across the ceiling.

"Near the base are sphaeralcea ambigua and hyptis emoryi, more commonly known as globemallows and desert lavender," she explained. "I set them up so the breeds would mix and create a brand new type of flower." She then pointed to a small blossom overhead—the only one yet to successfully mutate in this batch. "I named them lavenmallows."

"They are lovely," Rhoco said, examining the hybrid floret from a safe distance. He did not want to damage what she so carefully created. "Just like you."

"It's a shame blending breeds is a sin amongst the bouldes." She glanced at the new species of flower she birthed. "The results are magic. This is the second batch I've grown. These flowers have proven powers."

"What can they do?"

"They can make us feel." She gently ran her finger down his bare chest. "If you had eaten a lavenmallow, or if I had rubbed its petals on your skin, you'd have felt that."

For the first time, Rhoco craved the sensation of touch. He glanced up at the lavenmallow blossom, then back to Grette.

"More will grow?" he asked. She nodded in reply. He slowly placed his hand on the flower, ready to stop if she objected, but she said nothing and Rhoco plucked the blossom from the vine. He held the stem with great care, afraid his stone fingers might crush its tiny petals. She smiled up at him, eyes glowing with trust, and his confidence grew. She believed he could be tender; she did not fear his destructive nature.

She stepped closer and Rhoco traced her lips with the flower. The medicinal residue lacing its petals excreted onto her skin, seeping through her stone flesh.

He kissed her.

Grette smiled and then exhaled with marvel at the unfamiliar feeling.

"Your turn," she said before he wasted it all on her. She took the blossom and caressed his mouth with its petals. After its powers were expelled onto his lips, he pulled Grette close and kissed her again, more passionately this time. The strange phenomenon of feeling each other filled them with joy. This ecstasy was foreign and a tingling thrill took over their bodies.

Grette placed her palm, flower still in hand, over Rhoco's chest. His intensity tripled the moment the lavenmallow's medicinal magic seeped into his heart. She then grabbed his waistband to pull him closer and the flower fell into the front of his pants.

Rhoco's bliss instantly transitioned into lust.

"I love you," she whispered.

Rhoco grunted in agreement, unable to form a coherent sentence as the potent magic took over. The pleasure engulfed his consciousness. Covered in lavenmallow, Rhoco was no longer in control.

"Rhoco," she said hesitantly, alarmed as she watched the light leave his eyes. Blind and deaf to her terror, he entered a blacked-out state of intoxication as the chemicals reached his brain.

Grette suddenly understood what went wrong; there was too much lavenmallow coursing through his system. She reached into his trousers to retrieve the flower, but it was too late. He was gone, mind transported elsewhere, and he could not sense her dismay.

Pinned beneath his goliath form, she cried, but he could not hear her. The unfamiliar euphoria drowned every sense, except touch. She pressed the flower against his ribcage, hoping to soften an additional part of his body, then punched him as hard as she could, but the lavenmallow's magic was depleted. The petals were dry, no chemicals remained, and Rhoco did not feel the hit.

"I love you," he mumbled in a transfixed stupor.

As the final surge of magic from the lavenmallow coursed through him, he overwhelmed her with unreciprocated desire. Grette surrendered, helpless beneath the weight of his conviction.

Though an eternity elapsed for her, only a moment passed for him.

A prickling sensation sent chills throughout his body as the lavenmallow chemicals slowly wore off.

His senses returned to stone.

Rhoco exited his barbaric trance to find the girl he adored wholly broken. Tears stained her face, her expression was that of defeat, and her body shook with fear.

A small whimper accompanied each of her breaths.

Rhoco recoiled at the sound. Suddenly aware of what he had done, he was overcome with remorse.

Rhoco removed his body from hers, faster than he ever moved before, and freed her from his crushing company. The room went cold and the fresh, floral scent was replaced with that of sweat and dread. With the welcoming ambiance of the hut gone, the space felt unfamiliar. Grette sat up and pushed herself to the opposite side of the room. She cradled her wrist, which had accidentally cracked in his grip.

"What have I done?" he stammered, shell-shocked by the scene that greeted him.

Grette shook her head, unable to respond.

"You were there with me." Rhoco tried to recall what he struggled to remember. "Then it all went black."

"Couldn't you hear me?" she asked, gaze glued to the floor.

"What did you say?" His voice shook with lament, and she avoided his rueful stare. "Why won't you look at me?"

"I can't."

"The way you kissed me—" he said, still trying to understand how it all went wrong.

"You took it too far," she sobbed, unable to mask her devastation. "I wasn't ready."

"That flower," Rhoco faltered, "it took me away. I couldn't see, I couldn't hear; I could only feel. Why didn't it do the same to you?"

"You took too much."

"You gave it to me!"

"I didn't think it would turn you into a monster."

"I'm sorry," he insisted.

Grette shook her head.

Rhoco panicked. He just committed the worst possible betrayal against the girl he adored.

"I am so sorry," he repeated, aware these words meant nothing to her. His crime was unforgivable.

"Just leave."

"Please forgive me. I wasn't myself. I would never intentionally take advantage of you. I never meant to hurt you," he tried to explain, but Grette closed her eyes and refused to look at him. Tears dripped from their crevices and the more he tried to make things right, the faster they fell.

"I lost my head. I love you so," he confessed with bereaved honesty.

"Leave!" she screamed, finally making eye contact with him. The sparkle they once held for him was gone.

Tears welled in his eyes as he obeyed. He left, ravaged by a guilt that would live with him forever.

Chapter 1

The ocean beckoned.

Rhoco stripped down, stepped into the wake of the crashing waves, and walked until the water rose above his knees.

He took a deep breath and scanned his surroundings.

He was alone.

Entering the ocean was a death sentence for Bouldes. Rhoco couldn't swim—no one in Orewall could—but he was determined to learn. And if he could not learn, perhaps death would greet him as a friend.

A large, dark wave approached. Rhoco planted his feet, bent his knees, and prepared to absorb the impact. The water smacked into his body, barely moving him, and then broke along the shore. He did not fear the strength of the ocean, only its depth. Years of isolation taught Rhoco to welcome his fears as companions—they were his only friends after all. He walked until he was neck-deep, aware that he might drown. The water level rose and fell, sometimes covering his mouth, other times only reaching his chin. One more step and he'd be under.

Breath held, Rhoco took the final step and submerged. Feet planted on the ocean floor, he lifted his chin toward the dim, early morning sunlight shining through the water, then attempted to swim to the surface. Though it was only a few

1

inches away, his calcite bones were too heavy. He could use the muscles in his legs to push off the ground and jump to the surface, but that would defeat his objective. He wanted to swim, not use his strength to pretend.

He tried again, but the weight of his arms provided no traction and his body remained cemented to the ocean floor. The water level was rising and the surface was now even farther away. He would not succeed today.

Still underwater, he trudged toward the shore. About to run out of breath, his head breached the surface. He took a large gulp of the salty air, thankful to be alive, but disappointed to be thwarted. He hated the confinements of his being.

The morning sun crested over the black ocean. It moved slowly and the world remained dark, waiting for morning to bring it back to life.

Rhoco exited the ocean and sat naked atop the grassy knoll above his home. The approaching sun would not only dry him, but also revive his disheartened spirit. He tried not to let the defeat bother him, but he'd been trying to learn for an entire year with no success. He was beginning to believe he could not beat genetics.

The sediment of the knoll was coarse and soppy, and the grass grew in large, single strands. Rhoco plucked a thick blade and wedged it between his front teeth to free a remnant of his breakfast. His white dolomite teeth were capable of tearing through any material; the carnage left on his kitchen table was proof of their strength. The curious squirrel that wandered into his home that morning never stood a chance.

Orange light seeped over the horizon, warming his hardened skin. He was part limestone from his father and part malachite from his mother. Breeds weren't supposed to mix, but his parents broke the old laws and he was left with small craters throughout his green dermis. Most Bouldes saw him as handsome, many considered the Fused to be attractive, but Rhoco felt broken. He was alone and unable to determine where he belonged. Others gawked in awe when they saw him, jealous of his beauty, but none welcomed him into their circle because he wasn't a Purebred. He resembled neither side of his family. Those of limestone descent were beige, grainy, and rough, while those of malachite were emerald, shiny, and smooth. He fell somewhere in the middle.

Boulde children were abandoned and left to their own devices at age five, which proved as a double alienation for the Fused. Rhoco felt alone while his mother was around, but even more so when she left. He supposed she loved him as much as any Boulde mother could.

The best thing his mother ever did was refuse to coddle him. Before leaving, she helped him craft a tough exterior to survive beneath and he wore it to this day.

As a young man approaching his thirtieth year of life, he was most comfortable in his solitude and was happiest alone. Most Bouldes were. Rhoco did not need companionship to survive, or so he tried to convince himself.

Mid-morning arrived and he breathed in the salty air with contentment. The world was quiet outside the waves crashing along the pebbled beach and the sun cleansed him of his earlier defeat. Rhoco was at peace.

From his perch atop the knoll, he looked to the west and saw a sky-blue silhouette hobbling toward him. His neighbor, Cybelle Steen—an elderly lady made of ashy blue larimar and pink rhodonite—often visited his humble abode to check on him. Though he hadn't invited her and wasn't in the mood for company, he barreled down the hill and met her halfway, as he always did.

"You smell like seaweed," she noted with disgust.

"I'm a man of the ocean." He took her arm to help her traverse the rocky beach, but she protested.

"I can do it myself."

"Your knees are stone on stone. What kind of man would I be if I didn't help?"

"You're holding too tight," Cybelle groaned, so he loosened his grip.

His strength was a curse; he broke everything he touched. As a young Boulde, it caused him great dismay when things crumbled or snapped in his grip, but an even greater sorrow stirred when he discovered his strength also harmed the people he touched. Though his strength was no different than any Bouldes', Rhoco did not view the damage as normal. Underneath his hardened façade was a sensitive soul, and though he tried to curb his unyielding strength, he still hadn't mastered the art of tenderness.

Another reason he and all the other Bouldes were better off alone.

When he and Cybelle reached his house, she yanked her arm from his and limped to his kitchen table. She placed her basket of food next to the bloody remains of his breakfast. Her dusty blue hand touched the bushy tail and hovered over the spine, which remained intact.

"Eating meat will turn you savage," she warned.

"Hasn't yet."

"If the Royals ever find out, they'll force you into the river."

"I've been learning to swim."

"Bouldes can't swim," Cybelle scoffed.

"Maybe I'm different."

"There's no doubt that you're different," she said, amused, "but the laws of physics say we sink. We're made of stone, and stones don't float."

"I'll prove them all wrong."

Cybelle dropped the topic and returned her attention to the dismembered squirrel.

"Clean this up. It's an atrocious sight." Rhoco obeyed hastily, ashamed that she had seen his mess. "No wonder you don't have any friends."

"I don't need friends."

"Almadine visited yesterday to bring me blueberries. She talks about you often. I'm inclined to suggest her as a match, but every time I visit you I'm reminded what holds me back."

"All because I ate a squirrel?" he asked.

"And now you think you can swim. The meat is messing with your brain."

"I don't want to match with someone anyhow." Rhoco purposely didn't mention that he and Almadine already tried. "I don't want to bring another lonely child into the world."

"How could you say such a thing?" Cybelle protested. "It is our duty to procreate at least once in our lifetime."

"When was the last time you saw your child?"

"The same as any mother," she argued, trying to mask the guilt she had carried with her for the past century. "No one sees their child again after they fully aggregate."

"And as a father, I'd never see my child again after its birth. It's cruel and unusual."

"No, it's imperative to survival and builds character. We are the strongest of all the creatures in Namaté *because* of our self-reliance."

"It doesn't make it right. Hundreds of Boulde children die within the first few years after they are abandoned."

"Excavates the weak."

There was no arguing with Cybelle, she was too old and stubborn.

"Regardless," Rhoco finished, "No one wants my lineage passed on."

"You've lost your mind," Cybelle ridiculed. "Sure, you're not a conventional Boulde with Purebred roots, but the mixture of your genes is breathtaking. Any woman would match with you to make pretty babies."

"Unless the baby comes out as a Murk."

"Oh, you have a few generations before that will happen."

"I'd rather focus on learning how to swim."

"I'm sending Almadine over to talk some sense into you. She's the most stunning Citrine-Alexandrite I've ever seen. With your green and her yellow—" Cybelle gasped in excitement. "Oh, that baby would be beautiful."

"Don't send her over here," Rhoco pleaded, ignoring her enthusiasm for matters he cared nothing about. "She already stops by too much."

"Oh, does she?" Cybelle's light blue eyes gleamed with curiosity. "Tell me more."

"There's nothing to tell. Just don't make it worse for me."

Cybelle let the silence linger, waiting for him to elaborate, but when he didn't budge, she gave up.

"Fine. I'll just ask her. She doesn't keep secrets from me."

"Don't you know it's rude to meddle?"

"Don't you know I don't care?"

Rhoco laughed. "That, I know quite well."

"I'm old and bored. Get over it."

Cybelle dumped her basket of edible gifts onto his blood-stained table and marched toward the door.

"You need to find a hobby," he shouted as she left. "Something to occupy your time so you stop meddling with mine!"

"Someone has to look after you," she yelled back.

"I can look after myself!"

Cybelle ignored him as she made her way along the rocky beach toward her home.

Rhoco returned inside, slammed the stone door, and punched the wall. His fist dented the hardened clay. He was angry because he already handled the issue with Almadine and now Cybelle was likely to awaken what was already settled. He hated the interaction; he hated hurting people.

His hopes that Cybelle might stay out of his business were dashed when Almadine showed up at his door a few hours before nightfall.

"What?" he asked through the small grated slot carved into his door.

"We need to talk."

"No, we don't."

"You're being awful to me." Her bright citrine eyes glowed through the tears.

"We tried and failed. It's over. I'm done."

"We can still make something good."

"I don't want to hurt you again."

"It was an accident."

"I don't care if it was an accident. I'm not interested in feeling that way ever again." His eyes scanned her face. "That scar will never go away."

Almadine touched the long, orange mark on the side of her cheek. "These types of things happen when Bouldes mate. It's part of our reality. I don't blame you."

Almadine's persistence resurrected his past, uncovered shameful encounters he wished to keep buried. Rhoco shook his head, refusing to succumb to old guilt.

"I'm trying to be a better person," he confessed.

"Hiding away and refusing to interact with others won't make you a better person."

"I really wish you'd leave me alone."

"You're just going to cast me aside like I mean nothing to you?"

"I'm not worth the heartache."

"Stop acting like you're some kind of monster," Almadine demanded, tired of suffering because of his self-loathing.

"But I am. I warned you when we first met, and now you've seen it to be true."

"Tell me what happened," she pleaded, hoping he'd open up to her. "Tell me why you're so hard on yourself. Is it really so much worse than what any other Boulde has endured?"

"You'll find someone better," he replied, refusing to answer. "Another Citrine. It would be better for you."

"No one will want me. I'm tainted."

"I won't tell a soul."

"I want to finish what we started."

Rhoco finally opened the door so they could talk face to face, but refused to let her inside.

"We had noble plans," he told her. "But they were idealistic and unattainable. Even if we had a child and stayed with it, the Royals would have eventually found out and sentenced us to the river. Not only would our child have been abandoned, but also orphaned. No one would have loved them from afar and we would have doomed them to the loneliest existence possible. The whole plan was stupid, and I'm glad it didn't work."

"I hate you," she hissed through the tears. "You will die alone."

"I know."

Almadine stormed off into the shadows cast by the setting sun.

Rhoco's heart grew heavier, but he ignored the pain. He silenced his feelings for Almadine long ago and convinced himself he no longer cared for her, but even so, he did not wish to cause her distress—he already caused her enough.

He punched the wall, so hard he drew blood, but it didn't make him feel better. No pain could compare to that which he caused her.

Rhoco shook his head as he ran out his front door. He jogged along the shoreline, trying to clear this memory, when similar memories attempted to resurface. Memories he had buried long ago. With a growl, he shoved the recollections back into the pit of his mind.

He had to live with what he'd done.

Out of breath and miles from his home, he stopped, aware that no amount of self-punishment would change the past.

He turned to walk back to his dune and considered the vexing emotion that plagued his life. While love rarely existed amongst the Bouldes, it did not make them an uncaring species. When love did present itself, it almost never ended well, and because very few cases of reciprocated emotion existed in the history of their kind, most avoided the feeling altogether. As soon as Rhoco suspected that Almadine loved him, he retreated, aware that he wouldn't be able to prevent her heartbreak when he couldn't love her back. There was only one woman he loved and he lost that love long ago. Now, he cursed himself for engaging with Almadine in the first place. He knew the type of man he was: jaded and cold. He should have known better than to drag another into his dark, little world.

But Almadine had presented him with something beautiful— a chance for change, a chance to give a baby the childhood he always dreamed of having. To this, he wasn't strong enough to say no.

Now, he regretted his inability to see past the romantic notion and detect the situation for what it was: Impossible. Because of his momentary lapse in judgment, he was left with her fragile heart in his hands. He did not wish to hold it, he never wanted her love, and in his grip her heart would never be safe.

So he dropped it, knowing she would survive the fall. Hearts made of stone don't shatter.

Chapter 2

The bright red carrier cardinal arrived the following day, singing the song of the mines. Each job had a different song, but Rhoco always got mining. The Fused were given laborious jobs, careers that broke backs and tired souls. This was how King Alun encouraged Bouldes to procreate within their breeds. Cleansing a lineage after an inappropriate mixture of breeds took three generations, and most Bouldes were too short-sighted to achieve this. Bouldes were simple people, unconcerned with the future or acquiring the finer things in life. They were content with their strenuous but humble lives, and many did not think far enough ahead to plan a better future for their children.

King Alun and Queen Gemma were pure Amethyst. There was no mixing in either of their bloodlines. The skin covering their bodies was translucent crystal and their faces were a flawless purple. In the sunlight, they glimmered with regality. There was no denying their strength or power.

Rhoco was a first-generation Fuse, which was always the most striking. It usually took about five generations of interbreeding for the muddying to begin. Most Bouldes were smart enough to pick a line before this occurred, but many missed their chance to cleanse their line and ended up bringing a Murk into the world. It was well preached by King Alun that the genetics of Murks were compromised, causing them to be born weak with shrunken statures. No one wanted to match with a Murk except other Murks, which left their kind trapped and unable to reverse their fate.

The Royals confined Murks to the darkness, forcing them to reside in the mines and caves where Purebreds would not see them. The Murks obeyed because history proved they were unwelcome aboveground.

As a miner, Rhoco worked with many of them on a regular basis. He had no issue with those he worked beside, but he was also never forced to interact with them. They stayed in their tunnels, while he stayed in his.

The carrier cardinal chirped again, reminding Rhoco he had to leave for the mines.

"Alright, alright," he groaned. "I'm going."

The mines beneath Red Rock Valley were deep and rich with minerals. They had been worked for centuries, so most of the walls were stripped clean and the march to the fruitful areas took an entire day.

This week's task required the miners to travel underground to the eastern azurite field. The Royals were expecting a baby boy and wanted to build a nursery made of the deep, radiating blue rock.

The Orewall kingdom spanned a varying landscape. The heart of the country was Amesyte Valley, which was situated on a fertile field of wildflowers and encased in a circle of colossal mountain ranges. Large lakes and groves decorated the land set aside for the Royals and Purebreds, while beyond the mountains stretched dusty desert, bulging red rocks, and sprawling steppes.

On the outskirts of the desert, where the gritty terrain reached the coast, the landscape softened and gradually turned into grassy sand dunes and pebbled beaches. Most Bouldes lived in the deserts, but some, like Rhoco, chose to live along the shore.

No one, except carefully selected merchants, traveled beyond the Orewall coastlines. Other countries resided out there, with different species of people, but these foreigners were so far removed from the daily, laborious grind of the Bouldes that their existence was barely a consideration.

"Finally," Rhoco grumbled to himself as he reached his destination.

Rhoco and the other miners he joined along the way were finally at the azurite field. Only the largest Fused were summoned to work alongside the Murks in the mines. Most considered this an insult, but Rhoco preferred this assignment. If he wasn't in the mines, he'd be working construction aboveground, and he favored the dark, quiet tunnels over the steamy desert.

Better work visas were hard to come by, and very few of the Fused were granted permission to work inside Amesyte Valley alongside the Purebreds and in close proximity to the Royals. A circular mountain range protected the castle, and the Royals were selective about who they allowed inside the valley. Years of screenings and determination to pass the tests were required to obtain a Grade V work visa, which meant that the majority of the Fused were stuck slaving in the deserts and mines.

Rhoco unlatched his pickaxe from the strap he wore over his back and began hammering. A few of the Murks watched him as he worked. They were shadow creatures: scrawny, weak, and inferior. Rhoco tried not to judge.

"What?" he finally asked, annoyed with the two Murk men that stared at him in awe.

"You glow in the dark," one muttered, unaccustomed to speaking to non-Murks.

"No, I don't," Rhoco objected, but when he looked down at his bare chest he saw they were right. The firelight illuminating their workspace bounced off the azurite walls and reflected in the malachite tones of his skin. He didn't exactly *glow*, but his colors smoldered in the darkness, as they always did. "It's just the fire," he explained.

"It's beautiful."

Rhoco heard the defeat in the Murk's voice.

"It's not your fault you're muddied," he reminded them.

The Murks didn't reply. Instead, they dipped into the shadows and disappeared, just as they were conditioned to do.

Eighteen hours passed before they were given a break. Rhoco could have continued for another four hours, but when the Hematite guards walked by with tin mugs of water for the miners, he paused to accept the offering. The Hematites were so dark they could only be seen when the torchlight caught the iron speckles in their skin. Though they were Purebreds, the Hematites enjoyed the mines. Their iron-ore roots made the underground a natural fit.

After the break ended, the Hematite overseers resumed lounging comfortably, while the Fused and Murks hammered away.

By the end of their forty-eight hour shift, they had collected five hundred pounds of uncut azurite and were tasked with hauling the entire load all the way to Amesyte Valley. There were three passageways that led into the kingdom—each carved into the base of the mountain range. The miners delivered the azurite to the Obsidian guards stationed at the southern entrance, who then transported it through the tunnel and into the kingdom. There, skilled Purebreds would tumble, polish, and carve the azurite until its grading met the standards of the Royals.

Rhoco returned home. The three-hour walk through the harsh, arid desert was hot and unbearable, and he anticipated the moment he'd taste the fresh ocean breeze again. As he walked, the sun blazed down on him, attempting to scorch his stone skin, and it didn't take long for the heat to break through his rock-hard exterior and make him sweat.

When he finally reached his home, the sight of cool colors arrived as a gift. Rhoco inhaled the salty air and embraced the ocean scent before retreating into his clay nook. There, he made jelly toast with the supplies Cybelle brought him, but the moment he took a bite he wished he were eating rodent meat instead. He forced the food down anyway, eating for energy instead of enjoyment, and when he finished, he went outside to digest his bland dinner beneath the stars.

The evening was dark and brisk, just as he liked it. He walked down the sandy hill, over the large boulders at its base, and then across the smaller rocks until he reached the spot where the ocean sand merged with the pebbled shore. Rhoco sat down and let the waves come and go against his body, counting each surge.

Above him thousands of stars sparkled, thousands of worlds beyond this one. He thought of life elsewhere and what it might be like to be born as something foreign, as something other than this. Something better, something easier, in a place where feelings did not hurt. His imagination raced around possibilities far different from what he grew to know and accept, but as his ideas became irrational, his tolerance for such drivel halted him.

Nonsense, he thought. *Wild and utter nonsense.* He shut his eyes to stop the overwhelming notion of fascinating life in other pockets of the universe and instead enjoyed the rhythmic movement of the very real sea lapping against his legs.

When the seventh wave arrived, so did something peculiar. A heavy object slammed into Rhoco's hand, momentarily turning the darkness behind his closed eyes red.

An intense and unexpected surge of color. He opened his eyes, unsure what games the ocean played.

He searched for the root of this sorcery and found, amongst the rocks, a black heart. He leaned in to examine it closer, awe-struck and perplexed by this startling development in his typically mundane routine.

With care, Rhoco inched closer and determined that the heart was made of glass. He looked down the beach in both directions, curious if another Boulde was playing him for a fool, but no one was around. He looked down at the heart again, then out to sea.

This heart had come from a foreign land.

His own heart pounded with dread at the discovery of something so fragile and he was unsure what to do. He bent down to examine it again, hoping an answer would materialize.

Fine cracks covered the heart's casing; it was nearly broken. He wanted to pick it up, but feared his rough touch would harm it further. Then a large wave crashed against the shore, and the water's momentum rocketed the heart into a nearby boulder.

He cringed as it slammed into the large rock, and when the wave receded, the heart tumbled back toward Rhoco.

A twinge of guilt plucked his heartstrings; if he did not relocate the heart, it would surely shatter. Though he did not wish to engage, he was the only one who could protect the object, and his instincts insisted he must. With great care and concentration, he picked it up.

The moment his fingers touched the heart, a faint red glow simmered beneath its black casing. This revelation of life within the object came as such a shock, he let go, and the heart fell toward the rocks. Rhoco shook free from his astonishment and dove to catch it before it shattered. It landed on his stone palm, which wasn't as lethal as the rocks on the beach, but was still too hard for something so fragile. Though he prevented it from sure destruction, his rough catch created new fissures.

The heart smoldered in his grip.

Rhoco cradled the heart in his hands as he journeyed home, more aware than ever that he'd need to adopt a gentler touch. He wasn't sure what to do with this discovery, but leaving it amongst the crashing waves and rocks was not an option.

He placed the glass heart on his mantel and it turned black again the moment he let go. A curious feeling stirred in his chest. The heart appeared to need him, coming to life at his touch. Could he be trusted with something so fragile?

No, of course not, he thought, then cast the thought aside.

The black heart sat on his mantel as he readied for bed. For something so small, its energy was enormous, filling his entire home with its presence. He tried to ignore it, but found its company was inescapable.

When he finally descended into his cellar and got into bed, he could still feel the heart's pull through the wall. The feeling the heart gave him, as if he mattered, as if he were needed, was infectious. He could not rid himself of the thoughts that stemmed from such notions, nor of the desires he wished to have but knew better than to seek. If his past proved anything, it was that he was a menace to those who cared for him.

Rhoco got out of bed and marched up the stairs to the mantel. He lit a candle and stared at the heart with arms crossed.

He was stronger than this emotion and he reminded himself that he was happy without any ties. A few deep breaths and his mind cleared.

It was only a heart.

Chapter 3

Rhoco woke to find a yellow canary sitting on the sill of the only window in his home.

"Why aren't you in the mines?" Rhoco asked as he pushed the pane open. The window, which faced the ocean, was the small home's only source of fresh air besides the chimney.

The bird jumped off the sill and flew into his kitchen. It fluttered around the tiny room before landing on the stone table to eat breadcrumbs.

Rhoco considered eating the bird, as he hadn't eaten meat in a few days, but decided he couldn't. The bird was more than an animal; it was part of his work crew. Canaries detected toxic air long before a Boulde ever could.

A mixture of respect and gratitude shaped his decision to prepare a different sort of breakfast: blueberries and grains. The food wasn't ideal, but it gave him the energy he needed to start the day.

"I hope our brothers are safe down there," he said.

A knock came as he shoveled the last bite into his mouth.

"Who's there?" he hollered, cheeks full.

"Your only friend. Let me in."

Rhoco unlocked the door and Cybelle hobbled inside. The yellow canary flew out as she entered and Rhoco cursed at the exchange of companions. He preferred guests who could not speak.

"It's going to rain, you know," she said.

"So what?"

"Don't take so long to let me inside!"

"You're extra cranky today."

"Did you eat all the food I brought you?"

"Working on it."

"I have another batch of jams cooling in the mud. I'll bring a jar over tomorrow."

"Anything but strawberry."

Thunder roared and Cybelle raised an eyebrow. A strike of lightning followed. She made her way to the moss-covered, clay chair and set her achy body down.

Rhoco went to the window to watch the storm. Threatening black clouds took over the morning sky, which matched the shade of the sea beneath. As the world darkened, the only source of light came from bolts of sky fire.

Rhoco enjoyed thunderstorms. He closed his eyes and leaned forward so the mist of the rain caressed his skin. He imagined the feeling of the cool spray on his calloused face.

The spray brought with it some unknown form of deep relief. Despite their raucous nature, storms brought him peace.

"What's that?" Cybelle asked after a particularly loud rumble of thunder.

"What's what?" he replied. A flash of lightning illuminated the room and he saw his old neighbor pointing to the glass heart on his mantel.

"Just a heart."

Cybelle rose and charged toward the glass ornament.

"Just a heart? This likely belongs to someone!"

"A dead person, maybe," Rocco retorted, though he hadn't gotten the impression the heart was linked to death.

"Not necessarily."

"How could someone live without their heart?"

"Don't you read?"

"No."

Cybelle sighed. "Just because Bouldes can't live without their hearts doesn't mean other species can't."

"So you're saying the creature connected to this thing is alive somewhere, functioning without its heart?"

"Possibly. Where did you find it?"

"It washed ashore."

Her eyes widened in a combination of outrage and fear.

"Why did you bring it into your home?"

"Because it would've shattered out there. The waves would've knocked it against the rocks until it broke."

"As they should. You don't know what kind of trouble it will bring."

"It's just a heart."

"Don't you know the power of a heart?"

Rhoco shrugged, unsure what the big deal was.

"And this one has been separated from its owner," she continued.

"I thought I was collecting bones, not something someone out there might still have an affection toward."

"What's it made of?" she asked, afraid to get too close to find out for herself.

"Glass."

She nodded slowly. "Something terrible must've happened to cause such a removal. You ought to toss it back to sea. It won't bring anything but trouble."

"It hasn't yet."

"It will."

"I find no harm in the heart, so it stays."

"You'll come to regret that decision," Cybelle warned, backing toward the door. "I wish you well, but I must go."

"But it's still storming."

"I'd rather get wet than stay in the company of that *thing*. Be careful, Mr. Rhoco. There are powers in this world you have yet to uncover."

Before Rhoco could question her, she was gone. He glanced at the heart, brow furrowed.

"That was dramatic," he noted, unsure whether to take her seemingly sincere warnings seriously or to brush them aside as superstitions crafted in old age. "Are you here to cause me trouble?" he asked the heart.

The blackness simmered red in response.

"I hope that means no," he said with a heavy sigh, then whispered, "Who do you belong to?"

The unfamiliar feeling of curiosity got the best of him. He leaned in closer and peered into the glass heart. Though the red glow intensified, nothing within the glass casing revealed its intentions.

Rhoco surrendered, choosing not to take Cybelle's grave warning too seriously. He could easily defeat something so small and fragile—he'd simply smash it with his fist. Over and done.

He peered over his shoulder at the heart as he crossed into the kitchen. It was black and lifeless. He then glanced out the window and saw that the storm raged on. Rhoco looked for Cybelle's silhouette on the rocky shore, but he could see very little in the darkness. A pang of guilt rang through him.

With a grunt, he rushed out of his home to find her.

The rain lashed him so intensely he needed no concentration to feel the sting through the small craters on his calloused skin. He wasn't used to such uninvited sensations — in fact, other than the mist, he rarely allowed himself to feel any sensation at all.

The rain pelted his skin, searing him with each strike, and his concern for Cybelle's safety increased. It was a powerful storm and his old neighbor had a long walk home. He raced forward, jumping over the larger rocks along the shore. Still, he saw no sign of Cybelle. Her house was another five minutes away, so he darted toward it, hoping she somehow made it there already.

"Rhoco!" a voice bellowed through the wind. Rhoco stopped and tried to locate the voice through the darkness. "Rhoco!" it called again.

He darted toward the dunes and there, under a large boulder propped atop three smaller ones, crouched Cybelle, wedged in the tiny space between.

"You shouldn't have left," he insisted.

"Forget that, just get me home!"

Rhoco lifted and relocated the boulder blocking the narrow crawlspace, then helped her out of the crevice. He picked her up and ran the rest of the way with her cradled in his arms. When they reached her home, he put her down and she seized the long chain she wore around her neck. A large, ornate key dangled on the end. Cybelle opened the door and they both hurried inside.

"I haven't felt a downpour that fierce in decades," she gasped as she fell into her rocking chair.

"Thanks for dragging me into it," he complained.

"I never asked you to follow me."

"You planned to stay under that rock all night?"

"I did."

"You should be thanking me."

"Thanks, but I didn't need your help," she conceded stubbornly.

Rhoco sighed, defeated. "I'm going home."

"Back into that rain? Stay and I'll make you food. I don't have any squirrel meat," she teased in a disapproving tone. "But I do have jam."

"For the love of all that's right, no more jam."

"What's wrong with my jam?"

"Nothing, but if I eat another spoonful without something to break up the monotony, I fear my brain will turn to jelly."

"Better than the barbaric brain those squirrels will give you."

"I'm good. Not hungry, but thank you."

"How about mashed potatoes?" she tried again. It was apparent she didn't want him to leave and he sensed getting caught in the storm might have frightened her more than she let on.

"Fine. One helping of mashed potatoes."

"Great." She got to work, slamming her stone fist into a bowl filled with red potatoes, and Rhoco took a seat at her kitchen table.

Her home resembled his. It was dug into the side of a grassy knoll, had walls made of hardened mud and clay, and was small in size. By the shore, they dug into the dunes, while in the desert, they dug underground. Building a dwelling was a feat, but they often built their homes at a young age and never relocated again. Cybelle was over a century old, and the artifacts collected around her home spanned the decades.

As she cooked, Rhoco observed the ancient trinkets scattered around and thought of his own home. The only non-essential item in his home was the heart. It was the only piece he had added since building it. He shook his head, not wanting to let the heart consume his thoughts again.

Cybelle whipped up the potatoes in record time and placed two plates on the table. She opened the only window in her house before joining Rhoco at the table.

They ate the mashed potatoes in silence, for neither had much to say. An hour later, when the rain lessened, Rhoco departed.

He only had two days left before he returned to the mines and he wished to enjoy them alone.

His home usually provided a serene sense of solitude, but when he returned, the energy felt suffocating. Aggravated that his home did not offer the comfort he sought, he began slamming his fists against the walls, hoping to pound a sense of calm into the room.

Dent after dent in the earthen foundation fixed nothing. As he worked his way around the room, fist to clay, fist to clay, the feeling of another in his presence amplified. He landed his hardest punch next to the mantel, causing a crack to splinter across the entire wall. He lifted his gaze to examine the damage, only to see the glass heart pulsing with red light.

His fury intensified; he could not achieve the solitude he desired because of the heart. Its presence on the mantel filled the entire house.

Rhoco grabbed the heart and marched outside. The sky was still dark and the rain continued in a light drizzle. He carried the glass heart over the knoll to where the chimney protruded from the ground. He knelt next to the brick vent and started digging. His limestone nails collected wet dirt beneath their tips as he shoveled a hole for the heart.

Finally, Rhoco tossed it in the ground and covered it with soil. The act of separating himself from its unknown power was liberating. He did not hate the heart, he simply did not understand it.

Until he sorted out what it all meant, the heart would remain underground. He was the only one who knew where it was and within its grave it would be safe.

Chapter 4

Two days passed and Rhoco successfully stripped the heart from his mind. When the carrier cardinal arrived with its summoning song for the mines, he felt a peculiar sense of relief. He got dressed, slung his pickaxe over his shoulder, and began the trek to work. He was happy to leave, which was unusual because his alcove in the dune was the only spot in Orewall that ever felt like home.

But all of that was changing. Now, Rhoco was eager to leave and escape the confinement he used to welcome. He no longer felt at ease within those walls. The sudden change was disheartening and he hoped a few days in the mines would repair the damage.

Inside the mines, he found temporary clarity. Nothing here had changed and he embraced the comforting predictability of the underground darkness. The sweat, the exertion, the aches of hard labor; he greeted all of it with gratitude. He was a creature of habit and he appreciated consistency in even the most strenuous routines.

By the end of his work shift his hands were bloody and he was so sore he had trouble moving. He had worked even harder than usual and didn't realize it till the Hematites blew the end-of-shift whistle. The moment he stopped hammering, the pain set in. His hands were raw and stung ferociously. He clenched them into fists to prevent any air from brushing his open blisters.

As Rhoco and the other Fused marched in single file, the Murks stood along the walls. Rhoco avoided eye contact, as did the rest of the Fused.

"The Royals have scheduled a Murk lashing in the desert tonight," Carrick, the only co-worker Rhoco ever engaged with, informed. His blue topaz and sandstone skin shimmered like a moonlit lagoon in the torchlight. "Scheduled for moonrise."

"What's the crime?"

"Who cares?" Carrick said with a shrug.

He ran ahead, leaving Rhoco behind to ponder whether he wished to witness a lashing before bed. As he exited the mine, he noted that the sun was already setting, so stalling a bit in the desert wouldn't require too much effort. He hadn't seen a Murk lashing in years, but he still recalled the enjoyment the spectacle once gave him.

Rhoco followed the crowds to the nearest colony of Fused cacti huts and waited with them for the lashing to begin. Many came and went from the cacti huts located on the perimeter of the colony square. Rhoco had no place to go, so he waited patiently amidst the bustle of his fellow Bouldes. Though the desert was expansive, and most stretches were barren of life, the towns established throughout the land were far from dead. They were crowded and loud, with Bouldes bustling about and mingling.

All that socialization made him uncomfortable. It wasn't natural, and though everything he witnessed was surface interaction, it felt invasive from afar. Silently, he dreaded the moment another approached him to make small talk.

Carrick found him first.

"You came."

"It was on the way," Rhoco stated with a grunt.

"Should be a good one."

They stood in contented silence while they waited for moonrise. Slowly, others joined them in the colony square, forming a circle of solid bodies around the spot where the lashing would take place. The socializing ceased and the space quieted, except for a few mumbled conversations. The excitement in the air was electric as the crowd awaited the show.

The royal caravan arrived moments after the sun fully set. Obsidian guards yanked the accused Murk by his neck from the front of the convoy, while the largest of the Obsidian guards carried King Alun and Queen Gemma on a stone palanquin draped in purple silk. The sight of the Royals shocked Rhoco;

this Murk must have done something truly awful for them to leave Amesyte Valley and enter the desert slums.

The guards at the back of the procession carried a whipping post and when the caravan halted, they placed the contraption in the middle of the colony square. The Murk then had each of his wrists tied to separate posts, which stretched his body wide.

The Obsidian holding the whip dipped his hand into a pouch hanging from his belt and smeared white greasepaint across his face. The color stained his jet-black skin and his breathing grew heavy as he mentally riled himself for the main event.

The Murk cried, begging for anyone in the crowd to defend him, but no one stepped up. They watched with eager detachment as the torturer approached his victim.

"I did nothing wrong," the Murk insisted through terrified sobs. "I am innocent!"

"Let the lashing begin!" King Alun proclaimed from his mobile throne.

The guard unleashed the first crack. The salted, leather whip sliced through the Murk's dark skin, easily tearing through layers of stone flesh.

"I am innocent!" the Murk bellowed. Then, in his native tongue, he repeated, "E di inkocet!"

"Again!" King Alun commanded.

The whip struck the feeble Murk again, ripping a new lesion on his back. The Purebred guard grunted with savage satisfaction as he struck his victim a third time.

"Wyhe?" the Murk pleaded in Murkken, but no one here understood his language. "E di inkocet!"

Another lashing shredded a fresh section of his flesh.

None of the spectators knew why this man was being punished, and no one bothered to ask. The Fused Bouldes considered a good Murk lashing to be an acceptable form of entertainment. Obtaining enjoyment from such cruelty was a learned behavior caused by years of conditioned hatred that seeped into each new generation.

The fifth lashing brought the horror of this strange reality to the forefront of Rhoco's awareness. The whip wrapped around the Murk's face, tearing a gash through his eye. The injury was brutal, and when the Murk shrieked in agony, the crowd cheered for more.

For the first time, Rhoco saw the barbaric display for what it was: inhumane. He looked over at the king and queen, who watched happily, hands clean, and realized they were to blame for encouraging the acceptance of this atrocity. Tolerance of this cruelty was so ingrained into the Bouldes' psyches that they could not change their perception of the Murks, even when blatant injustice was being demonstrated directly before them.

Looking around, Rhoco wondered how many of the other Fused silently acknowledged their prejudice in this moment.

Still, he said nothing, just as he was conditioned to do. He did not step forward to defend the Murk or question the justness of the punishment.

The lashing continued until the Murk became silent. When the victim could no longer cry out in pain or profess his innocence, King Alun instructed the Obsidian guard to stop.

He waved his hand, which was made of the purest amethyst, and a different pair of guards stepped forward. They placed stone buckets at the Murk's feet and then maneuvered each foot into the contents. The Murk awoke as the searing pain of ore-eating lichen latched onto his skin and spread up his legs.

"Yekî mirî," Rhoco gasped beneath his breath. In addition to banishment to the river and decapitation via whip, strains of this lichen were a death sentence in Orewall.

The yekî mirî ate the Murk's flesh until nothing of him remained. Shins, gone. Thighs, gone. When the lichen reached his waist, King Alun finally spoke.

"A reminder," he warned the crowd of onlookers with ominous confidence.

No one replied. The Murk wouldn't die until the yekî mirî reached his heart, but still, as a final insult to his existence, the guards left him tied to the beams and dragged him, facedown, in the coarse desert sand as they carried him away. The royal caravan departed as swiftly as it came, leaving the crowd in adrenaline-fueled shock.

"He didn't do anything wrong," Rhoco mumbled beneath his breath.

"Surely, there is more to the story," Carrick replied.

"Who cares?" a nearby man injected. "Who cares about a lowly Murk? His life means nothing here."

"They shouldn't be allowed to punish people without reason," Rhoco countered, unsure why he suddenly cared to defend a stranger.

"You're a Murk-lover?" the man taunted.

"No, but how would you feel if one day they turned on the Fused for no reason?"

"That would never happen," the man spat. "They need us."

"Living by the sea has salted your brain," an elderly woman jumped in, sniffing the air around Rhoco. "You stink like seaweed. No one with any sense would live in such a bedeviled place. That ocean is home to monsters, home to creatures you couldn't imagine in your worst nightmares. Go back to the dunes where you belong, before you lure the devils inland."

"Happily," Rhoco retorted, annoyed by the woman's archaic delusions. Not much rattled the Bouldes, but when it came to superstitions and paranormal oddities, they were highly precautious. They believed in fate and sorcery, celestial folklore and Karmandel, the goddess of fate. If a Boulde detected any ounce of magic in a situation, their superstitious nature was revealed.

He stormed toward the shore, angry and confused. Witnessing the lashing was both exhilarating and infuriating. It had never before awakened such profound thoughts, but now he found he could not stomach the gross injustice.

"Wait," Carrick called out, chasing after him.

"What?"

"Why are you mad?"

"That was wrong."

"Maybe, but what can we do about it?"

Rhoco paused, realizing Carrick was right, and his fury deflated in surrender.

"They are Bouldes, too," Rhoco said. "We're all made from the same matter and vulnerable to the same perils. Why are they treated like they are less than us?"

"It's always been that way," Carrick replied, with a shrug.

"It's a shame."

"You might be right."

A light turned on behind his fellow miner's eyes. This was the first time Carrick had been forced to assess this situation for what it truly was.

"See you in the mines," Carrick said before darting back to the cacti colony in the direction of his hut.

Alone with his thoughts, Rhoco started toward the dunes. Everything felt off: his outlook, his reactions, his values. What was once solid was now dithered and he wasn't sure how these revelations would change him.

He thought of the Murks and a surge of anger rose inside him. He shouldn't care, but he did, and the unwanted emotion aggravated him. Mentally, he fought to retreat to his old, simpler ways—ways that did not torment his conscience.

By the time Rhoco reached the dunes, his unsettled views surrounding the Murks had passed and thoughts of his simple life returned.

Pain coursed through his muscles and he remembered the raw sores on his palms. Pure, searing agony. He hated feeling anything. It was unusual, unwelcome, and reminded him of shameful times.

As luck had it, Cybelle's talents stretched beyond jam-making. She also brewed medicines—healing ointments that Rhoco rarely needed. If the pain did not cease soon, he'd seek her out for a cure.

When he arrived at his front door, Almadine was there waiting for him.

"What are you doing here?" he said in greeting.

"We're friends, aren't we?"

"I don't have any friends."

"Then what is Cybelle?"

"My neighbor."

"You're too stubborn for your own good."

"Maybe. Do you need something?"

"I was hoping to spend some time with you."

"I just spent forty-eight hours in the mines. I am beat up and in pain. I will be terrible company."

"I don't mind."

"That was my polite way of declining your offer."

"Well, I'm not leaving."

Rhoco groaned, unlocking the door and allowing her to follow him inside. He didn't have it in him to fight her right now. He marched toward the hatch where he stored his ice and Almadine took a seat on the mossy, clay chair in his living room.

"What happened here?" she asked, shivering.

"What do you mean?" he shouted from the small cellar.

"Your house feels different and cold."

"Really?" His head popped up through the door. "I've been experiencing the opposite. It's been too warm for me lately."

"It's frigid," she disagreed, looking concerned. "Perhaps you're sick."

"I'm not sick." Rhoco dipped back beneath the floor and reemerged a moment later with ice. He placed the bucket on the kitchen table and dunked both hands into its contents. A sigh of relief escaped his lips.

"Come here," Almadine demanded. He did not move. "Bring the ice," she insisted.

He begrudgingly obliged and she motioned for him to sit on the floor in front of her. She began massaging his broad shoulders, temporarily soothing the aches he felt. With her strong grip, she kneaded the muscles around his neck. Lost in the moment, he unintentionally allowed her heavy touch to loosen his senses and open him up to feel everything. Almadine's fingers moved in circles around the top of his spine, then traveled downward. She pressed on his back, tilting her body into his as her hands worked their way to his tailbone. Her nose was inches from him and her breath warmed his skin.

She leaned in to kiss his neck, but the moment her lips touched his skin, Rhoco recoiled.

"What's wrong with you?" he demanded, tensing up and defiantly shutting down his sensory nerves.

"It felt right."

"No."

"I love you!"

"Well, you shouldn't, so stop."

"You can't just *stop* loving someone," she said, tears in her eyes.

"This is wrong." Rhoco sprang to his feet, angry with himself for allowing Almadine into his home. "It's my fault. You have to go."

"Don't make me leave."

"Get out!"

An icy chill swept through the room causing the tears on Almadine's cheeks to freeze. Her eyes widened with alarm as she wiped the frozen droplets off her face.

"What was that?" she asked.

"What was what?" Rhoco did not feel the chill. His senses had returned to stone.

"Look." She showed him the tears in her hand. They were quickly melting in the heat of her palm.

"You're crying. Trust me, I'm aware. I already told you I never meant to hurt you."

"No. They froze to my face. Something is haunting your house."

"Haunting? Like a ghost?"

"How else would you explain frozen tears?"

"I didn't feel any chill."

"You better be careful."

"Just leave already."

The supernatural shock was enough to suppress Almadine's heartache; rejection stung a little less when her mind was consumed with supernatural questions.

"I hope they don't mean you harm," she warned as Rhoco slammed the door behind her.

He was alone again, but not completely. Almadine wasn't wrong when she sensed a strange presence.

Rhoco sat in his clay chair and tried to ignore the uncomfortable warmth filling his house. It was sticky and humid and made breathing hard. There was no reason for such conditions; the weather outside was cool and the air was fresh.

The longer he sat there, inhaling the thick air, the more hypnotized he became. Before he had a chance to realize what was happening, he was spellbound. It was too late to crack the window, too late to open the door. He was captured.

Eyes glued to the ceiling. Paralyzed. His heart raced, unsure what had come over him. Was there truly a ghost occupying his hut, haunting his existence? Had someone snuck a charm cursed with black magic into his home? But with no adversaries he could think of, that notion was unlikely.

The spell tightened around his neck. His chest pounded with fear. The muggy air clogged his throat, blocking his breathing. He was choking; he was dying.

The heart.

The moment he remembered the heart, the spell lifted and he was released. But his chest still pounded and he couldn't quite return his breathing to normal. His entire demeanor was rattled.

He glared upward. A few feet above the ceiling was the heart, buried—unwisely—above his dwelling. Rhoco cursed himself for choosing such a foolish place to bury the relic.

He stormed out of his house, ascended the knoll, and found the fresh patch of dirt covering the grave. Kneeling, he shoveled with his hands and soon reached the heart's resting place.

As soon as his finger brushed the glass casing, the heart came to life. He watched as it glowed brighter than ever. When he leaned away to examine it, its light dimmed. He leaned in again and it smoldered. The heart beckoned for his touch.

Aggravated, he lifted the heart. Upon contact, everything that felt wrong was suddenly restored: his home felt like home again, his stress vanished, his comfort returned. The drastic change should have caused him unease, but instead, he felt contentment similar to that which he felt prior to finding the heart. Was it false? Was it another illusion cast by the glass heart?

Rhoco did not know, nor did he have the mental strength to fight through the overwhelming serenity that washed over him. Cautiously, he carried the heart back into his home and returned it to the mantel.

The moment he let it go, his senses returned. He saw clearly again, yet the clarity did not bring forth any new alarm. His house still felt like home, his stress was still gone, his comfort did not disappear; everything that had been restored remained.

The entire ordeal was peculiar and perplexing. Though Rhoco could not make sense of it, there was no doubt that the heart was more powerful than he ever realized. Cybelle's warnings were warranted, he saw that now, and though it worried him, his inclination to offer the heart protection outweighed his revulsion. He wasn't sure why or how this had come to be, but he felt confident that if he kept the heart safe, it would cause him no further harm.

Chapter 5

Rhoco spent the following day outside. He attempted to swim again, with no luck, and then spent the remainder of the afternoon lying in the wake of the crashing waves. The water lapped over him repeatedly, sometimes merely caressing his body, while other times submerging him completely. He remained motionless for hours, unconcerned by the changing tides.

"You're a strange one," Cybelle said, announcing her arrival, and Rhoco moved for the first time all afternoon to see his visitor approach. After acknowledging her presence with brief eye contact, he resumed his position in the wet sand. A wave crashed over him, covering his entire body for a moment.

"I'm not joining you there," she remarked after the water cleared.

"I didn't suspect you would."

"Almadine tells me you have a ghost?"

"I don't."

"It's the heart, isn't it?" Rhoco's failure to respond answered her suspicions. "I told you it was trouble."

"Well, there's not much I can do about it now. I'm stuck with it."

"You are *not*," she insisted. "Toss it back to sea."

"I tried to bury it, but it found me and suffocated me until I dug it back up. If I discard the heart, I will die."

"Don't be foolish. Its magic can't locate you once it's carried away by the tides."

"But what if it does? If I throw it out to sea, I have no way to retrieve it and stop whatever lethal spell it casts over me. I have to keep it safe. The only way to save myself is to protect the heart."

"So you're resigned to harboring that atrocity in your home?"

"I have no other choice."

"You *could* turn it over to the authorities."

"That would be an act of betrayal against the heart. I'd be a dead man if I did."

"You might be a dead man if you don't. The Royals hate the Glaziene, so they better not catch you with it."

"They hate the what?"

"The people made of glass. The Kingdom of Crystet." Rhoco's expression revealed his ignorance. Cybelle continued, "Typical Boulde, you know nothing."

"I've heard of the Glaziene, I think. It sounds familiar."

"You're sheltering the heart of our enemy. If King Alun finds out, you'll be labeled a traitor and sentenced to the river."

"I don't even know who the heart belongs to."

"It doesn't matter, possessing it is still an act of treason. If what I've read about the power of the heart is true, then there's no telling the trouble it will cause."

"I don't understand how something inanimate can hold such power."

"On its own, apart from its owner, a heart is one of the most powerful relics on the planet. It holds magic and abilities most only dream of. Without ties to the brain, without a bodily casing, it is free and capable of anything. Be it noble or malicious, a heart has no bounds."

"Is it still connected to its owner?"

"Always, but it acts on its own accord once separated. It still recalls who it was when it lived inside its owner, but once removed, the heart blossoms and achieves its full capabilities."

"Why don't these people die without their hearts?"

"It's how the Glaziene are built. *Our* hearts need to be carved out of our bodies if they are to be removed. There's no other way to get to them and the process of heart carving is lethal. No Boulde survives it. Ancient Boulde kings tried to find a way so we could fight back against our enemies, but they learned very quickly that we weren't equipped for that type of warfare."

"I don't understand the point of removing a heart. Why do it at all?"

"Each species has different reasons, but not all species can do so and survive. Bouldes for instance. Also, not all species receive magic when they remove their heart." Cybelle paused, then scolded him. "Why haven't you taught yourself any of this?"

"How?"

"Ask!" Cybelle clicked her tongue in outrage. "Too many Bouldes stopped caring about the world outside of Orewall, and it's a damn shame. You all just accept your miserable existence without a care for what else is out there. Your generation has no concern for the dangers beyond our borders, and you all live like there are no outside threats to our existence. But there are— there are many! King Alun has all of Orewall whipped into believing he's invincible, but he isn't, and I hope we never see the day outsiders challenge his rule because if they do, he'll have nothing but benighted soldiers trying to save his kingdom."

"I've been alive for almost thirty years and there hasn't been one conflict involving foreigners."

"In my time, there were many."

"Why'd it stop?"

"King Alun declared that the Bouldes no longer had interest in the Great Fight."

"What fight?"

"For the scepter of alchemy. Whoever possesses it reigns supreme. King Lucien of Elecort currently possesses it. The Voltains have had it for centuries." Rhoco's face showed his lack of comprehension and Cybelle sighed. "The Voltains of Elecort are born from electricity."

"Why did King Alun stop the Bouldes from participating in the Great Fight?"

"He was afraid of what the Voltains would do to him if they ever caught him acting in accordance with the revolution."

"How don't I know any of this?"

"Because you don't ask."

"Even so, I've never heard anyone talk about this war, nor our part in it. I'd have thought it would have been mentioned in conversation by now."

"As someone who lived through it, it truly feels like our entire society somehow forgot. It's strange seeing new generations born without any awareness of all that was sacrificed to obtain peace. I guess I can't really blame any of you, seeing as they burnt down all the libraries." Cybelle tapped the side of her head. "Not all knowledge has been lost, though. In the old days, children were abandoned at age five so that they could train with the Orewall Army. Boys and girls were sent to battle by age fifteen, and many never returned. In those days, all adults were not only obligated to mate within their breed so that the children were strong Purebreds, but also to have as many children as possible. The army needed a continual replenishment of soldiers."

"Why were we so bad at war? We are made of stone, we ought to be invincible."

"We're a simple people. Though we are big and strong, we are not calculating. Our war tactics and strategies paled in comparison to our competitors. We never stood a chance."

"I have a lot to learn," he commented, his tone full of defeat.

"Don't sound so glum. Like I said, luck provided you with me as a friend. I'm a knowledge pirate." She lifted the cloth covering her basket to reveal the corner of an ancient book. Once he caught sight, she quickly covered the illegal artifact. "Between my brain and my stash, you've got the best resource Orewall has to offer. But first, you need to get rid of that heart. As much as I hate the collective ignorance under King Alun's reign, keeping the rest of Namaté at a distance does let us live in peace. And since that's how we survive, that *thing* is not welcome here."

"I can't just discard it." Rhoco sighed and Cybelle glared at him disapprovingly. "I already explained why."

"Well, you need to figure something out."

"I will." He stood, sopping wet. "I need to dry off."

He headed for his house and Cybelle followed, carrying her basket. Still fearful of the heart, however, she entered his house with caution. She remained in the kitchen as Rhoco retrieved the towel that hung on the pegboard near the fireplace. As he rubbed himself dry beside the mantel, the black heart began pulsating the faintest of reds.

"What's it doing?" Cybelle gasped from the kitchen. Rhoco stepped away, hoping to silence Cybelle's fears, but he only managed to heighten them. The heart returned to black.

"Holy boulders, it does that for you?"

"It probably does that for anyone," he offered lamely. Cybelle marched toward him and placed her finger on the heart.

It stayed black.

"No wonder this place feels haunted. The heart has bonded to you."

"Bonded?"

Cybelle retrieved the book from her basket and handed it to him.

"It's time you learned some history."

Rhoco never held a book before. It felt old and fragile in his grip. He placed it down before he accidentally cracked the withered leather cover in half.

"I'm not good at reading."

"Practice will make you better," Cybelle insisted, picking up the book and thrusting it back into his hands. Then, as she exited his home, she declared, "I'll be back tomorrow to answer any questions you might have."

He had no time to object or refuse. She was gone.

Rhoco looked down at the soot-covered book; it appeared no one had opened it in years. He placed it on the table with a little too much force. The filth from decades of neglect burst into the air and hovered over the book. The fog of dust was thick as Rhoco swatted the cloud away.

He glanced over his shoulder at the heart before surrendering and opening the book. It was time to learn where the heart came from, and hopefully, what it wanted from him.

Chapter 6

Over the next two days, Rhoco took his time reading the history book Cybelle gifted him. He was a terrible reader and it took a while to get through each page. He often found himself rereading the same line countless times until its meaning sank in and he understood what was being conveyed.

The book, titled *Beyond Orewall*, taught the basics of the different regions of Namaté — the planet upon which they existed. Each race was made from a different type of natural material. The Bouldes of Orewall were made of stone, but he knew little about the countless other people who resided beyond the horizon.

Each page was crammed with words and Rhoco was overwhelmed by the end of page one. He began flipping through the pages, unconcerned with lessons about other lands, and instead, he focused solely on that of glass.

After breezing past seven chapters focused on other lands and their species, he finally reached the chapter on the Glaziene of Crystet.

When he turned the chapter's title page, he was greeted by an elaborate, breathtaking drawing of a glass city. The sunlight, which reflected off the jagged architecture, cast beams of light in all directions. And although he found it difficult, he took the time to carefully read the details describing the Glaziene.

The Glaziene were fragile, yet sharp, so every touch had the potential to slice. Though made of glass, the material was interlaced into plush skin, which meant they bled through the cracks. He scanned the sketched images of the Glaziene and could not find one individual without a fracture. Most were covered with them. Through the blushed, glass-laced skin, he saw each person's colorful insides, which were the only source of color amongst the white and gray landscape draping the city.

Though they were stunning creatures draped in diamonds and crystals, they carried a heaviness with them that Rhoco felt through the pages. Years of pain plagued Crystet, crafting a populace too cautious and guarded, too quick to draw blood from others to safeguard their own. The distrust was rampant, as was the gloom. He turned to look at the heart on his mantel and felt great empathy for it—it came from a land cloaked in sorrow.

He then wondered why *this* heart was removed from its owner. In the next paragraph, he found some clues.

THE GLAZIENE HAVE ETERNAL LIFESPANS—EVEN WHEN THEY SHATTER THEY CAN BE REBUILT IF THE BUILDER HAS ALL THEIR PIECES. USING HEAT, THE PIECES ARE WELDED BACK TOGETHER, LEAVING

HORRIFIC SCARS, BUT ALLOWING THE INDIVIDUAL TO RESUME LIFE.

IF A GLAZIENE SHATTERS BUT PARTS OF THEM ARE MISSING, THEY DIE. IN RARE CASES, IF MISSING PIECES ARE FOUND, THE DECEASED CAN BE RESURRECTED YEARS LATER, BUT THESE OCCURRENCES ARE UNCOMMON.

HOW DO PIECES GO MISSING? WHEN A GLAZIENE IS READY TO DIE, THEY THROW ONE OF THEIR PIECES OUT TO SEA, OR BURY IT IN A CLANDESTINE LOCATION. THIS SYMBOLIZES THEIR DESIRE TO REMAIN BROKEN. THEY WILL REMAIN ALIVE WITHOUT THEIR MISSING PIECE UNTIL THEY SHATTER.

DUE TO THE SELFISH AND NARCISSISTIC NATURE OF THE GLAZIENE, IT OFTEN TAKES CENTURIES BEFORE MOST ARE WILLING TO SURRENDER AND END THEIR LIVES. THE ELDERLY ARE WALKING FOGS, WITH SO MANY GLASS FRACTURES FUSED TOGETHER THAT THEIR COLORFUL INNARDS ARE NO LONGER VISIBLE.

WHILE THE GLAZIENE RARELY SACRIFICE THEMSELVES, IT IS COMMON FOR ONE TO CUT THE LIFE OF ANOTHER SHORT. ACCUSTOMED TO A GREEDY EXISTENCE AND A RAVENOUS DESIRE FOR SURVIVAL, THE GLAZIENE TAKE NO PAUSE WHEN ENDING ANOTHER'S LIFE IF DOING SO SERVES TO ENHANCE THEIR OWN. THE MOST COMMON REASON

FOR MURDER IN CRYSTET IS JEALOUSY AND
HEARTACHE.

Once again, Rhoco looked at the heart and wondered which
fate it suffered. Had someone ripped this organ from an
unsuspecting victim? Or did the heart's owner willingly toss a
piece of themself out to sea? According to the book, no Glaziene
readily ended their life, so he had to assume this heart was the
victim of another's selfish cruelty.

Rhoco realized then that he had developed a soft home for it
within his own heart.

If what he read was accurate, then pain was abundant in
Crystet and the repercussive sadness was blinding. The
Glaziene reacted out of emotion, and such reactions resulted in
lifelong consequences. The heart was protecting itself the only
way it knew how: intimidation and terror.

He caused it pain when he buried it, and it retaliated. He
understood its defense mechanism, as he too often answered
pain with more pain.

"I forgive you for threatening me with magic," he said aloud.
"I probably would've done the same."

Rhoco no longer feared the heart's magic. Instead, his
empathy toward the peculiar relic increased — an empathy that
heightened his original intuition to protect the heart.

A knock sounded at the front door.

The moment he cracked the door open, Almadine barreled through.

In her arms was a basket full of black magic, a sling packed with tools, and a stone mallet. Raising the hammer, she marched toward the heart.

Chapter 7

"Stop!" Rhoco demanded, chasing after her and grabbing her forearm before the mallet smashed the heart.

"It's haunted," she shouted. "I will rid you of its charm!"

"It's not here to harm me. It just got lost at sea."

"It froze the tears to my face," she countered. "It possesses dangerous magic. It will plague your life if you let it stay."

"I cannot let you destroy it."

"Why not?"

"Well, to start with, it would kill me. I suspect its magic will live on, even with a shattered casing, and since it chose me to protect it, I will suffer the consequences of its demise."

"Not if I disarm it with my own magic. I brought tools, potions, and spells to properly neutralize the heart. These charms will set you free."

Rhoco ignored her and continued his train of thought. "More importantly, I *want* to protect it. It needs me—I am choosing to keep it safe."

"I won't let you," she insisted as tears formed in her citrine eyes.

"You don't get a say in the matter."

Almadine's eyes narrowed as she shoved her hand into a pouch in her basket, retrieving a fistful of mint-green powder.

"What's that?" Rhoco asked.

"Your redemption."

She turned and tossed the powder onto the heart. The moment it touched the glass shell, a shrill shriek filled the air.

"What have you done?"

"I am saving you," Almadine insisted.

The screeching filled his small home. The sound was so awful, a chill cut through his hardened nerves.

"You're hurting it!"

He snatched the heart from the mantel. Afraid to apply his rough touch to the glass, he gently blew the powder off instead. The more he managed to remove, the less it shrieked. Finally, once he blew away the last remnant, the heart quivered in his palms. He turned to chastise Almadine, but she was on the floor, convulsing.

He placed the heart back onto the mantel, then raced to Almadine's side. Orange blood poured from the corners of her eyes and her body shook violently. Not knowing how to help her, he cradled her head in his arm and held her, hoping her pain would cease soon.

He glared up at the heart, understanding that it caused Almadine's sudden affliction.

"Leave her be!" he shouted at the heart. A faint buzzing sound became audible. As it grew louder, Almadine's condition grew worse and neon citrine blood began trickling from her ears. "You're hurting her!"

A chilling hiss joined the loud buzz that filled his home.

Chastising the heart was not working. He carefully placed Almadine's head on the floor, then stood to confront the heart.

He stared at it for a moment, breathing deeply as he contemplated what to do. The deafening noise disturbed him to his core: it was unnatural, it was otherworldly, and it sent a shiver through him that he feared he'd never shake.

Finally, Rhoco stooped so he was eye-level with the heart and spent a moment there with his nose so close to its casing, his breath fogged the glass. It continued its shrill wails of self-defense. He looked down at Almadine, who was covered in glowing, dark orange blood, and then back at the heart.

"I won't let her hurt you," he promised, surprising himself.

The unsettling combination of hissing and buzzing lessened, but it did not stop.

"I won't let *anyone* hurt you."

The heart went still, and so did Almadine. Fear entered his heart, afraid that she was dead, but as the black glass heart glowed red, Almadine's chest began to move, matching the rhythm of pulsating color. The heart kick-started her lungs and gave Almadine life until she was able to breathe on her own again.

He lifted Almadine's weak body and carried her outside. Once atop the dune, he placed her onto the gritty soil and waited. The long grass blew in the wind, tickling her face, but she did not feel it. The grass was too tender, too slight a touch.

As he waited, the sun set beyond the shiny, black ocean, and the red light in the sky complemented her coloring. When she finally awoke, it was of her own accord, and the orange specks in her yellow irises sparkled in the glow.

"What happened?" she asked, still shaken.

"You tried to hurt the heart and failed. It retaliated, quite successfully."

"I feel weak."

"You lost a lot of blood."

"How long have I been out?"

"A few hours. Once I got the heart to stop assaulting you, I thought it best to let you recover out here."

"So you remove me from your home when I'm at my weakest instead of removing the heart?" she snarled.

"I stayed with you the whole time."

"Your priorities are twisted."

"Stop being a martyr," Rhoco grumbled. "You needed the fresh air."

"Just admit it. That devilish *thing* is more important to you than I am."

"You want me to say that?"

"Is it the truth?"

He sighed. "I already told you my decision regarding us. Nothing has changed. Why do you need to hear it again?"

"This is different. This is about our friendship, which should still matter to you."

"We can't be friends," he repeated, exasperated because he already told her this multiple times. "You can't let go of our past."

"I'm done being rejected by you. I deserve better."

Rhoco's eyes narrowed. "Then why did you try to kiss me the other day?"

"It was a mistake." She was visibly embarrassed. "I'm sorry for doing that, but I came back today with no ulterior motives. You need a friend now more than ever. You can't handle this heart alone—though you're trying to, even though I'm here, willing and begging to help. I can't stand by and watch it destroy you."

"I can absolutely handle the heart on my own. I know more about it than you ever will. I wish you would leave me be." He was being harsh and was very aware of the brutal boldness of his words, but subtleties did not work with Almadine. If he was not brash, she would not understand.

"I see," she mumbled.

The confident finality of his words cut through her stone-cold senses, tearing apart the fleshy nerves beneath. He chose the heart of a stranger over her.

Almadine rose and departed, saying nothing more to him. Her efforts on him were wasted and she would try no more.

Rhoco was ashamed for hurting her once again, but remained unsure how it could have gone any other way. She gave him no choice. He never promised to catch her every time she fell, yet she returned repeatedly, pushing a love on him that did not exist. Hoping that if she carried his half of the love long enough, he'd eventually realize he felt it too. It was a burden she placed on herself and tried to force upon him.

She felt abandoned, but he gave his apology, his reasoning, his truth, and he no longer owed her anything. Their quest for love was over.

Despite his conviction, the heart's extreme behavior angered him. It was unacceptable, and though he intended to continue protecting it, he could not have it sharing his home. It had him tiptoeing around broken glass, living in fear that one wrong step would be his end, or worse, the end of someone he cared for.

The map of lands in *Beyond Orewall* appeared in his mind as he stared at the dark ocean. Crystet was far, but not unreachable.

The best thing he could do for the heart was to take it home.

Chapter 8

The carrier cardinal should have returned to summon Rhoco for work, but it hadn't. Though this wasn't common, it wasn't unheard of, so he embraced the extra time off.

He approached the heart and paused. Handling such a delicate object still unnerved him. Cautiously, he picked it up and sat down in his moss covered chair, cradling it in his hands.

"Do you want to go home?" he asked the heart.

In response, the heart attached itself to him. A layer of glass melted into shards that latched to his palms.

Everything went black.

He started to panic, afraid he'd gone blind, but then the image of a woman floated across the blackness. She was tall, slender, and effervescent. She glowed within the darkness and her radiance carried a mesmerizing warmth. Her skin caught the reflection of an unseen sun, bouncing off her as hazy rainbows and momentary flashes of blinding light. Glorious in her beauty, Rhoco was entranced.

She smiled at him and approached with open arms. He welcomed her embrace, but the moment they were about to make contact, she was yanked backward. Her body lurched dramatically, as if she'd been grabbed by the spine, and the once confident and gleaming woman was now shaking on her knees, paralyzed by fear.

Behind her quivering frame, a towering shadow rose and crept a hand over her shoulder. Its lanky fingers slithered between her breasts. She held her breath, staring at Rhoco imploringly, but he wasn't really there and could not intervene. He was merely witnessing a memory that belonged to the heart.

With a light thud, the shadow sent a crack down her chest. It carefully clawed its way through the fracture and reached inside. When it withdrew its hand, it held a dazzling, red heart—the same glass heart he currently held in *his* hands.

The woman collapsed in defeat as the shadow straightened and brought the heart to its lips.

Its kiss turned the heart black.

Rhoco tried to scream, tried to chase after the shadow that now sauntered away, but he was mute and unable to move. He was forced to watch this atrocity without the ability to help. His body trembled with rage and his limbs fought their invisible constraints with such force that the heart pulled him out of the memory before he could break free and permanently alter the moment. He was torn from her side and the image of the tearful woman was forever scarred inside his mind.

"Why'd you stop me?" he demanded of the heart. "I would have saved you!"

The heart could not answer.

Aggravated, he carefully returned the heart to the mantel and hurried outside to calm down.

His assumptions were correct — the heart was the victim of a heinous crime. It had been stolen from the radiant woman and discarded into the ocean. He sensed she was still alive out there, but without her heart, she would die the moment her pieces broke apart, either by accident or by force. And when he recalled the warmth of her presence and the beauty in her aura, he was more certain than ever that returning this heart to its owner was his responsibility.

But he had no idea how. The memory and his inability to change the past still sat like a rock inside his chest. He needed to calm down before determining his next move.

Rhoco stripped off his trousers and strode into the ocean until the sea reached his chin. He sucked in as much air as he could, hoping to make himself lighter, but his body wouldn't float. So he walked a little farther until the water rose above his head.

Sunlight pierced the sea, its rays splintering in the water. He aimed his body toward the light, but no matter how energetically he waved his arms or kicked his legs, his body remained stationary. Gravity refused to let him swim. His oxygen began to run thin, but he kept trying.

When he couldn't hold his breath any longer, he conceded and trudged along the ocean floor until his head crested above the water. Another failed attempt.

He exited the ocean, put his pants back on, and then sprawled out on the sand. The heat from the burning sun dried his body.

"Why do I always find you like this?" Cybelle suddenly scolded above him. "Are you hoping the ocean washes you away?"

"I already told you. I'm trying to learn how to swim."

"You're wasting your time."

"Maybe."

"Why aren't you at work?" Cybelle asked, realizing his schedule was off.

"The cardinal never came. The current work shift must have been extended for some reason. Maybe they were in the middle of a good dig."

"Hopefully everything is all right. The Royals have been quiet lately."

"What do you mean? They're always quiet. They rarely leave Amesyte Valley to address us, and they never let us in. Until that recent Murk lashing, I hadn't even seen the Royals since I was a kid."

"Yeah, but they *do* trickle messages down to us. If you stopped wasting your free time at the bottom of the ocean and socialized in the desert, you'd hear their messages."

"Not interested."

"Clearly."

Rhoco sat up. "I'm going on a quest," he divulged, abruptly.

"A quest? Where to?"

"Crystet. I read the book you gave me and it shouldn't be too hard to get there with a boat."

"All that meat has rotted your brain."

"I haven't eaten squirrel in weeks," Rhoco lied.

"The effects creep up on you."

"My brain is fine."

"Then why do you need to go to Crystet?" she scoffed. "Is this because of that heart?"

"Of course it is. I need to return it to its owner."

"You do not."

"Someone's life depends on its return."

"But that's not *your* problem."

"Yes, it is. For once in my life, I want to be good. I want to do the right thing." His tone was desperate.

"You are good. You don't need to risk your life to prove that to anyone."

"I need to prove it to myself," he replied in a quiet voice.

"You're searching for forgiveness in all the wrong places."

Rhoco glared up at his old neighbor, unable to see the truth in her words.

"You don't know me as well as you think you do."

Cybelle raised her ashy blue eyebrows. "I know more than you realize." She then tied her shoulder length, wispy blue hair into a ponytail, revealing a faded crown tattoo on the side of her neck.

It was the mark of a chosen Fused.

"Since when?" Rhoco asked, shocked.

"Since always. You never ask questions."

Rhoco's heart slammed violently against his ribcage. "Which village?"

"Karxane."

"You were a royal botanist?" Rhoco asked, all color drained from his face.

Cybelle nodded and Rhoco buried his face into his hands.

"You aren't a bad person," Cybelle gently stated.

Unable to process this unexpected revelation rationally, Rhoco stood and began to pace, eager to turn the subject away from his shameful past.

"The heart chose me," he began, "and it has been dishing out violent reminders of our bond. It almost killed Almadine last night and it has threatened me with its magic multiple times."

Cybelle accepted his silent request to leave the past in the past, and entertained his change of topic. "I gave you that book to educate you on the dangers of Namaté, not to inspire a foolish quest, and definitely not to convince you to save that thing. It's holding you hostage. You need to destroy it!"

"I don't want to destroy it. Almadine came here last night with a basket full of tricks, intending to demolish the heart, and I stopped her."

"Why?"

"Because I am trying to do the right thing."

"If you stopped Almadine, why did the heart still attack her?"

"Because before I stopped her, she managed to blow some powder onto it that made it convulse. It responded in self-defense."

"And now you're *defending* the demon relic? It's absurd. It almost killed that lovely girl!"

"I know. That's what inspired me to take it home. It doesn't belong here, and the only way to keep *it* safe and everyone, including myself, from harm is to return it to its owner. Obviously it doesn't want to be here. It's not my fault that it picked me as its guardian."

"You're going to get yourself killed," she warned. "How do you plan to get a boat?"

"I haven't figured that out yet."

"Sounds like you haven't thought much of this through. The only boats in Orewall belong to the Royal Guard. Good luck convincing them to let you borrow a boat so you can traipse off to return a glass heart and save the life of some unknown Glaziene. What if it belongs to a nefarious soul? What if the person you're saving ought to be dead? Maybe whoever stole that heart and tossed it out to sea was doing it for the good of everyone."

Rhoco ignored the bait. "The heart's owner is innocent."

"How could you possibly know that?"

"I just do. I can sense it." He did not want to tell her about the vision. It would only heighten her alarm.

"Even after it attacked you and tried to murder your friend?"

"I told you, it was self-defense. The first time, it was protecting me because Almadine made me uncomfortable. It misread the situation and thought I was more upset than I actually was. And last night, Almadine attacked first."

"It doesn't matter how you try to explain it, the heart is better off dead."

Rhoco gave up. "I shouldn't have told you."

"But you did, and now I think you're more of an idiot than I did yesterday."

"It's the right thing to do."

"You didn't learn anything from that book! If you had, this quest wouldn't even be a consideration. I personally don't think you'll make it past the Royal Guard, but if you do somehow steal a boat and attempt this journey, you can't be sure you won't run into other species along the way. You're sheltered, like all Bouldes are, and you're uneducated about the ways of the world. You don't understand the hierarchy of cultures or the customs necessary to stay alive when interacting with foreigners. You'll get eaten alive out there!"

"I studied the map in *Beyond Orewall*. If I aim my boat right, I can make it to Crystet without ever touching another shore."

"One read through *Beyond Orewall* doesn't make you an explorer. We aren't the only land with boats."

"I'll be one man, alone in a boat. Why would they care what I'm doing?"

"The world is full of mistrust."

"Then I'll tell them the truth."

Cybelle threw up her hands. "Your mission to return a discarded heart to Crystet won't be seen as noble, it will be seen as suspicious or foolish, both of which will get you killed."

"It shouldn't be that way. Maybe I am the man to bring about change."

"One man can't decide on a whim to change what's been the way of the world for eons," she chastised him. "And what if your boat sinks? You'll drown."

"It won't." He fell backward and resumed his position of resignation on the sand.

"I'm done here," she conceded. "Take a few nights to really think this through and you'll see just how senseless this reckless quest is."

She stepped over him and continued her morning walk.

"I won't change my mind," he shouted without sitting up. She ignored him and he quietly observed her departure. Her silhouette shrank the farther away she walked.

Cybelle disappeared into the foggy shoreline.

Rhoco was alone again, his thoughts more burdened than usual. His decision was set; he would go on a quest to Crystet, but the sight of Cybelle's crown tattoo and all it implied had nestled into the recesses of his mind.

He wasn't a monster—he would prove it by saving the owner of the glass heart.

Chapter 9

The carrier cardinal arrived, singing its work song, demanding that Rhoco be at the mines within the hour. It was an impossible request because the walk to the mines took a minimum of three hours, but he got dressed anyway, grabbed his pickaxe, and began the trek.

He mulled over the wrath he'd face from the Hematites for arriving late. Memory of the public lashing of the Murk was still vivid, and since he did not wish a similar form of torture for himself, he started to jog. He hated running. His heavy body wasn't built for such an activity, and with every leap, he landed with a terrain-shuddering thud.

A half hour into the journey, he encountered Carrick at the edge of the desert. His ashy blue skin stood out amidst the red-toned landscape. Like Rhoco, Carrick was a first-generation Fused. His mixture was quite stunning and he often received uninvited fawning, particularly from those who also viewed their Fused status as an affliction. Rhoco and Carrick frequently commiserated about their blessed misfortune with humor. For outcasts who just wanted to live simple lives, the gift of handsomeness was a curse.

Carrick appeared to have been running too, but he was already out of breath.

"You better hustle, Car, or you'll be at the end of the Heemies' whip. You know how much they enjoy thrashing that thing around," Rhoco warned as he jogged past his companion. Carrick picked up his pace and jogged next to him.

"I ran the first hour. I'm dead tired. Cardinal came late."

"Yeah, I thought we might've been given an extra day off."

"No such luck, huh?" Carrick spat between heaving breaths. "We should've known better."

They jogged in silence for a while, saving their breath for the great distance they had left to travel. Living along the outskirts of Orewall, they'd likely be the last to arrive.

And they were. Though they arrived only fifteen minutes later than the other stragglers, the Hematites were not happy.

"You're late," Bedros barked, making a note next to their names on his checklist.

Carrick tried to explain. "The bird was late—"

"No excuses. Face the wall."

As Rhoco turned, he noticed that the majority of his fellow miners also bore wounds from the salted, leather whip Bedros used to tear through their stone skin.

"Good day for you, huh?" Rhoco remarked sarcastically.

Bedros replied with the first of ten brutal lashings. Hematite whips were designed to cut through stone flesh, and each strike carved out deep back wounds that would take weeks to heal.

When Bedros finally stopped, Rhoco was covered in his own lime green blood, while burnt orange blood dripped down Carrick's torso.

"Next time, you won't be late," Bedros remarked before walking away.

"Next time, I won't show up at all," Rhoco retorted under his breath. Only Carrick heard him.

"I wish there was a way to get out of this work for good. Only the Purebreds get so lucky."

"Unless we make our own luck. I've been thinking about stealing a boat."

"A boat?" Carrick asked, a little too loudly. "Where would you go?"

"Far from here." Rhoco wasn't ready to reveal the entire truth yet.

"Do you even know how to sail?"

Rhoco hadn't thought of that. "No, but it can't be too hard if the fat-brained Obsidians can do it."

"Where are you going to steal one from?"

"Not sure yet. They are docked along the north shore. I just need to figure out the security schedule and when the best time to steal one would be."

"I bet the Murks would know. I've seen them in the desert lugging boats from the east to the north."

Rhoco was intrigued, but with the Hematites circling, he didn't want to risk facing the whip again. He let the idea flourish quietly as he hammered for diamonds.

Rhoco slowly inched his way toward the corner where the Murks were located. He had never held a conversation with one of them before, so instead of offering a greeting, he opted to work beside them silently.

He slammed his pickaxe against their designated wall. They glanced up cautiously at him, but did not question his unusual proximity. Rhoco could sense they did not want him there, but they said nothing. Instead, they kept hammering and glaring at him with displeasure, continuing like this for half an hour before the oldest Murk finally broke.

"Bahn de boe!" he exclaimed angrily. Though his skin was as dark as the shadows, his glowing irises revealed his rage. He raised his pickaxe and repeated himself. "Bahn de boe!"

Rhoco stopped mid-swing and stepped back, afraid the Murk's raised pickaxe might come down on him. He lifted his hands in surrender.

"Bahn de boe!" the old Murk said again.

"Seok, stop." A younger Murk stepped in, blocking the space between Rhoco and the furious Murk.

"I don't understand what he's saying," Rhoco said to the younger Murk.

"Of course you don't. You're not a Murk, so you don't speak Murkken," he answered.

"You also speak Boulde?" Rhoco asked.

"I'm a first-generation, so I'm a little less hardened than Seok. He understands Boulde too, he just refuses to speak it. This archaic brute found me floating down the river in a basket when I was a day old."

"That's terrible."

The Murk shrugged. "They could've tossed me into the river *without* the basket."

"I guess. What's your name?"

"Pedr."

"I'm Rhoco. What was he shouting at me?"

"He wants you to go away," Pedr explained. "We all do."

"I see."

"Why aren't you over there?"

"Because I wanted to be over here."

"But this is *our* zone. You can't take this from us too."

"I wasn't trying to take anything from you. I was just trying to mingle. I didn't realize I wasn't welcome here."

"We aren't welcome most places aboveground, so you're not welcome in our corner of the underground," a third Murk objected.

"I understand. I'm sorry for the way things work up there."

"No, you're not. No one cares."

"The Fused care, they just care quietly inside their minds."

"Worsch lech," the ancient Murk spat.

"I'm not your enemy," Rhoco pleaded, unsure what Seok had said but certain it wasn't kind.

"Might as well be," Pedr argued. "If you can't defend us, then you're standing against us. Silence is the greatest weapon of all."

"You're hollow like a Woodlin," the third Murk spat, then turned away.

"What's a Woodlin?" Rhoco asked, unable to hide his curiosity.

"Figures you know nothing about our neighbors."

"You know about the lands beyond Orewall?"

"We know about everything," Pedr responded.

"What do you know about Crystet?"

"Enough." Pedr had no interest in sharing his knowledge, which was one of the few valuables exclusive to the Murks. While the rest of the Bouldes fell into a state of oblivious apathy, the Murks held on tight to their history. It made them who they were, for better or worse.

"Well," Rhoco began, seeing his opportunity. "I need to leave Orewall."

Pedr laughed. "No one leaves Orewall."

"I'm going to."

"Why?"

"I'm in possession of something that does not belong here, and I need to return it before it causes real trouble."

"Turn it into King Alun."

"That might get me sent to the river."

"By our merciful king? Preposterous!" Pedr's tone oozed with sarcasm.

Rhoco persisted. "Plus, he might break it. It's very fragile."

"What is it?"

"I can't tell you."

Pedr shrugged. "Then I can't help."

Rhoco saw he would have to take a gamble. "Tell me how to steal a guard boat and I'll *show* you what I have."

Pedr glared up with intrigue at Rhoco's determination. There was more to this quest, Pedr could sense it, and the Murk's stubborn refusal morphed into cautious curiosity.

"Trouble, trouble," he purred with unexplained fascination.

"Trouble?" Rhoco repeated, confused.

Pedr scrutinized him before conceding. "Fine, I'll help, but you won't succeed if you try to steal one of the guard boats. There is always an Obsidian posted in the watch tower. You're better off building your own."

"How am I supposed to do that?"

"With your hands," Pedr replied condescendingly.

Rhoco looked down at his hands, unsure where he'd even start.

"How do you think the boats are made?" Pedr asked, exasperated.

"Murks?"

"Naturally. There is a gigantic volcanic rock quarry beneath the east shore. It reveals itself during low tide, which occurs between moonset and sunrise. Since it's mostly made of rhyolite and pumice, it's perfect for boat carving."

Rhoco wanted to ask Pedr to help, but he felt guilty burdening the Murk with yet another thankless task.

"Okay, I appreciate the information."

"Just don't let the Obsidians catch you. They patrol the east shore after sunrise and sail those waters through moonrise. Building a boat is likely just as punishable as stealing one."

"Great, that's very helpful."

"I'm aware. When will you tell me what you're building this boat for?"

"Once my boat is built."

"Bahn de boe, nieh," the ancient Murk interjected, ready for Rhoco to leave now that he had his answers.

"Are we done here?" Pedr asked.

"Yes, thank you. Wish me luck."

Pedr nodded, but offered no well-wishes.

Rhoco was on his own, but he was used to that arrangement and preferred working in isolation. He still did not know how to build a boat, but what he had learned brought him one step closer to returning the heart to its rightful owner in Crystet.

Chapter 10

The Murks watched Rhoco closely as he worked beside Carrick. He opted not to bother them again; he suspected they wouldn't offer any additional help. Murks were highly suspicious creatures, incredibly untrusting and guarded, and because they did not speak up out of fear of punishment greater than that which they already endured, their overly cautious nature had given them their reputation of weakness. The Fused or Purebreds *could* stand up for them, but after speaking with the Murks, Rhoco realized that the Murks were smart enough to stand up for themselves. Their submission seemed spineless, but Rhoco did his best not to judge. They survived for centuries as timid creatures in the shadows; perhaps he'd have turned out the same if he'd been born that way. Perhaps *he* was spineless for staying quiet. He let the notion go. It was too much to contemplate with so much to do to prepare for his quest.

Carrick interrupted Rhoco's train of thought. "I suppose you're wondering about the fresh wounds I wear," he said between swings.

"I noticed," Rhoco replied, knowing that Carrick, who was an uncharacteristically talkative Boulde, would eventually tell him. "No need to share the details."

"It's a travesty, really," Carrick went on, ignoring Rhoco's disinterest. "The desert hut I built as a child—gone. Lightning tore it in two, leaving me shelterless during the worst storm Orewall has seen in years."

"I'm sorry to hear that."

"Wanna know what's even worse?"

"Not really."

"In addition to rebuilding my home, I also have to build a home for Rubi. She's having my baby next month and her hut isn't big enough for two. It's also rotting; she hasn't replaced the walls since she built it as a kid." His tone was disapproving. "And since I won't let my child live in a moldy or odorous home, it lands on me to build something new. Between that and hours spent here, I barely have time to breathe."

"That is a lot to take on," Rhoco commiserated on Carrick's behalf.

"I'm so overwhelmed, I almost bear-hugged a poisonous cactus while collecting materials to rebuild the walls. Lucky for me, Rubi shouted in warning before I made contact, but still. Close call."

Rhoco was not particularly interested in hearing the details, but he let Carrick carry on without interrupting. Graciously, he listened as Carrick somehow managed to talk about his unfortunate predicament for the duration of their shift.

The walls of desert huts were cacti; the inside portions were de-thorned and the roof was made of braided tumbleweed. Most desert huts were made of similar materials. They were easier to build than the sand dune homes, but equally dangerous. While sand dunes occasionally collapsed on young Bouldes, burying them alive, those who built cacti huts risked choosing poisonous varieties. Even if they did avoid the lethal breeds, all cacti in Orewall sprouted titanium thorns that ripped through Boulde flesh at the slightest touch. They varied in width and length, but all were capable of harm. Young Bouldes were inevitably pierced multiple times while digging up and replanting cacti for their walls, and if they weren't careful, a simple prick from a poisonous thorn would be their demise. Those who survived the bloody piercings were forever left with the marks of their labor. One could always tell who lived in the desert by the scars they wore.

Carrick not only had marks on his hands, but also on his forearms, chest, and stomach. It appeared as though his young, strong self had used his entire body to relocate his cacti. The marks from his younger days were healed and glossy now, but Rhoco winced every time the sun reflected off Carrick's scars.

After all of Carrick's oversharing, Rhoco wondered if he should tell his workmate about his own trials. He suspected Carrick went on so excessively about his hut in hopes that

Rhoco would reciprocate by divulging what he had going on, but Rhoco wasn't ready to share, so the topic went unaddressed.

Bouldes were taught that prying into the lives of others was offensive and distasteful. This social taboo meant that everyone minded their own business and kept to themselves, except for Cybelle, of course, who poked into everybody's business.

Rhoco used to like it this way, but now wondered if this custom made the Bouldes hardhearted and ignorant. After finding the heart, hearing Cybelle's account of the war, and reading just a small section of *Beyond Orewall*, he realized a wealth of knowledge was yet to be discovered. This world was much more interesting than he ever fathomed. They *should* be asking questions and taking an interest in the world around them, be it their neighbors or those in far-off lands. Living simply was fine, but it was no excuse for ignorance.

Rhoco recognized his growth; his mind was expanding. A few weeks ago, he would have cursed such a complex revelation, but now that he was thrust into the truth, he accepted the shift in his outlook with gratitude.

When they left the mines, Carrick ran ahead without saying goodbye. He had a hut to rebuild.

The Murks kept their eyes glued to Rhoco as he departed. He could sense their glowing glares of mistrust and dislike on his back. Though their overall disposition toward him was negative, he detected a sense of wonder too. They were curious about what he kept hidden and what could inspire a dense, simple-minded Boulde to leave the comfort of home—they wanted to know what kind of object could send a man made of stone out to sea.

Rhoco was starved. Nothing tasted better than swamp squirrel, so he detoured to the marsh before returning home.

Catching rodents there was easy, as places for them to hide were few.

All life scattered as he arrived. He approached the nearest tree, which was skinny and brittle. Once next to it, he stood as still as possible, becoming a stone statue, and after a patient wait, life returned. Bugs crawled out from the mud and from under leaves, birds in the highest branches resumed their songs, and mice left their hiding places among the tall blades of grass.

A scrawny squirrel crawled from the hollowed-out center of the tree next to Rhoco. He hoped a better-fed member of the pack would emerge, but when no others left the tree, he broke his statuesque pose and seized the squirrel by the tail. He held the critter at eye level—close enough to examine his meal, yet far enough so its flailing claws could not scratch his face. It was skinny, with little meat on its bones to eat, but he likely scared the other squirrels into hiding for the remainder of the day.

With a shrug of resignation, he used his thumbs to restrain the squirrel's limbs and bit off its head. A quick death.

Rhoco spit the head into the marsh and trudged through the shin-deep water. He picked the squirrel apart as he went, starting at the neck and peeling off its fur-covered skin like a banana as he worked his way down its body. He sucked every morsel of meat from the critter and chucked the squirrel's tiny bones over his shoulder after he had licked them clean. Just as he suspected, there was minimal meat, so he consumed the nutrient-rich blood as well, despite its foul taste.

When he reached the rocky beach in front of his home, all that remained of the squirrel was its skin and tail. He contemplated throwing the carcass over a fire and eating it later, then imagined all the fur inside his mouth. The thought made him gag, so he tossed the carcass into the ocean. His face and hands were still covered in blood, so he knelt on the sand and let the waves wash him clean. The blood cleared, staining the water temporarily as it was carried away. No one would ever know.

A desperate excitement plagued the air inside his house; the heart was happy he was back. Rhoco walked over to the mantel and exhaled deeply. The complex emotions he experienced in the short time since the heart washed ashore were more than he felt in his entire lifetime. Though he recognized some noticeable good in this forced awakening, his mental exhaustion often overshadowed the glimmers of progress he saw within himself.

The heart craved his attention, but he could not provide. He was drained, with no patience for its suffocating needs. When he turned to walk away, the room iced over. His breath became visible and the temperature was so cold he felt its chill through his stone flesh.

"Relax. I have a plan," he told the heart over his shoulder. It intensified the freeze in response. Rhoco's dolomite teeth rattled with a shiver. "I'm going to take you home."

The heart contemplated his announcement, but as it considered the meaning of his offer, the cold got worse. The sediment between Rhoco's joints froze, trapping him in place.

"Please stop," Rhoco begged before his mouth froze shut too.

The heart delayed for a moment before it conceded, releasing him and his home from its consuming grip.

As soon as Rhoco thawed, he rubbed his kneecaps and elbows until the tingling sensation disappeared. He glared over his shoulder at the heart.

"You need to stop attacking me. I'm on your side. You should be grateful." The heart pulsated a faint glow. "If you had bonded to any other Boulde you'd be smashed to pieces by now. To be honest, I don't know how I've controlled my temper this long, but I have, and you ought to be thankful. See the dents in the walls? All created by me." He held up clenched fists. "My patience is short and I don't like to be bothered. I should've left you on the beach, but I didn't, for reasons still unknown to me."

He approached the heart and leaned in close. "Whoever is listening, either the lady in that vision or some other source of power, I hope you can hear me because my tolerance for your games is at an all-time low," he seethed, clouding the glass with his breath. "I can't do magic, but I sure as hell can use my fists. I want to help you, but if you threaten me with violent hexes again, I will obliterate you."

The heart went black. Nothing radiated from it—neither anger nor understanding. It was blank. Rhoco preferred a docile heart and accepted its lack of response as an improvement.

He retreated to the cellar to sleep.

Morning arrived and he missed his first opportunity to start work on his pumice boat. Though the heart was plainly visible on the mantel when he walked up the cellar stairs and into his kitchen, the space between them was vacant; the energy of their bond was missing.

"Good morning," Rhoco growled, aggravated and confused.

The heart remained black.

He marched over to it, frustrated that it ignored him.

"Anybody home?" he asked, peering into the glass. The darkness remained, as did its sudden emptiness.

Rhoco did not understand the change. Before last night, he could not escape the heart's suffocating presence, no matter how angry he was. Even when he buried it, he still could not evade its grip. But now, the heart seemed vacant, which only infuriated him further. *He* should have the upper hand after all the harm the heart had caused, yet he still floundered beneath its will.

He grumbled under his breath and surrendered, then stormed out of his house to escape the tension. Though he recognized that the heart had taken over his home and that he shouldn't be the one to leave, he did so anyway. Rhoco was stuck in a strange place between who he was and who he was becoming. The heart kept him in a constant state of confusion.

He decided to walk along the east shore to assess its layout and see what he'd be dealing with when he visited in the early morning hours. He never bothered walking the shoreline before; he did enough walking to and from the mines every few days.

When he arrived, he was surprised to see no shoreline, just tall, jagged cliffs with ocean water crashing against its walls. Obsidians from the Royal Guard were stationed at the top of the cliff, heads turned toward the horizon. They weren't guarding the shore from the civilians of Orewall, they were guarding their borders from outsiders. A few weeks ago, Rhoco would not have understood why they faced east, but after seeing the map, he realized the most powerful lands resided in that direction.

He opted not to scale the rocky hill that would bring him to the ledge where the guards stood. There was no point. Instead, he turned around and went home. His reconnaissance was futile; the tides were too high.

When he arrived home, Cybelle was waiting by his door.

"Have you reconsidered your foolish idea?"

"No."

He gently pushed past her to unlock the door, and she followed him inside.

"You ought to."

The house was vacant. The heart was still avoiding him.

"Stop pestering me," Rhoco demanded with more anger than he actually felt toward Cybelle's incessant presence. The heart's stubborn behavior was getting to him and he hated that he missed its company. "Your interest in my life is unnatural, you know."

"Your life is unnatural, hence my interest."

"I have a plan. Just leave me be."

Cybelle huffed in aggravation, but resigned from sharing any additional opinions on the matter. When Rhoco happily accepted her silence, she marched out of his home as boldly as her old knees allowed.

She left the door open behind her, so Rhoco closed it, locking the bolt and closing the small, grated window. He was separated from the outside world, secluded with only the heart as a companion. When he glanced at the mantel, the heart remained dark and vacant. He cursed beneath his breath before turning toward the door to leave again.

He headed for the marsh, deciding a healthy dose of swamp squirrel would settle his temper. When he arrived, he did not stand still and wait for the animals to drop their guard. Instead, he trudged through the murky water, directly toward the tree where the squirrels hid, and reached his arm into the trunk to snatch the first body he connected with.

The fat squirrel squirmed in his grip and the others clawed at his skin, hoping he would drop their friend, but he could not feel their tiny lashings. All that mattered was the meaty creature he pulled from the tree trunk. It bit his finger, so he bit off its head. The critters inside the tree mourned in a chorus of squeaks as Rhoco spit the head into the swamp waters. He sat on a mushy mound and devoured the squirrel right in front of them.

Blood covered his face as he sloppily ate the animal, bones and all. His temper was inflamed and the only remedy was destruction. The squirrel served as a calming agent; the harsher its death, the better he felt. No matter how sick and twisted the cure was, it always worked.

By the time he had nothing left in his grip but a bushy tail, his anger had subsided. He inhaled deeply, returning to the present and assessing the damage he caused. A group of squirrels sat on the highest branch, looking down on him. They watched as he ate their friend.

"Sorry," he mumbled up at them. "I lost my head for a minute."

He tossed the tail into the marsh. He was thankful squirrels couldn't speak, otherwise, his indiscretions would have been reported to the Royals by now. Usually, he was far more cautious when he ate meat, as he didn't want to get caught, but today was different. His frustration was too great to use caution. He needed to eat; he needed to heal. The heart had control over him, even in its absence.

The situation baffled Rhoco, and now that he was calm and could think clearly, it made no sense. He should be happy that the heart chose to leave him alone, but instead, he was scorned and bitter. He shook the feeling, burying it temporarily.

He returned home, ready to ignore all the unwarranted disdain projected his way, but he found ignoring the heart was impossible. Instead, he sat in silence for hours, staring at the heart, willing it to break, channelling more stubborn frustration at it than it could possibly return. The longer he sat there, behaving like a fool, the more he wanted to smash the heart with his fist. He wasn't sure what stopped him.

When night fell, he relented, unsure who won the battle. He suspected the heart was the victor since it still sat in muted contempt, but he refused to admit defeat to an object that in any other scenario would be inanimate.

Moonset was only two hours away and his timeframe to begin building his boat was approaching. Rhoco grabbed his pickaxe and laced his boots.

"Maybe I won't come back," he threatened the heart, breaking the silence between them, but it remained black. Then, as he turned toward the door, the heart pulsated the faintest red and its phantom tentacles seized his heart. It latched back onto him, begging him not to leave. Magic yanked him back into the room and the air reeked of desperation and fear.

"I forgive you," he reassured the heart.

Its grip loosened.

Rhoco departed with more confidence in his control over the situation. He was treading in uncharted waters, but something in its depth felt familiar. He was doing the right thing, he was sure of it, and no amount of backlash from the heart would stop him from doing what was best for them both.

Chapter 11

Rhoco arrived at the east shore right before moonset. The guards were gone and the ocean had receded. A large stretch of rocky terrain replaced the waves and Rhoco climbed down the shortest side of the cliff to explore.

The Murks were right; the ground was pure pumice and rhyolite. Rhoco gazed toward the distant sea, wondering where the volcano that produced this solid rock was located. The earth beneath the ocean on this side of Orewall was pure rock with no sand or pebbles like his shore, and the natural phenomenon baffled him. No one had ever spoken of a volcano or its proximity, and he wondered if it was close enough to cause the Bouldes harm one day. Glancing up at the cliff wall behind him, he supposed its height kept them safe when the lava flowed their way.

Large, rectangular ditches indicated where the Murks had previously dug up stone blocks to carve into Royal Guard boats. Rhoco detached his pickaxe from his back and struck the ground near the edge of an old cavity.

His heavy and powerful hit only made a small dent in the rock. Confused, he tried again, striking the rock with greater force, but his effort yielded the same result. With a sigh, he continued making tiny dents, outlining the area he wished to remove.

By the time he finished marking his work area, the sky began to lighten. The sun was about to rise and his time was up. With minimal time separating moonset from sunrise each day, Rhoco feared it would take months before he had a boat ready to sail.

He didn't want to stop working, but the tide already shifted and the lapping waves now reached his work area. When he made his final strike of the night, the water touched his feet.

He glanced at the top of the highest cliff, but no guards were in sight. He swung his pickaxe over his shoulder, walked to the southern side of the cliff where the incline was less steep, and climbed. By the time he scaled the boulders and reached the top, the sun was already peeking over the horizon. Its yellow and orange glow illuminated the black ocean and the glare off its ice-like surface was blinding. Rhoco turned away and headed home.

Each night not spent at the mines was spent at the east shore carving out his chunk of rock. He was unsure where he'd store the massive rock after he finished extracting it, but he had time to figure it out. Invigorated by spontaneity, Rhoco questioned how he survived so long in his old, mundane routine. The mere memory of his old life before the heart's arrival bored him, and when the carrier cardinal arrived two days later, he begrudgingly put his project on hold to fulfill his duty as a citizen of Orewall.

The mines felt more claustrophobic than usual. What was once a comfortable routine now felt like a suffocating prison. Rhoco supposed the change might stem from his new outlook on everything. He was finally living for something greater, reaching for more than what was given. His hopes were bigger than these walls and his eagerness to leave and return to his mission was overwhelming. The confinements were unwelcome, but he worked without complaint.

Carrick hammered nearby. He hadn't asked about the boat, but Rhoco could tell he wanted to. He contemplated updating him, but opted to wait. He didn't want to drag others into his mission for fear they'd rat him out, or worse, ask to join. He didn't want any tagalongs when the departure date arrived.

Carrick mostly talked about the cacti hut he was building. It was fixed and the one he was building for Rubi was nearly complete. Carrick spoke with pride regarding his progress. He was proud of all he accomplished, especially since his lover was nearing her due date. This hut would shelter his baby, and though he would not live with them, he wanted to give them the best home possible.

The Murks watched him closely throughout the shift, but maintained their distance. Their suspicions were high, and though they greatly mistrusted the whole endeavor, their curiosity was undeniable. Rhoco could detect the willpower they exerted while withholding their questions. They wanted to approach, wanted to pry into his progress, but they restrained themselves from revealing their interest. Intrigue was a weakness and they would not let Rhoco gain the upper hand.

After Carrick divulged all he possibly could about his home reconstruction and Rubi's pregnancy woes, he went silent. The remainder of the forty-eight hours in the mine passed without much conversation at all.

When the final whistle rang, Carrick darted to the front of the exit line. Rhoco held back in order to avoid the chaos. The Fused pushed and shoved to leave first and the Hematites intervened with their whips to break up the frays. Rhoco did not want to cause any trouble, or be reprimanded for others' tempers, so he waited his turn.

He started his walk through the desert surrounded by a pack of miners making their way home, and the farther he traveled, the less he was surrounded by others. The size of the caravan dwindled as individuals broke off from the main path. By the time Rhoco reached the edge of the desert, he was alone. Carrick ran ahead hours ago and the few miners who lived in the dunes had already dispersed toward their sections of the shore.

Rhoco arrived home to the heart: his dark and forbidden secret. After spending several dozen hours confined with simple and unsuspecting Bouldes, he grasped the magnitude of what he kept hidden. His life had taken a wild turn, one that most wouldn't understand, and he was in the middle of a transformation he still had yet to fully appreciate.

The heart welcomed him home with a faint red glow that simmered in the darkness of his tiny living room. He paused to greet it briefly, then went right into the cellar to sleep.

He had no alarm, so he rustled awake often to check the moon's position. When it finally appeared to be setting, he emerged and left for the east shore.

The indentations from his previous work were still there but were now smoothed over by the ocean. This meant he'd need to trace the outline again and redo what he had already done. The four hours passed too fast, and when the sun began to rise, Rhoco felt like he barely accomplished anything. He cursed as the waves touched his feet and he was forced to quit for the day.

This project would take forever if he didn't find a way to make faster progress each night.

When he returned the following night, he was armed with the energy provided by five squirrels. He worked hard and fast, deepening his outline by a few inches. Progress.

His final night at the east shore before returning to the mines for two days was sluggish; his over-indulgence in squirrel meat had caught up to him. He was angry with himself for making such a foolish mistake, but he performed through the stomachache. Though he made less headway than the night before, he hoped he was carving the lines deep enough that the ocean wouldn't erase them again.

The moon had almost disappeared beyond the cliffs when Rhoco sensed he was being watched. His nerves stiffened.

"Who's there?" he shouted into the darkness, but received no reply. "I demand that you show yourself," he continued.

He raised his pickaxe and marched toward the shadows, ready to strike the moment the spy was revealed.

"Slow down there, little sludge," a familiar, hoarse voice called from the darkness.

"Cybelle?" Rhoco asked, bewildered. He lowered his weapon.

"Yeah, ya brute," she said as she exited the shadows. "I told you the squirrels would turn you savage."

"I haven't eaten a squirrel in months," he lied. "You can't just sneak around on a person and expect them not to defend themselves."

"I had to know what you were up to. Looks like you're trying to *build* a boat?"

"It's none of your business."

"I suppose that's wiser than trying to steal one, but at the rate you're moving, it'll take you years to finish this project."

"Great, you got your wish. No need to spy on me any longer."

"Of course I still need to. What if the guards catch you one day? Someone needs to know what became of you."

"I'm not your child. Stop mothering me." Cybelle pursed her lips, offended, and Rhoco realized he hit a nerve, so he continued more carefully. "How about instead of spying on me, you act as a lookout so I *don't* get caught. Then you'd actually be of good use."

Cybelle shrugged. "I don't want to get too involved."

Rhoco shot her a nasty glare of disbelief, but Cybelle paid him no mind. She was very aware of her actions and felt no need to address his cynicism.

"How many nights have you lurked in the shadows, spying on me?"

"The past three. Just goes to show how terrible you are at sneaking about. I have no doubt the guards will stop your foolish mission before you finish building that boat."

"So you're rooting against me?"

"You'll be better off in prison than out at sea."

"Rotten," Rhoco spat, then picked up his pace and left her behind.

"I know more than you!" she called after him. "What lies beyond Orewall will do you no favors. Returning that heart is a fool's errand and I'm just trying to prevent you from being the fool."

Rhoco ignored her.

When the carrier cardinal arrived the following morning, he obliged begrudgingly.

Halfway through the shift, Pedr approached while the Hematites patrolled a different corridor.

"You're a slow builder," the Murk hissed.

"How would you know?" Rhoco asked, startled.

"You're still here."

"I'm new to boat-building."

Carrick overheard and couldn't suppress his mounting curiosity any longer.

"Now you're *building* a boat?" Carrick asked in disbelief. "I thought you were going to steal one."

"I decided against that and opted to build my own."

"But are you, *really*?" Pedr asked, remaining in a shadow.

"I'm making progress." Rhoco's defenses were up. He didn't like that Pedr doubted his ability.

"If you say so."

Pedr walked away and Rhoco realized that he did not understand the Murk's motives. Pedr offered him no help, even though he knew he'd only learn Rhoco's secret after a boat was built and ready to sail. Maybe they didn't take him seriously, or thought he'd give up before he ever finished.

"I can help you," Carrick offered.

"You have a cacti hut to focus on."

"That's almost done."

Rhoco observed the fresh wounds covering Carrick's glossed-over scars, surprised he was considering the offer at all.

"If I get caught, I don't want you to go down with me."

Carrick shrugged. "That doesn't concern me too much." Then he sighed heavily. "I've been thinking a lot since we talked at the Murk lashing. What you said makes a lot of sense and I've been finding it hard to enjoy this complacent life. There's more to live for, to fight for, I'm certain of that, and I'd happily risk my life for an adventure."

Rhoco sympathized with this sentiment, but the secret he held was too dear; he still desired to conceal the heart's existence.

"What about your baby? It will be here soon."

"Might hurt less to abandon it if I never get to meet it at all."

Rhoco understood the rationale, but hesitated. "I'm not sure."

"Well, if you ever change your mind, you know where to find me. If you don't want to tell me what the boat is for, I swear not to ask questions. I'm more interested in the thrill of doing something forbidden."

"I'll think it over."

Carrick nodded and returned to work. They hammered the wall in silence and departed after their shift without any further mention of the boat.

When he returned to the east shore, his previous work was not ruined at all. In fact, the trenches appeared slightly deeper. He looked around, confused.

A song echoed through the sky and he snapped around to find Cybelle strolling along the edge of the cliff. She whistled a melody as she located a spot where she could comfortably watch over Rhoco.

He got to work, perplexed by the old lady's stubbornness. At the end of the shift, he waited for Cybelle to meet him at the base of the cliff.

"Thanks for acting as a lookout," he said.

"What are you talking about? The air is just fresher up there."

"Why can't you just admit that you're helping me?"

"Because I'm not," she insisted.

"I suppose you also didn't help keep my trenches carved while I was in the mines?"

"Of course I didn't."

"Then who did?"

"You really have no sense of your surroundings. Haven't you noticed the Murk who's been watching you every night?"

"A Murk?"

"Yes, he hides in the shadows, studying your every move." Rhoco stared at her, astonished. She went on, "Your obliviousness is how I know the outside world will eat you alive."

"Why didn't you tell me last time?"

"Because the Murk poses no threat. He's the one who helped keep your trenches fresh."

"How many?"

"Just one."

Rhoco looked over his shoulder, but saw no one. It couldn't have been Pedr; he never left the mines, nor did the others he worked beside. Why would a Murk help him? And why was this individual staying hidden?

He returned to the east shore each night and hammered away from moonset to sunrise with no sign of the snooping Murk. His progress remained slow and he considered asking Carrick for help when he saw him again.

The sun crested over the horizon, indicating it was time to leave. He turned toward the cliff wall, saw Cybelle leaving her post atop the highest ledge, and prepared to depart too, but when his gaze lowered, a blur darted past in his peripheral. He tried to identify the source, but it moved too fast and disappeared into a cave he hadn't noticed before at the bottom of the cliff. Rhoco was certain it was the Murk who had been spying on him and he wondered if Pedr put the sneaky fellow up to the task.

Rhoco cursed himself for revealing his plans to so many individuals. He would have to work faster so he could depart before anyone divulged his plans to the wrong person.

Chapter 12

Back at the mines, Rhoco kept a close eye on the Murks. He didn't like that they were sneaking around behind his back, spying on him. He considered confronting them about it, but never found an opportunity to hash it out with them privately. The Hematites rarely left their corridor and a group of older Fused were stationed directly beside the Murks on this particular shift. The tanzanite mines were tight and narrow, so there was very little space to spread out.

When the shift passed without the much-needed discussion, Rhoco decided he would confront whoever hid in the shadows when he returned to the east shore.

After taking a brief nap in his cellar, he woke in the wee hours of morning to resume his work. Just like last time, the trenches were not smoothed over by the waves.

"Who's out there?" Rhoco shouted into the darkness.

He received no reply except the echo of his own voice bouncing off the cliff walls.

Then he looked up and saw Cybelle pointing toward a dark corner of the cavern. Rhoco raised his pickaxe and walked in that direction.

"I don't want to hurt you, I just need to know who you are," he warned as he trekked slowly toward the spy's location. He stopped where the moonlight drew a line on the land. Whoever was there remained hidden in the shadow of the cliff.

"Come out, or I'll charge," he advised.

As Rhoco crouched, preparing to attack, he heard movement in the darkness.

"Show yourself," he demanded.

A skinny, mud-colored body limped out of the shadows with its arms overhead to protect itself from Rhoco's rage.

Pickaxe raised, Rhoco examined the spy.

It was a male Murk, much scrawnier than those he'd met in the mines, and one he did not recognize.

"What's your name?"

"Feodras," the Murk sniveled. He appeared far more timid and scared than the Murks Rhoco knew.

"How did you know I'd be here?"

"I heard rumors," Feodras explained, continuing to cower beneath Rhoco's raised weapon. Rhoco lowered his pickaxe, realizing the Murk was not a physical threat.

"Do the Murks in the mines know you're here helping me?"

Feodras shook his head. "They cannot be trusted." He then stepped forward to hand Rhoco a tool he'd never seen before. Rhoco stared at it for a moment before Feodras snatched it out of his grip.

The Murk lowered himself to his hands and knees and rapidly jabbed the tiny tool into the ground. He leaned in as he worked, moving the tool in short strokes. After a moment, he sat back so Rhoco could see his progress.

Amazed at the depth Feodras had carved in such a brief amount of time, Rhoco joined the Murk on his knees. Feodras handed him the tool, which he examined closely.

"Is this made of cacti thorns?" Rhoco asked.

Feodras nodded.

Rhoco studied the tool. "Of course titanium cacti points would work better on the rock than my steel pickaxe. Is there a diamond coating over the gathered thorns?"

Feodras nodded again.

"Thanks for sharing this with me."

Feodras said nothing and Rhoco got to work. Bouldes were strong enough to use chisels without the aid of a hammer, so Rhoco used his arm strength to propel the tool in and out of the stone.

When the sun began to rise, his usual progress had been doubled. He sighed with relief; this project wouldn't take nearly as long as he feared. He turned to thank Feodras, but the Murk was already scurrying toward the cave tucked within the cliff wall. He disappeared into his dwelling before Rhoco could express his gratitude.

114

"Don't worry, he'll be back," Cybelle shouted as she strolled away from her lookout spot to join Rhoco.

"Have you ever seen a tool like this before?" Rhoco held up the unpolished, yet effective, chisel.

"Murks have all sorts of tricks. They're a resourceful batch of Bouldes."

Rhoco agreed and secured the chisel into the waistband of his pants, point up so that it did not tear apart the skin on his thigh.

The following night, Feodras returned with a second chisel and helped Rhoco carve.

"What's this tool called?"

Feodras ignored him.

"You don't talk much," Rhoco noted before returning to work.

A few moments later, Feodras spoke.

"Cachise," he said.

"What?"

"Cachise." Feodras held up the cacti-point chisel.

"I see."

Feodras dropped his gaze and continued hammering his cachise into the stone. They were moving along nicely and it would only take a few more shifts before the block could be removed.

On Rhoco's final night off before he needed to return to the mines, he and Feodras began hammering into the base of the block, separating it from the surrounding pumice and rhyolite. They freed a third of the block before the water began to rise, flooding the cracks of the block and forcing them to leave.

Feodras hurried back to his cave without saying farewell and Rhoco walked to the south and met Cybelle back on the main land.

"I did some digging," she confessed.

"Of course you did."

She ignored his cynicism. "The Murks are divided into work forces, just like the Fused and chosen Fused. Your buddy Feodras is a carver. Carvers build boats for the Royal Guard and deliver them to the kingdom docks along the north shore. When the need for boats is low, as it is now, they are assigned to carving tasks within the kingdom."

"Why is he helping me though? I don't understand."

"That, I cannot answer."

"The Murks in the mines gave me no indication that they knew I was being spied on. I thought maybe they set him up to help move my progress along since they want to know my secret so bad. Don't they communicate within their group? Or is Feodras truly working alone?"

"You plan to tell them about the heart before you leave?"

"It was part of the deal. They help me find a way to depart and I reveal *why* I am leaving. They traded their secret for mine."

"Unfair trade if you ask me. Sure, they told you *where* to build your boat, but they left you to do the work all by yourself. I wouldn't tell them anything if I were you."

"I'll be gone, what does it matter if they know?"

"You never plan to come back?"

"Sure I do."

"Well, they could do a lot of damage if they tell the wrong person about the heart while you're gone."

Rhoco paused; he hadn't thought of that.

Cybelle continued, "You might be better off never coming back if that happens. Assuming the ocean or sea bandits don't kill you first, you'll likely come home and be sent straight to the river."

She was right.

"Maybe I won't tell them."

"I wouldn't. You have plenty of time before you finish your boat. Think up a crafty lie."

They walked without talking for a while. Cybelle broke the silence as they reached her home.

"How's the heart?"

"Fine."

It wasn't a lie. The magic the heart used against him had mellowed and he was always at the mines, the east shore, or sleeping, so he hadn't spent much time with it lately.

"Of course it's fine," Cybelle retorted. "It's got you as its slave and has you risking your life to carry it home."

"This was my choice, not the heart's."

"Don't be a fool. You said it yourself, it gave you no other choice."

"I want to help," Rhoco insisted.

"You're brainwashed."

"You don't know what I know."

"Then tell me."

"You'd never understand."

"Try me," Cybelle dared him.

"I said, no!"

"You're a coward."

Cybelle stormed off, hobbling away on creaky knees.

Rhoco seethed internally, unapologetic for keeping the vision the heart shared a secret. It was none of Cybelle's business. He never asked her to get involved.

He marched into his home and approached the heart. It glowed fondly at his return. Despite his aggravation, he picked it up carefully so his rough touch would not create new cracks, then sat with it in his lap.

118

"Who are you?" he asked, his palms secured to the glass casing, hoping it might show him more. It merely glowed brighter in response.

"A name would help."

Nothing.

He exhaled heavily, ready to surrender, when the heart's casing latched to his skin, just as it had last time. When his sight went black, he braced himself, unsure what was to come.

He stood in a gray room, naked and alone.

The woman from the last vision glided into view. Her eye sockets were empty holes filled with white light and a large fracture snaked down her bare, glass chest. Beneath the crack was a dark crater where her heart should have been. She seemed vacant, void of life.

Rhoco felt her gloom creep into him. He wanted to know the purpose of this vision, but all he received was an overwhelming grief he wished to escape.

Her empty eyes caught sight of him and their beams locked into his gaze. Her body slowly turned and glided toward him. She was neither alive nor dead, she was something in between.

When she reached him, she grabbed his hand and placed it on her naked chest. In this space, he felt everything. Every nerve in his body awoke and the smooth surface of her skin registered.

He attempted to stifle his arousal, but when she guided his hand over her breast and began moaning, it was impossible.

The woman moved his hand over the side of her ribcage and down to the small of her back. Then, she pressed their bare bodies together and the heat from the contact inflamed him to the core.

"What do you want from me?" he gasped between heavy breaths.

She traced her lips over his with the gentlest caress. Perceiving her tenderness, he wished to seize the moment, but restrained himself. He did not want to repeat old mistakes, even if this was only a dream. And though his primal urges were awakened, his logic sensed that none of this was real.

Despite the realization that this could end at any moment, he surrendered to her will. She invited him in and stimulated the entirety of his being.

Excitement aroused his senses as he realized he could not hurt her here, not in this safe space. For the first time, he felt connected to another soul without the dampening fear of breaking what he touched.

"Tell me what to do," he begged, unable to stop himself from pressing his body harder against hers. He had never before felt such ease in an intimate embrace.

"Drain me," she ordered. With her words came an immense sorrow that draped the moment and washed his senses cold.

"What do you mean?" he asked, releasing her and stepping back.

"Does my darkness frighten you?"

The shadows in the room intensified and the warmth they shared froze. It was a trick, a sick game, and he was the fool.

"Why did you do that to me?" he demanded.

"I want you. Come closer." The lights in her eyes captivated his heart; her body was the answer to all his urges.

He was tempted, he wanted her, but he could no longer lose himself in this false passion. As much as he wished it were real, it wasn't.

"Tell me what happened to you," Rhoco pleaded. *"Let me help."*

"You'll find those answers once you're inside me," she purred, grabbing his hand and placing it between her legs. His insides caved as his fingers touched her wet glass-flesh, and an uncontrollable heat radiated through his groin.

"I have to have you," he stammered, brain in a stupor.

He leaned in to kiss her and she was gone. Angry, embarrassed, and confused, his heart raced.

"What kind of game is this?" he shouted into the nothingness of the room. An omnipresent voice echoed in response.

"I carry the sorrow of a thousand souls. My darkness will swallow you whole."

Chapter 13

Reality returned and Rhoco fumed.

He returned the heart to the mantel and waited outside for the carrier cardinal. His confidence in the heart wavered; the last vision was an enormous tease, a game that he did not want to play.

Still, he could not deny that he enjoyed what the heart made him feel. Every past moment of intimacy paled in comparison to what the heart evoked. He actually *felt* her tender touch. He was inclined to hate the heart for this tantalizing bait, but couldn't. If anything, it made him more drawn to the heart.

Rhoco never realized how desperately he wished to feel something, to feel *anything*, again. He spent his youth forming mental callouses, numbing himself, and shunning every chance to feel, but when it came to the heart, he couldn't help but soften. He wasn't a wrecking machine, destroying everything in his path. He was not so hardened that he couldn't feel the world around him. He was changing for the better, and the intoxication of the tender moments was overwhelming. The heart, and all it offered, was worth fighting for.

When the carrier cardinal arrived, singing its summons, Rhoco departed. The long walk to the mines proved necessary, as he was still shaking the aroused tingle from his nerves. By the time he reached the entrance to the tanzanite mine, his stone-cold senses had returned.

"Any thoughts on my offer?" Carrick said as he approached from behind. It was unlike him to pry and the uncomfortable nature of this question read plainly in his expression.

"I haven't thought much about it."

"Well, are you making good progress?"

Rhoco glanced over his friend's shoulder to make sure no Murks were around to overhear.

"Lately, yes. A Murk has been helping."

"Which one?" Carrick squinted into the darkness, looking for the group of Murks they worked with.

"No, not one of them. A Murk from a different group that carves for the Royal Guard. He's letting me borrow his tools, which work much better for a task like this than my pickaxe."

"So you don't need my help?" Carrick looked disappointed.

Rhoco sighed, then reluctantly replied.

"If you want to see what I am building, come to the east shore right after moonset. Not a minute earlier, or the guards might see you."

Carrick's expression lifted. "I'll be careful. Don't worry. I won't mess this up for you."

Rhoco hoped that inviting another to join him wasn't a terrible mistake, but excluding Carrick from what might be the only excitement he'd ever experience felt cruel.

They began work extracting blue tanzanite for the royal nursery. The prince would arrive in a few months and the miners had been digging for gems to decorate the child's bedroom since the pregnancy announcement. Rhoco hoped he was gone by the time the little boy arrived and that the thrill surrounding the birth of a new prince would prevent anyone from noticing his absence.

After the last vision, he was more eager than ever to meet the heart's owner. He hoped that after he restored her heart, she'd remember him and the bond they shared.

His deepest desire was that she'd be willing to make him feel something again, a sensation as strong as what she manifested in his mind, but he kept that wish buried, aware that what they shared in the visions was not real and that the living, breathing woman on the other end might not desire such intimacy with him.

Still, the fire of her touch lived on inside.

Bedros rounded the corner and cracked his whip against Rhoco's back. The stinging pain snapped Rhoco out of his wandering thoughts, which had brought his work to a temporary stop.

"No breaks allowed," he bellowed before lashing Rhoco a second time. Green blood poured from the new wound on his shoulder.

He raised his pickaxe and slammed it against the wall. A large chunk of grainy tanzanite crumbled to the ground. Bedros retrieved the piece, grunting with approval, then tossed it into Rhoco's wheelbarrow. The Hematite walked away, looking for another worker to torture.

When the ending whistle blew, the group was more weary than usual. They had hammered straight through the forty-eight hour shift with no breaks and the exit was painful and sluggish.

Unfortunately, their shift was not yet over. Though they were not always tasked with bringing their hauls to Amesyte Valley, when the loads were as large as they were today, their shifts extended. The Fused miners wheeled the heavy tanzanite haul to the guards manning the southeast entrance into the valley. Only after the load was inspected and approved and the guards had transported the rocks inside were the miners free to leave. As always, this exchange added an extra two hours to their shift and Rhoco's walk home would now take even longer. He'd barely get any sleep before he needed to return to his work at the east shore.

"I'll see you later," Carrick said at a low volume when they reached the edge of the desert, then turned and headed for his cacti hut.

When Rhoco reached his dune, he decided to nap atop the grassy knoll instead of sleeping inside. Though the heart provided him with marvelous growth, he was still hesitant to get too close too frequently. His guard disintegrated in its presence and he did not yet trust who he was without his shield, nor did he trust or understand the heart's mysterious motives. He wanted to remain in control, and if that meant keeping the heart at a distance, then that was what he would do. The heart bonded to him and meant him no harm, but the woman in the vision wallowed in anguish. She appeared hopeless and counteracted her despair with bizarre and destructive behavior. Though he craved another vision like the last, he needed to focus on his immediate task.

His priorities were straight, his intentions pure. Another bout of unrestrained desire would serve no favors to either of them. The woman, though stubborn and despondent, needed his help, so he could not let any distractions prevent him from saving her life.

Sleeping atop the dune made it easy to detect moonset. When the moon began to fall, he rose and headed toward the east shore.

His unlikely crew of helpers waited for him. Cybelle sat at the highest peak, legs dangling over the edge, Feodras was in the ravine hard at work, and Carrick waited where the cliff's decline met the shore.

"I was a little early, but there were no guards in sight," Carrick explained.

"No need to worry, my other 'helpers' are already here too." He tried not to sound aggravated, but he could not shake his persistent desire to do this alone. He swallowed the irritation, aware that they each served a valuable purpose.

"Feodras," Rhoco said to the Murk, "Meet Carrick. He is here to help."

Feodras looked up at Carrick, blinked a few times while inspecting the newcomer's appearance, and then returned his attention to the rock.

"Feodras doesn't like to talk," Rhoco explained.

Carrick accepted the Murk's silence and let Rhoco explain the project. They didn't have an extra cachise for him, so he hammered away with his pickaxe. Still, the extra set of hands proved useful because by the time the water began to rise, the block was detached from the terrain.

The following night, they combined their Boulde strength to relocate the pumice and rhyolite block into Feodras's cave. The ceilings were high, with a manhole in the center to let light in, and the floor was elevated, so they did not have to worry that the ocean water would drown them when the tides changed. Though the water would not reach the platform, it would surely block the exit, so Rhoco and Carrick departed when the water trickled in.

Cybelle waited for them at the base of the cliff.

"Halfway there," she commented, trying to mask her disappointment.

"Your duty as lookout will be over soon."

"These assumptions that I'm your lookout are dangerously inaccurate. You ought to know that I take naps while you work."

"That's great," Rhoco retorted sarcastically, though he knew she was lying.

"I have to run ahead," Carrick explained. "I'm almost done with Rubi's hut."

"Okay, thanks for your help," Rhoco said.

"I'll be back tomorrow," Carrick promised, then darted forward.

"How nice," Cybelle commented. "A young Boulde with friends."

"He's just attending to his responsibilities."

"At least he allots time for others. I have to seek you out if I want a moment of your company."

"Sorry for being so awful."

Cybelle huffed at his stubborn sarcasm; they both knew how much they cared for each other.

"How's Almadine?" he asked. Though he did not regret rejecting her, he still thought about her often.

"You don't get to ask me about Almadine."

"Does she know I'm leaving?"

"Yes, I told her."

"She hasn't come to see me."

"Oh, do you miss her now that she's gone?"

The answer was yes, but he'd never say that out loud.

"I just thought she'd visit to say goodbye."

"Why should she? You've been rotten to her every other time she's stopped by."

"It's complicated."

"No, it's actually quite simple. You pushed her away and you're not allowed to want her back now that she's gone."

Cybelle was right and the weight of what he'd done to Almadine finally hit him.

"I might've loved her," he said, mostly to himself.

"There's no *might've* in love. You either do or you don't."

"Maybe I was wrong."

"She deserves better than maybe."

"You're right." Rhoco paused. "I don't think I know what love is."

"I think you do," she countered, glaring up at him knowingly.

Rhoco sighed.

Cybelle continued, "Don't let the lure of this heart fool you—it isn't real if it's only happening inside your head."

Cybelle marched away and Rhoco was left stunned—she really did know more than she revealed.

And it was true; what the heart offered wasn't real until its owner expressed the same sentiment. His feelings for the heart were created by magic, time, and illusions.

Rhoco was reminded that keeping his distance from the heart was imperative. He could not grow too fond of it. That was not the purpose of his quest. All his efforts were not an attempt to find love, they were an attempt to save a life.

He repeated this reminder silently until he was convinced.

Chapter 14

Rhoco and the others spent the next two nights inside the cave, carving the block of stone into a boat. Feodras had brought a third cachise for Carrick and took the lead. With chalk, he drew guidelines all over the block to indicate where Carrick and Rhoco should carve, and the men got to work.

By the end of the third night, the boat was beginning to take shape. Rhoco was pleased with their progress when they left at dawn and suspected it wouldn't be long before he could set sail.

Back at the topaz mines, the Murks hovered. Whenever Rhoco switched his workstation, the Murks followed. Halfway through the long shift, they finally confronted him.

"We heard you're nearly done," Pedr hissed between pickaxe blows. Rock dust clouded the space, entering their every orifice, but they'd grown accustomed to breathing soot.

"You heard wrong," Rhoco lied.

Dim torchlight flickered on Pedr's face, illuminating his suspicious glare. "I hope you haven't forgotten that you owe us a secret."

"I have months to go before I'll be done."

"That's not what the bees said."

"The bees?"

"The mud bees."

"You talk to bees?"

"We are keepers of the bees," Pedr explained with clear distaste for Rhoco's continued ignorance. "The queen resides safely underground with the Murks and her worker bees travel aboveground to collect pollen. We trade secrets for the queen's continued safety. They tell us what goes on aboveground, and we make sure the queen's labyrinth of tunnels in our walls remain untouched."

"You can talk to bees?" Rhoco repeated, incredulously.

Pedr was perturbed. "You're missing the point. The bees don't lie and they say you're almost done."

"Well, you must have interpreted this bee language wrong, because I'm *not* almost done. In fact, I'm so tired from working non-stop, I can't even see an end in sight."

"Welcome to the life of a Murk."

Rhoco thought of Feodras, who spent four hours helping him every night. "What about Murks in other professions?"

"How should I know? I haven't left the mines since I was assigned here as a young boy."

"Sorry."

"Don't do that," Pedr scoffed.

"What?"

"Apologize when you aren't sorry."

"I am though."

"I have eyes on you," Pedr threatened. "Your secret will be mine."

The Murk returned to his work.

Pedr's conniving temperament was a complete contrast from that of Feodras's. The carving Murk was quiet, focused, and hardworking. Though he was timid and scared, he was driven. He offered Rhoco help without asking for anything in return.

Rhoco made a mental note to watch for bees around his home. He did not need meddlesome bugs discovering the heart—that secret was still his to keep.

When the shift ended, Carrick found Rhoco after transferring his haul into the shared bin. A thick layer of rock dust masked the scars he had collected over the years.

"Did you see any bees flying around while we worked at the east shore?" Rhoco asked, rubbing mine grit out of his tired eyes.

"Bees? Do bees go near the ocean? I've only ever seen them around the wildflowers outside Amesyte Valley."

"Apparently the mining Murks have been spying on us through the bees."

"How? And why?"

"I promised to tell them *why* I was leaving if they told me *how* to leave. I never would have known to build from the rock beneath the ocean on the east shore if they hadn't told me, nor would I have known the safe times to carve."

"I see. Will you tell them?"

"No."

"They'll likely rat you out once you're gone. No one is allowed to leave Orewall. It's the law. They may not know why you left, but they can still tell King Alun that you built a boat using his rocks."

"Let them. I don't care."

"Aren't you planning on coming back?"

"That was the goal, but the more I think about it, the less possible it seems."

"Whatever you've kept hidden must be dangerous."

"It is, in its own way."

Carrick nodded, aware that Rhoco would reveal nothing more.

That night, instead of returning to his cacti hut, he joined Rhoco at the dunes. He slept atop the knoll, while Rhoco slept inside. When the moon began to set, Rhoco emerged and rustled Carrick awake, and together, they made their way to the east shore.

They arrived early, so they crouched behind a large boulder to spy on the Obsidian guards, who stood tall along the edge of the cliff. Their ebony-hued skin blended with the darkness of night and all that was visible in the remaining moonlight was the white paint smeared beneath their eyes. Around their torsos, each wore a salted, leather whip, which they were trained to use with skill.

As a young boy, Rhoco had witnessed two guards dueling and the way they made their leather dance was both beautiful and terrifying. With the right amount of force and a proper flick of the wrist, they could decapitate even the sturdiest Boulde.

When the guards finally left their posts, Rhoco and Carrick emerged from their hiding spot and climbed down the rocky hill to the ocean floor. The water had receded, revealing the ravine of pumice craters. They darted around the large holes and hurried to Feodras's cave.

Rhoco sprinted inside first with Carrick close behind. The Bouldes were big and strong, but not very agile, so their dash into the cave and subsequent climb took a toll. By the time they reached the top, they were winded.

"Feodras," Rhoco shouted into the darkness.

"Where'd all the light go?" Carrick asked. They both looked toward the cave ceiling and saw that the manhole that had previously let light in was now blocked.

A moment later, Feodras emerged from the depths carrying two torches. The space was illuminated and Rhoco was amazed at what the firelight revealed. The boat was nearly finished.

"Did you do this all on your own?" he asked.

Feodras nodded.

"Why?" Rhoco asked. Though he was grateful the ship was carved, he was also angry that Feodras continued without his supervision.

Feodras did not answer. Rhoco snatched a torch from the Murk and circled the boat, shining light over every inch to examine the result.

The stern was tall and rounded, thinning out as the back of the boat tapered. The bow also had height, but was square in shape. The wide bottom of the boat was deep, with more room than he'd need for a solo mission. The gunwales were high, so he could not see over and into the boat, but what he could see was the tall pole wrapped in a furry sail, as well as a covered platform that towered at the front of the boat.

"Will this float?"

Feodras nodded.

Rhoco's suspicions mounted to an all-time high when he noticed the beautiful, complex patterns and markings that covered the entire hull. The decorative addition was a true mark of Feodras's craftsmanship—but completely unnecessary. The detail was absurd for the purpose of his mission.

"Why did you do this?" Rhoco asked, pointing to the patterns. "It's too much."

Feodras did not reply.

Rhoco was fed up. "Why did you help me?"

"So I can leave, too." Feodras spoke for the first time since revealing his name.

"No. Absolutely not."

"But you wouldn't have this boat if it weren't for me," Feodras countered meekly. He was right, but Rhoco never asked for his help.

"You should have told me your intentions. If I knew the cost of your help, I would have refused."

Feodras remained timid, but resolute in his stance.

"This is my boat, too."

"What could you possibly want beyond the borders of Orewall?" Rhoco asked, "What's out there for you?"

"A place where I am welcome. I don't want to be a slave anymore."

"You'll be an outsider anywhere you go. What makes you think it will be any better out there?"

"It can't be worse than here."

"It very well might be. I am doing this because I *have* to, not because I *want* to."

A stubborn silence lingered between them and Feodras's eyes flickered with muted rage.

"I can turn this boat to dust just as fast as I made it," he threatened in a whisper.

The intensity startled Rhoco, forcing him to concede. "Fine. You can come, but don't get in my way. *I* am the captain."

Feodras nodded and scurried into the shadows.

"That was unexpected," Carrick chimed in.

"That was not part of the plan. I should've known better."

"It might be good to have a companion," Carrick offered with a shrug.

"A Murk?"

Carrick sighed in agreement. "What if you leave while he's sleeping?"

"I doubt he'll take his eye off this boat for one second. He'll destroy it if I try."

"True. Guess you have no choice but to take him."

"This is awful. He is sneaky and knows more about the workings of Namaté than I do. What if he outsmarts me and takes me off course in order to satisfy his own needs? This could alter my entire mission."

"I could join you," Carrick ventured. "To watch over Feodras and make sure he doesn't undermine you."

"You'd do that?"

"I've come to think this whole ordeal might be a death sentence, either out there or upon your return, but I've helped you this far and I'd like to see it through."

Rhoco hesitated. "I'd rather not drag you further into this mess."

"It's too late for that," Carrick laughed. "I still have little interest in whatever you're hiding and figure you'll tell me at some point if you want to."

"What I'm hiding might keep me stuck where we land. I might not want to come back to Orewall."

"If that's the case, then I'll return with Feodras. It's the adventure I seek."

Sensing that Rhoco still did not trust him, Carrick switched his stance to ground himself and raised clenched fists. "I'll make a dust pact to prove I'm trustworthy," he offered.

Rhoco never made a dust pact with anyone before. It was a serious commitment and he never had need for such a promise. Bouldes rarely made this vow, but when they did, it was understood that any agreement made was binding till death.

Rhoco mirrored Carrick's stance, prepared to make the pact. The men leaned in till their foreheads touched, and then connected, fists to fists. Once in position, both men pushed into the other with all their might, creating intense pressure at each point of contact. The force between them was strong, but neither budged, and they absorbed each other's strength despite the pain.

"Do you promise not to betray my secrets, those you currently know and those you may discover along the way?" Rhoco asked through clenched teeth.

"I promise not to betray you in any way, ever. Before, during, or after this quest, regardless what happens throughout," Carrick vowed. Sweat dripped down the side of his face. Their contact remained concentrated. "And I'll make sure Feodras doesn't stop you from getting where you want to go," he added.

"I promise the allegiance you show to me will be equally returned," Rhoco stated. "Pact sealed."

"Pact sealed."

The men broke apart, revealing rock dust in their previous spots of contact. The skin beneath each pressure point had eroded.

Carrick bowed his head and Rhoco licked the rock dust from his forehead. He then smeared his own limestone and malachite sediment over the spot his tongue had cleared.

Rhoco then bowed his head in turn and let Carrick do the same to him. After Carrick consumed Rhoco's dust and covered the spot with some of his own. The ritual was complete.

The ancient formality was oddly personal, which made Rhoco feel uncomfortable, but after sharing such a moment, he found he did, in fact, trust Carrick more.

"Great," Carrick resumed briskly, seemingly less affected by the intrusive transaction than Rhoco. "When will we leave?"

"Tomorrow. I need a night to collect my thoughts."

"Same. I have a few things to attend to."

"Just don't tell anyone that you're leaving."

"Of course not," Carrick reassured him before climbing down the ledge and darting out of the cave.

Feodras returned with a packed duffel bag. He tossed it over the side of the boat, then fixed a serrated knife into his belt.

"Will you make a dust pact with me?" Rhoco asked. "Promising you will not interfere with my mission?"

"What is a dust pact?"

Rhoco was inclined to explain, but then decided it wasn't worth the hassle. If Feodras didn't already know the significance of such a promise, the ritual would mean nothing to him. Nothing Rhoco explained would make him take the vow seriously.

"Never mind. We aren't leaving until tomorrow night. Carrick and I both have matters to attend to before our departure."

"Understood."

"The Murks in the mines have been spying on us, did you know?"

"The bees came to me first. I knew nothing of your plans, so they just watched us build. I asked them not to tell the others I was helping you."

"Why?"

"I don't trust the miners."

"Why would the bees obey you? Seems to me they owe more loyalty to the miners, since they house the bees' queen."

"Yeah, but they like us more," Feodras replied with quiet conviction. "The bees will follow when the carvers leave. The king and queen will regret how they treated us when all their flowers die."

His evident dislike for the Royals made Rhoco feel a little better about allowing him to join, though he still did not trust the Murk.

"My only condition is that you let me get to where I'm going before you embark on your vendetta."

"The sea will determine our path."

"Surely the boat can be steered?"

"Yes, but once we set out to sea, our fate resides with Gaia, mother to nature and overseer of the universe. There are greater powers at play, deities shuffling our pieces on their playing boards, and if my quest is a priority, the ocean will see to it that I get where I need to go."

"Just don't interfere," Rhoco demanded—he did not believe in gods or fate.

"I would never."

They parted ways and Rhoco went home to collect his thoughts and prepare for his departure.

Cybelle sat on the step leading to his front door. On her lap was a basket full of supplies.

"This came about a lot sooner than I anticipated, but I did my best to pack what I thought you might need."

She held up the basket and he accepted her parting gift.

"What's in here?"

"Food and tools to help you survive. No squirrel meat though, sorry."

He laughed. "Didn't think there would be."

"There's also a bit of magic in there, courtesy of myself and Almadine."

He silently scoffed at their superstitious nature, but made no comment.

"Will she stop by before I leave?" he asked.

"I highly doubt it."

Rhoco nodded in understanding.

"I also brought you this," Cybelle continued, pulling a satin drawstring pouch from her pocket. "I suggest the heart remains your secret."

Rhoco took the small, black pouch with gratitude. He too thought it wise to keep his possession of the heart private. Neither his comrades nor those they might encounter along the way needed to know what he kept concealed.

"Thanks."

Cybelle nodded. "I'll be on my way."

"Will you see us off?"

"If you want me to."

"I do."

"Then I'll be there."

This gave Rhoco relief. Though he hated to admit it, her presence provided comfort. He understood now that she was his truest friend and having a proper farewell from her was most important.

Cybelle departed and Rhoco entered his home. He placed the basket of gifts on the kitchen table and turned to face the heart, which fizzled with a faint red glow at his return. He hadn't touched it since the last vision. The place it brought him to, the desires it awakened, the way it made him feel—it was all too much. He wanted to return the heart to its home before it latched onto him any further. He had never intended to care so

145

deeply for it, and once again, he resolved to do everything in his power to keep himself detached from the lure of the glass heart.

Chapter 15

Rhoco spent the day leading up to his departure preparing. Cybelle had provided him with many useful items, such as an overloaded medical kit, various edged blades, a compass, a telescope, a few bottles of potions, and three history books, one of which contained a world map of Namaté hidden behind the cover. He packed the tools and non-perishable food into two separate duffel bags, then retrieved his barely used fishing gear from his cellar and set it by the front door.

The time to leave had come. He approached the heart, and without touching the glass, placed it into the satin pouch. He pulled the strings tight and then placed the pouch into the pocket of his pants. The heart was safely tucked away, unable to touch him, unable to make him feel. His focus was sharp and he was ready to go. With the mission clear, he wouldn't let anything take him off course.

When he arrived at the east shore, Feodras and Carrick had already relocated the boat so that it sat atop the rock in the vast ravine.

"You could've waited," Rhoco announced. "I would've helped."

"You were late," Feodras explained.

Rhoco grunted and tossed his bags and fishing gear over the tall sides of the stone boat.

"I have bad news," Carrick whispered as he pulled Rhoco aside. "I can't go with you."

"Why not?"

"Rubi's hut collapsed. I'm not sure what I did wrong, but the whole thing caved in last night. Thankfully, she hadn't relocated there yet. The baby will be here any day and I have to get her out of her condemned hut before its birth. I have to stay behind and finish building their new home."

"I get it, that's noble." Though he was being understanding, Rhoco's energy was tense. "Since you can't watch over Feodras while I travel, can you keep a close eye on the mining Murks instead? They can't tell the Royals I'm gone."

"Absolutely. Our pact still stands and I will do my best," Carrick promised.

"Thank you."

"I brought you extra food and a spear gun. They're already on board," Carrick informed. "Best of luck. I'm rooting for your safe return."

Rhoco wasn't sure if he'd ever make it back to Orewall, or if he even wanted to return, but he appreciated the sentiment.

"Thanks. I hope your situation turns out well too."

"I'm praying they both survive."

"As am I," Rhoco said, returning the sentiment, even though he wasn't the prayerful type.

Carrick placed his right hand on Rhoco's left shoulder, indicating that they were friends and equals, and Rhoco echoed the gesture. They shared a moment of silent understanding that they'd remain as such even with oceans between them. Nearby, Feodras watched them, but said nothing.

Although the day remained overcast and dim, light from the sun crested the horizon, indicating their time was running short. Cybelle arrived just in time and hobbled toward the boat.

"Thought you forgot about me."

"Never," Cybelle replied. "I just didn't want to drag this out. I hate goodbyes."

"I'll see you again," he assured her, but neither were sure if that was true.

"Just promise me you'll be safe out there."

"I promise."

"And that you won't fall in love with that heart," she added in a whisper.

"I won't," Rhoco replied, aware it was likely too late for that.

"I hope you come back in one piece, but I'm prepared for this to be the final time I see you." Cybelle exhaled deeply. "I fear I'm going to miss you."

Rhoco laughed. "I'll miss you too."

She wrapped her arms around him and they hugged for a full, silent minute before she let go. She then lifted her right arm and placed her hand on his left shoulder, just as Carrick had done. Rhoco mirrored her stance. They shared a moment of quiet understanding and at the last moment, right before they disconnected, Rhoco took her hand and placed it over his heart.

"Family," he said to her. Happy tears welled in her bright blue eyes. She grabbed his hand and kissed his knuckles before letting go.

"Take care of yourself," she said as he climbed the ladder and boarded the ship.

"Same to you. I need you here when I return."

"Return with marvelous tales."

"For you, I will."

The water began to rise. Cybelle and Carrick retreated to the cliffs to watch from a safe height as the waves lapped against the boat. When the water was high enough, the boat began to float and the tide took them out to sea.

Rhoco looked over his shoulder as he sailed into the sunrise. Carrick had an arm around Cybelle, who continued to wave until they were a mere spot on the horizon.

He turned and set his sight on the rising sun, hoping its light might blind the fear that had crept into his heart. He hadn't been nervous until this moment. Cybelle was right; he did not know what the world beyond Orewall had in store, and for the first time, he felt wildly ill-prepared.

He placed his hand on the pouch that housed the glass heart.

This is for you, he thought before joining Feodras at the bow. A long, unpredictable journey lay ahead and Rhoco's nerves teetered between thrill and terror. The ocean beckoned and he was finally answering the call.

Chapter 16

Before the sun had fully risen, a storm rolled through and darkened the morning sky. It hadn't started raining yet, but the clouds blocked the sun from shining through.

Atop the boat's stone platform, Rhoco sat with his map, compass, and telescope. He looked out to sea, but saw nothing except smooth, black water, vacant of life. The waves were mild, but the storm brewing overhead would change that soon.

He removed the map of Namaté from the history book and unfolded it, careful not to rip the thin paper. This map was far more detailed than the smaller sketch in *Beyond Orewall*. Though he didn't know much about navigating, he knew he wanted to travel east, so he got his bearings while he could still see the eastern coast of Orewall and checked his compass to make sure they were heading in the correct direction.

"A little more to the right," Rhoco called down to Feodras, who pedaled wooden slabs that moved the paddle wheel at the back of the boat.

Feodras looked around, assessing their location before responding.

"That's unwise."

"Why?" Rhoco called down.

"The underground volcanoes."

Rhoco climbed down from the ornate platform and marched over to Feodras with the map in hand. Without Carrick to act as a second set of eyes, Rhoco's distrust of the Murk was even more heightened than it was before they left Orewall.

"Volcanoes? Where?" he asked, shoving the map in the Murk's face.

Feodras snatched the map from Rhoco and pointed to the long stretch of water between Orewall and Crystet.

"This entire area of water conceals an active volcanic range. That right there," he went on, moving his skinny finger to an unnamed island southwest of Crystet, "is an aboveground volcano. The entire area is plagued by fire and death."

"I don't care. This is the quickest route to Crystet. We're taking it."

Feodras eyed Rhoco suspiciously; this was the first time he mentioned his destination.

"What's in Crystet?" Feodras questioned.

"Don't worry about it."

"Except whatever drives you is now putting *me* in danger."

"You promised you wouldn't interfere," Rhoco reminded him.

Feodras huffed, but obliged, adjusting the handheld rudders that moved slabs located beneath the boat as he pedaled.

After the boat was redirected, Feodras abandoned his station to raise the squirrel-hide sail. He yanked on the rope until the fur-covered sail was up, then knotted the rope to keep the sail in place.

Rhoco admired the sail, which was made of a hundred different squirrel carcasses stitched together to make one massive sheet.

"When did you have time to collect and stitch together all these squirrel hides?" Rhoco asked.

"I've been patching this sail together for years," Feodras explained as he resumed his spot near the pedals and rudder handles. "You think your revelation to leave was the first time I ever thought about escaping?" he went on with a raised brow.

"I guess not," Rhoco considered. "So, why didn't any of the other carvers know we were there? I thought that's where you all worked?"

Feodras sighed, clearly annoyed that Rhoco kept talking.

"We sculpt more than just boats. Our recent shifts have been focused on building a room, toys, and play areas for the little prince. Once the polisher Murks finish smoothing out the stones and gems given to them by the miners, we incorporate the precious stones into our carvings."

"But how did you find out about my project if your assigned work of late has been inside Amesyte Valley?"

"They don't let us *stay* in the valley. We aren't even allowed *into* the valley unless it's imperative. We do most of our work in underground rooms beneath the castle, then return to our dwellings at the end of each shift. You were hammering loudly right outside my home," he replied, as though the answer were obvious. "Then I asked the mud bees to investigate. They filled me in on what they could and I decided your mission could also be my mission."

"This is *not* your mission."

"You've made that clear."

"Why didn't the other Murks hear me hammering?"

"I have the only cave dwelling within the cove facing the east shore mining field. All the other carvers have caves situated along the coast, but they are on the other sides of the cove walls. There, the caves don't flood with water every time the tides change."

"You're the only Murk who has a cave that floods?"

"Such is my luck. My time spent with you was my sleeping hours," he explained as he pedaled slowly.

Rhoco relented a bit. "If you're tired, you can take a break and I'll pedal."

"I'm fine. Murks rarely sleep, we just don't let the Royals know that. If we did, we'd never get breaks."

"I see."

Rhoco realized he was prying, which was out of character. He clammed up, ashamed of his inquisitiveness.

"No more questions?" Feodras asked in a snarky tone.

"I only inquired because understanding you will help me better protect myself from your sneakiness."

"So I am expected to answer your questions, to better educate you, but when I ask you something, you give me nothing."

"That's how this works, Murk. Get used to it."

"Well, I detest talking. Get used to *that*."

They had hit a wall. Both were too stubborn to bend in order to find common ground. Feodras did not want to be bullied into talking if Rhoco would not compromise by providing his own wealth of knowledge, and Rhoco refused to view Feodras as an equal he could trust.

Just then, Rhoco noticed the bumblebee latched onto the back of Feodras's earlobe.

"What is *that*?" he asked, appalled.

"Leave me alone."

"You brought a spy?" Rhoco roared.

"She is my friend, Erlea," Feodras explained.

"No. Absolutely not."

"She can be trusted, I swear."

"Send it home!"

"No."

Rhoco grabbed Feodras by the neck and lifted him into the air. He then extended the scrawny Murk's body overboard and growled, "Send it home now, or I'll drop you into the ocean."

Feodras hesitated before conceding. He let out a high-pitched hum and the bee flew away.

Rhoco dropped the Murk back onto the stone deck.

"You'll regret that," Feodras declared between coughs as he caught his breath. "Erlea was our only tie back to Orewall."

"We can't have *any* ties back to Orewall right now. If the wrong person finds out what we're up to, we're dead men."

"She won't tell anyone."

"I'd rather not take the risk," he seethed, hating the idea that bees were an intelligent species.

"You're unwise to leave the mining Murks unattended."

"Carrick is watching over them, making sure they don't snitch."

"Your friend cannot warn us when they inevitably evade his watch."

"But your bumblebee could? How could she possibly tell us what is happening there while she is here with us?"

"Bees telecommunicate. No matter the distance, they can hear each other."

"Regardless, if the mining Murks rat us out, there's nothing we can do about it from here, whether we are aware of their actions or not. King Alun might not receive our return with kindness, but he's not going to send out a fleet to retrieve an unimportant Fused miner and a Murk. I built this boat, it's mine, and I haven't done anything to threaten his kingdom."

Feodras glared at Rhoco silently.

Rhoco continued, answering Feodras's unspoken complaint. "It is *my* boat, no matter what you think. I did not ask for your help, so you cannot claim ownership."

Feodras shook his head and turned away, forcing Rhoco to assume there was more hidden beneath the Murk's silence.

"What aren't you telling me?" Rhoco demanded.

"Nothing," Feodras replied apathetically. "You've got it all figured out."

"Of course I do," he shouted at him from the opposite side of the boat. "And I hope we never see that treacherous bee again!"

The men separated in anger, remaining as far apart as possible for the rest of the day. When it began to rain, Rhoco relocated beneath the platform to read. To his dismay, Feodras was already there, taking shelter.

He did not acknowledge the traitor in his vicinity and returned his attention to the books. Though he wasn't sure what information might prove useful in his travels, he was confident his time spent reading was worthwhile. His main focus was Crystet. He wanted to learn everything he possibly could about the Glaziene before he arrived at their land. He expected they'd get there soon, so he read every detail the books offered about the people made of glass. With a critical glare, Feodras watched Rhoco struggle to read.

"We have a long way to go before we reach Crystet," Feodras finally remarked. "You should be educating yourself on the danger we'll encounter along the way."

"You told me about the volcanoes. I get it, but you also realize stone doesn't burn, right?"

"There are far worse dangers than volcanoes."

Rhoco eyed him intently, waiting for more information, but Feodras abruptly stopped his verbal assault.

"I suppose these dangers can't be so threatening if you aren't willing to divulge the details."

"I am a Boulde of his word. You are the captain and I said I would not interfere."

"You're a mulish thorn in my side."

"As Erlea would advise, damned if you do, damned if you don't."

"We were getting along just fine until I learned you were harboring that stupid bee."

Feodras fumed, but maintained his silence.

Rhoco slammed his book shut and abandoned the shelter of the platform. He stood in the rain and tried to calm his breathing by staring out to sea, but the sky was still blanketed in storm clouds and it was impossible to see anything. Everything was black—the sky, the water. He could hear the waves lapping against the side of the boat, so he focused on that. As it lulled him into a state of serenity, he thought of the heart, which remained safely tucked away in his pocket. If he held it in his hands, it would surely ease his frustration, but he couldn't. Too much was at stake to let the heart distract him with its unpredictable magic.

Rhoco's gaze remained on the dark sea as his thoughts twirled around the heart. A faint, red glow emanated as he pictured the glass heart on his mantel. The burning radiance intensified and the image of the heart grew larger in his mind. Its heat began to bubble at the surface and Rhoco could no longer separate what he was picturing from reality. The warmth of the heart invited him closer, so much so he could actually feel the heat radiate through the stone-hard skin on his face.

The intense temperature ripped him from his reverie and forced him back into reality. An enormous pocket of lava boiled beneath the sea and rose steadily. His senses seized with dread as the bubble rocketed in his direction. As the lava burst through the ocean's surface and lurched toward him, he was shoved hard from behind and knocked out of the way. The liquid fire exploded like a firework, splattering in all directions, before disappearing back into the ocean.

"I told you this would happen," Feodras shouted. "No one sails these seas except the Voltains and Metellyans. They are the only ones with boats equipped for this type of natural attack."

Rhoco looked at a piece of lava that had landed on the deck. Apparently stone *could* burn. The chunk of lava seared the rock until it cooled enough that it could damage the stone no further.

Rhoco stood and saw that the entire ocean was imploding. The surface was covered with bursting pouches of liquid fire and the horrific explosions illuminated the night sky.

"We need to get out of here," Rhoco stressed as another glob of lava landed on the deck and began burning through the stone.

Feodras had already begun pedaling the paddlewheel and redirecting the rudders.

"Grab the ropes for the sail and do what I say," he instructed Rhoco, who obeyed without dispute.

Another patch of lava ruptured and bulleted through the sail. It passed straight through, leaving a smoldering hole that grew from miniscule to large in a matter of seconds. The wind and rain from the storm stopped the fire from destroying the entire sail, but the damage was done.

"We are going to sink," Rhoco hollered as hunks of molten fire rained down on them.

"Not today," Feodras mumbled, upping his pedaling speed. The tides ripped at their boat, trying to tug them back into the fire, but with great effort, they fought the current and were able to navigate away from the lava cesspool before the bottom of their boat melted and they sank.

The tides had turned and keeping the boat on track amidst the wild currents was far more difficult.

Rhoco pulled out his compass. "We're headed the wrong way."

"Unless you want to head back into that volcanic minefield, we have to find another route."

Rhoco let Feodras take charge for the time being. He needed to consult his map to figure out the best alternate route to Crystet.

Feodras regained control of the boat, so Rhoco dipped beneath the platform to study his map.

But before he could settle down and dive into the book, Feodras began yelling from the back of the boat.

Rhoco returned the map and the book into his duffel bag and emerged to investigate.

"What's wrong?" he shouted over the howling wind.

"It's bad, it's bad," Feodras mumbled as he pointed at the looming mist in the distance and tried to steer the boat in a different direction.

"What is *that*?"

"Vapore."

Vapore was home to the Gasiones, who were mysterious creatures that thrived within the natural material gas. No one knew what they looked like or the basic functionality of their species, as they remained hidden within the fog of their land.

"Maybe they can help us," Rhoco offered.

"No, they will not help. We must not enter."

Though Feodras did his best to redirect the boat, there was no altering the tides. The ocean current sent them straight toward the misty dome encasing Vapore.

Rhoco tried to adjust the sail, but to no avail.

The wind picked up and within the whistling squalls was a melody. It was subtle, but audible, and the tune was quite enchanting. Rhoco stopped to lean over the edge of the boat and listen. The song grew louder and he could now hear the voices within the melody.

"Do you hear that?" he called back to Feodras, who still frantically pedaled.

"Hear what?"

"The song."

Feodras stopped pedaling abruptly and his face drained of color. He looked ill as he absorbed Rhoco's discovery.

"Much worse. Oh, so much worse," he muttered.

"Worse?"

"Much." Feodras gulped. "The cecaelia have found us."

Chapter 17

Feodras joined Rhoco at the edge of their stone boat and peered into the water. The song was now louder than the wind and the previously mumbled voices were clear. The lyrics echoed from the sea.

Sailor, sailor,

come to me.

I'll handle you quite recklessly.

If you let me crawl inside

I promise I will make you mine.

Surrender, sailor,

for I fear

you do not belong here.

The last line rang the clearest of them all.

"Who is singing?" Rhoco asked.

"The cecaelia," Feodras answered, his eyes wide with fear.

"What's a cecaelia?"

"Half octopus, half human. The women feed on souls and the men eat whatever's left. We must reach Vapore."

As he said those words, the boat lurched away from the mist of Vapore.

"They are pulling us away!" Rhoco shouted. He grabbed the spear gun Carrick had given him and aimed it at the surface of the black ocean. The gun was their best bet; with its titanium cacti pointed arrows that could pierce stone, it was lethal to most creatures.

Rhoco frantically looked for a target to shoot, but yielded nothing. "I can't see them."

Man of Gaia,
come to me.
You reek of sensuality.
A death laced with erotic glee
will satisfy both of our needs.
I am the temptress of the sea,
and now your soul belongs to me.

A whimper came from Feodras; the head cecaelia had crawled aboard. Her eyes, black marbles beneath feathered eyelashes, bore into Rhoco with desire. Despite his fear, he found himself drawn to the monster. Though an encounter would be his demise, a death entangled by her ravenous passion suddenly seemed worthwhile.

The octopus temptress beckoned him with a devious smirk. Feodras shouted something at him, but Rhoco could not hear; he was too mesmerized by her beauty. Her long, ink-black hair barely covered her pale breasts. Her sallow skin had a purple undertone, while her bottom half was jet-black. Sight of her oily, slick tentacles snapped him out of his hypnotized stupor.

"Shoot her!" Feodras shouted, entwined within the tentacles of a second cecaelia. Rhoco heard him this time and aimed his spear gun at the cecaelia, who abandoned her passive seduction and sped toward him with fury.

He released an arrow as she tackled him to the deck, knocking the gun out of his hand. The arrow pierced her hip and she shrieked with pain, but her massive tentacles still pinned him.

The other cecaelia mimicked her howl of agony, sending a chorus of bereaved cries into the gloomy air—a horrifying symphony.

The arrow remained lodged until she yanked the wooden spear from her hip. Black ink poured out, painting the boat's stone deck.

"You'll pay for this," she hissed. She leaned in so that her lips hovered over his, then stabbed the spear into his shoulder. It cleared his skin and came out the other side. The cecaelia cackled as green blood gushed from his body.

"She's too strong," he shouted to Feodras, who slipped in and out of consciousness in a cecaelia's clutches. She sucked on his neck while he lay there, unable to fight back.

His mission was ruined. He had failed and the heart would be lost at sea with these monsters.

As he thought of the heart, his left pocket heated against his thigh. He wasn't sure why until he remembered that the heart was still wrapped up in the pocket of his pants. The heart was magic; maybe it could save him. He struggled beneath the weight of the creature, freeing his arm and reaching into his pocket. He unlaced the pouch as the cecaelia began to lick his face, burning his stone flesh with her acidic saliva. The moment his fingers touched the glass, he was transported to a dark room.

"No!" he shouted. "Take me back!"

The woman in white appeared in the distance and glided toward him with speed. She radiated in the dark space. Once she was upon him, she placed both of her hands on his face and he melted beneath her warm touch.

"No one can have you but me."

She kissed him with passion. He closed his eyes in submission, and when he opened them again, he was back on the boat.

The cecaelia were gone, and Feodras was curled up, motionless.

Rhoco shook the aftermath of the kiss from his senses and pulled the arrow out of his shoulder. Green blood poured down his body, but he ignored the pain. Feodras was in far worse shape and needed medical attention, but Rhoco had no idea how to help him.

He scrambled for the book Cybelle gave him that he had yet to open: *Creatures Beyond Orewall.*

Information on the cecaelia would surely be in it, as well as details about healing a cecaelia's kiss. Rhoco tore through the pages, flipping them hastily, visibly concerned by his ignorance of all the monstrous beasts that existed in the world. When he arrived at the chapter dedicated to the cecaelia, he scanned the information with acute brevity.

A kiss from a cecaelia became lethal if not treated in time. Sketches depicted the varying degrees of damage a kiss could cause. If a cecaelia latched on for a few seconds, the wound was small and inflamed. Looking back at Feodras, Rhoco saw that his neck wound was black around the raw central point where the cecaelia tried to suck the soul out of him.

He checked the book for a diagnosis. A kiss that lasted a few minutes created a sore that was black around its edges. A kiss that lasted longer than ten minutes would cause the victim to not only stop breathing, but to suffer permanent psychological damage. Any longer and the victim would not survive.

Rhoco placed a finger under Feodras's nose; he was still breathing.

He scanned the pages for a remedy and found one a few paragraphs beneath the logistics of their kiss.

- *Two leaves skunk cabbage*
- *One cinnamon fern*
- *Three pinches black lava salt*
- *½ spoonful rice vinegar*

Muddle until ingredients form a paste.

Rhoco collapsed to his knees, utterly defeated. He did not have any of those ingredients. Feodras shivered in his unconscious state and Rhoco no longer saw him as a threat. Feodras was a Boulde, just like him, who currently suffered from terrible pain. Rhoco had to help him.

Cybelle's potions! he remembered, then grabbed Cybelle's basket and prayed some of the ingredients were in there. Though he wasn't well-versed in the art of medicine or magic, he imagined the list contained common ingredients. He dug to the bottom of the basket and found a vial of green mush. When he held it up, botanical fragments within the glass sparkled in the moonlight. He read the small tag tied to the vial's neck:

Since you're certain to encounter cecaelia. Good for one use.

-C

Rhoco gushed with silent appreciation for Cybelle as he uncorked the vial and shook the contents onto Feodras's neck. He rubbed the mixture into the wound, covering the mouth-sized sore completely. Once the wound was masked, he sat back and waited.

Their boat drifted farther into the mist of Vapore as the medicine worked its magic. Rhoco stood to assess their new predicament. He peered over the ledge of their stone boat and saw that the cecaelia had followed them in the shallows. They glared up at him through the surface of the sea, eyes black and menacing in the light of the moon.

A cough came from behind and Rhoco turned to find that Feodras had regained consciousness.

"Are you all right?" Rhoco asked after dashing to his side.

Feodras shook his head. "What happened?"

"I planned to ask you the same thing. Did you see anything before you passed out?"

He nodded. "You scared them away."

"Impossible," Rhoco argued. "I was knocked out too."

"The cecaelia had you pinned, but you managed to hold up some glowing, red weapon, I'm sure of it. When she saw it, she retreated, beckoning all the other cecaelia to follow, and they slithered back into the ocean. Once they were gone, I let myself slip away. I don't know what happened next."

"I woke up and found you like this."

"So, you did all that while unconscious?" Feodras asked, still struggling for breath.

"I guess so," he replied, aware that the heart did all the work, not him.

"What was that weapon you used?"

"Your guess is as good as mine," Rhoco lied. The heart needed to remain his secret.

"I thought I was dead." Feodras was too shaken to press the issue.

"You were. Lucky for us, Cybelle provided us with one dose of healing salve for a cecaelia kiss."

"And you used it on me?"

It hadn't crossed Rhoco's mind *not* to save the Murk, but he couldn't let his compassion appear as weakness. "Who would pedal and steer the boat if you were gone?"

"Thanks for saving me," Feodras offered, reluctantly.

"This doesn't make us friends."

"I didn't suspect it would. Where are we?"

"Not sure."

Feodras looked around and his expression returned to one of dread. "We are in Vapore."

"And the cecaelia have followed us here," Rhoco warned.

"They won't surface. It isn't safe for them in Vapore, but we also can't leave the boat."

"Why not?"

"The Gasiones of Vapore are aellas, and they hate outsiders."

"What's an aella?"

Feodras sighed, not wanting to explain, but realizing it served him better if Rhoco was educated on the dangers they faced. "No one really knows. They come and go as a whirlwind. If one snatches you, you're gone forever. Those who live to tell of their journey to Vapore have only ever seen their eyes— Gasiones hide within the mist of their land, but they cannot hide their phosphorescent eyes."

As he finished speaking, the boat thudded against the shore. Rhoco looked over the side to see that they were securely docked in the clay of the swamp banks.

Early morning was upon them, yet the landscape remained a thick shade of gray. Silhouettes of trees were visible, but all their details were lost in the fog. Rhoco concentrated harder and detected the sets of eyes Feodras had mentioned.

It appeared that all of Vapore was alert to their arrival. A sinister shriek echoed through the morning air.

"Should we leave?" Rhoco asked.

"Yes, but not yet. The cecaelia need time to forget about us. I doubt they've eaten a Boulde in centuries; it will take a while for them to release our scent. Until they do, we are safe here."

"How does *anyone* sail with those monsters out there?"

"Pacts and treaties. We are unclaimed meat, so our lives are fair game. You have to pay the cecaelia if you want to live."

"With what?"

"They like pearls and opals."

"You should've told me that before we left. I could've gotten opals easily."

"There are other ways. I thought I had it covered."

"Go on," Rhoco prodded.

"I carved warding runes into the hull, but I guess I didn't get them right."

"Can you fix them?"

"I'm not sure."

Rhoco clicked his tongue with disapproval, then realized he was being too harsh on the Murk. Without Feodras, he'd know nothing except the minimal information gathered from his dismal attempts to read.

Feodras was not only helpful, but intelligent as well. He was worthy of respect and it frustrated Rhoco that his habitual instincts continually shaped his behavior toward Feodras as unkind. Despite his unmanageable attitude and inability to admit the truth to anyone but himself, Feodras's value grew in his subconscious. He recognized the Murk's worth, even if years of conditioning prevented him from acknowledging that aloud.

"I'm not sure what I did wrong," Feodras continued, "but the Woodlins can help us fix them. They live in Wicker—a land west of Orewall."

"No. That's another pit stop in the wrong direction. I have to get to Crystet."

"If you want to arrive at Crystet alive, I suggest we stop in Wicker first."

Rhoco huffed, but said no more.

The day passed with restless patience. They barely spoke, but took turns watching the cecaelia swim circles around their boat. When night arrived, the foggy dome above them grew dark and the blazing eyes of the Gasiones became more apparent. Their intense gazes remained fixed on their stone boat.

"Will they attack?" Rhoco asked in a whisper from where he tried to sleep.

Feodras did not reply.

Rhoco rolled over, punched the Murk in the arm to wake him up, and asked again. A distant Gasione released a rancorous howl into the night sky.

"Will they attack?"

Feodras groaned. "Only if we get off our boat. They don't eat Bouldes, just cecaelia and sylphs."

"What are sylphs?"

Again, Feodras did not wish to explain but was wise enough to know that Rhoco was more useful when educated. "Sylphs are protectors of the air. They are tiny, fairy-like creatures that flutter through the sky like fireflies."

"They sound pretty."

"Pretty, yes. Harmless, no. They are worse than the cecaelia. Their mouths have ten rows of razor-sharp teeth and they attack in swarms. There's no surviving a sylph attack after it's begun."

"Will they try to harm us?"

"They won't bother us here. Just like the cecaelia, they do not enter Vapore. The Gasiones would devour them if they did. But once we're back on the open sea, I'd imagine so. We are men, after all."

"What does that have to do with anthing?"

"They only feast on the flesh of men."

"Why haven't they attacked us yet?"

"How should I know?" Feodras grumbled. "Go to bed, why don't ya?"

He rolled over and buried his head beneath his blanket. Rhoco exhaled deeply, feeling overwhelmed and underprepared. This world held grave secrets he had not anticipated, and if he wished to survive, he'd need to uncover them all.

Chapter 18

The alluring chant of the cecaelia's lullaby woke them before the light of the sun illuminated the foggy dome. The chant enticed them to jump overboard, tempting them to enter the water and meet their fate.

Though Rhoco found himself inclined to obey, the heart kept him grounded. It sat in his pocket, suddenly as heavy as one thousand stones.

Its refusal to let him leave gave him the time he needed to shake the enchantment away and regain clarity. Once he had a solid grip on reality, he noticed Feodras wasn't faring as well. In a dazed state, his Murk companion crawled toward the edge of the boat.

"Stop!" Rhoco shouted, but Feodras could not hear him. He tried to stand so that he could constrain the Murk physically, but the weight of the heart kept him in place.

"Let me go," he insisted, but the heart would not lighten itself. It stubbornly kept him pinned to the deck. He reached into his pocket and grabbed the pouch concealing the heart, but he could not move it, and he did not dare touch the heart with his bare hand.

Feodras had reached the edge of the boat and was attempting to stand so he could fling his body overboard.

Rhoco was running out of time. Thinking quickly, he removed his pants to escape the weight of the heart and lurched toward Feodras, who was already leaning over the edge. Rhoco grabbed his ankle and held on tight as a cecaelia tentacle gripped Feodras's forearm.

"You can't have him!" Rhoco shouted, clinging to the Murk's foot.

"*But we must,*" the cecaelia hissed in melodic unison.

A shrill screech came from the forest, followed by a spear that pierced the cecaelia's exposed tentacle.

She immediately released Feodras's arm and submerged. Rhoco pulled the scrawny Murk back onto the deck and slapped his face hard. Feodras blinked rapidly as the hypnosis faded, and then both men returned to the edge of the ship to see a pool of black ink in the gray water.

"She's gone," Rhoco said with relief, but Feodras shook his head and pointed to a rope in the water. It ended somewhere in the forest.

A moment later, the rope tightened and the hooked cecaelia was yanked ashore. The rope near the end of the spear was newly frayed, as if her colleagues under the sea had attempted, but failed, to cut her free. She was tugged onto the marshy beach, wailing in terror. Her high-pitched cries sent waves of pain through Rhoco's skull.

"Don't let them eat me," she begged once she caught sight of the Bouldes watching her from the safety of their boat. "I guarantee you safe passage if you save me," she bribed.

Rhoco looked to Feodras, who shook his head without breaking his gaze from the harrowing scene. Rhoco returned his focus to the cecaelia, whose pathetic begging rapidly morphed into hostile threats.

"My sisters are watching and they will feast on you the moment you leave Vapore. My death will bring forth yours!" she screamed as her body was heaved into the shadows of the trees. The glowing eyes disappeared momentarily once the cecaelia was out of sight, and the sound of grunting and loud chewing accompanied her dying screams. When the Gasiones were done feasting, they resumed their guard and the eyes in the forest returned.

"You saved me again," Feodras murmured.

"Only because I dislike *them* more than I dislike *you*."

Feodras sensed his reply was a shield, but said nothing of it.

"How will we get to Crystet now?" Rhoco asked, worried that the cecaelia's resentment toward them would become even more vicious.

"I already told you how. We ask the Woodlins for help."

"Won't they get to us before we reach Wicker?"

"Not if they are waiting for our departure on the other side of Vapore. They think we are headed east; Wicker is to the west, and it's only a two-night sail."

Rhoco grunted. "Fine. To Wicker we'll go."

They remained in Vapore another night. The oppressive, swamp-like atmosphere seeped into Rhoco's pores, clamming up his ability to breathe as he slept. He awoke with a gasp, alive and working hard with each respiration. Dawn brought with it a chorus of horrible screeching from the Gasiones. No morning lullaby from the cecaelia to greet them, just the earsplitting shrieks of aellas.

"Looks as though the sea devils have retreated," Rhoco commented as he examined the shallows below. The shiny, black eyes of the cecaelia were gone and the water appeared vacant of monsters.

Feodras looked for himself. After scrutinizing the black water for countless minutes, he finally replied.

"If the water remains still by nightfall, we can leave tomorrow morning."

Rhoco agreed with anticipation, eager to leave this misty hell.

He spent the afternoon reading about the sylphs. *Creatures Beyond Orewall* depicted them as miniature women, pastel-colored with glassy wings made of a shiny, delicate membrane that shimmered like opal in the sunlight. The wings resembled those of the bumblebees the Murks loved so much. Next to an average-sized female Boulde, the sylphs were the size of a single finger. Tiny in stature, but lethal in capabilities.

When docile, the sylphs were quite lovely, but in the images where they were aroused with anger, they were terrifying. Their mouths opened to unimaginable widths, revealing teeth designed in a nightmare. Their fingers sprouted needle-like talons, sharp on all sides and able to slice through any material. They could tear apart the burliest Boulde with ease. They attacked in packs, swarming their victim and devouring creatures five times their size in minutes.

Rhoco had read enough. He closed the book, hoping the Woodlins knew how to ward off the sylphs too.

They slept on the stone deck, stewing uncomfortably in the thick, humid air, and awoke to the morning screeching of the Gasiones. Feodras examined the water and determined it was safe.

"They are gone. We can leave."

Rhoco exhaled with relief. After three days in Vapore, he was eager to return to his mission. As they prepped the boat to depart, he had a thought.

"It's a shame we can't exit the boat. This swamp has most of the ingredients we'd need to make another batch of the remedy for a cecaelia kiss."

"It's not worth the risk. The Gasiones are extremely possessive over their land. We are lucky they let us stay this long on their shore."

Rhoco did not press the issue. With the long oars latched to the walls of the boat, they managed to dislodge themselves from the muddy swamp bank. The strenuous effort took an hour to complete, but finally, they were back on the open water and heading west. To Rhoco's dismay, the world was still overcast, as it had been since they left Orewall.

As they left the mist of Vapore, Rhoco looked behind to watch it grow smaller as they sailed away. He would not miss the dank abyss.

The consistent drone of the barbaric Gasiones remained audible, even when the boat was a few miles beyond the fog wall. The occasional shriek of murder echoed louder than the steady hum of grunts and growls. Then a particularly loud predatory howl radiated into the sky, drawing Rhoco's attention to the top of the dome.

A black and gray whirlwind twisted up into the air. As he tried to define the sight in his mind, it morphed into a naked man with enormous, black falcon wings. The creature darted headfirst toward a small, hovering light, snatched the light in its mouth, then nose-dived as a whirlwind back into the mist of Vapore.

Rhoco stared, mouth agape.

"Did you see that?" he asked, turning to Feodras, who faced the opposite direction.

"See what?"

"The aella!"

"You saw a Gasione?" Feodras snapped around to face Rhoco.

"I think so. It soared above the dome, as a whirlwind at first, then transformed into a man to catch an orb of light in its mouth. Then it dove back into Vapore."

Feodras paused to consider this description.

"If it's true, you might've just witnessed a Gasione hunting sylphs. It looked like a man?"

"Yes, with giant, black falcon wings."

"Interesting." He turned back around and watched the sea ahead.

Rhoco didn't understand his indifference.

"Don't you care? I saw a Gasione and lived to tell about it. You told me yourself that never happens."

"Yes, and you told me. Time will tell if either of us ever gets the opportunity to tell another."

Rhoco scowled at the Murk's pessimism and retreated to the top of the platform.

Night arrived without any conversation between them. Despite all they'd been though, their apparent disdain for one another continued. The time of quiet reflection with no setbacks allowed Rhoco to remember all the things he disliked about the Murk: that bumblebee, his ulterior and unknown motives, his superior intellect. He tried to recall the positives too, but found he couldn't. By the time he realized that his outlook had tanked, he was swimming in destructive thoughts. Only sleep would help reset his frame of mind.

The sun returned the following morning. Atop the platform, Rhoco awoke and peered over the edge to locate Feodras. The Murk was still asleep, however, completely cocooned in his blanket.

Rhoco checked his compass; they were still heading west toward Wicker. He climbed down the ladder and headed for the bow. He sat on a stool near the edge, staring at the open sea, enjoying the calm, until Feodras interrupted his quiet.

"We'll arrive by nightfall," he informed.

Rhoco turned to reply, but was shocked into silence. It was the first time he had ever seen Feodras in sunlight. In fact, it was the first time he had ever seen *any* Murk outside of dismal darkness.

Feodras's skin, which normally appeared as shades of brown, green, black, and gray smashed together into an ugly, drab hue, was now the loveliest skin tone he'd ever seen. The light changed everything. Feodras appeared radiant, despite his usual slouch and shifty eyes. Rhoco had no words; he merely stared in bewildered awe.

"It's why they keep us in the dark," Feodras explained after catching Rhoco's astonished stare. "If others knew the blending was so appealing, everyone would do it."

"Why would the Royals keep this a secret? They paint Murks as hideous, uneducated miscreants. But it's so untrue. Why have they done this to you?"

"Because we are more powerful than them."

Rhoco's confusion increased. "How so?"

"Not only does the fusing of breeds make us look like this, it also gave us magic. There's a lot we can do that the Royals can't."

"Like what?"

He hesitated. "Why should I tell you?"

The trust was still missing.

"Fine. Don't."

Though Rhoco was intrigued and Feodras wished to divulge, they were both too stubborn and neither was willing to bend yet. It didn't matter that they had almost died together, or that they both took turns saving the other's life—the deep-rooted mistrust remained.

A buzzing whir approached from the north. Feodras heard it first.

"The sylphs," he whispered in terror.

Rhoco turned to gauge the threat. There was a patchy luster in the sky that steadily grew larger as it moved toward them. The noise became clearer, too. The high-pitched whine contained a hundred tiny voices that squealed with excited hunger.

"What do we do?" Rhoco asked, desperate to avoid being eaten by fairies.

Feodras leapt into his chair and began pedaling as fast as he could.

"You should have let Erlea stay," he scolded Rhoco as he pedaled. "The sylphs don't eat females."

"She is a just bumblebee!" Rhoco countered.

"Still, she could have spoken on our behalf. The sylphs might have listened to her. We are men, so our words mean nothing to them."

The coast of Wicker was in sight, but the sheen was already upon them and the sylphs circled the boat. Their shrill chatter was deafening, bringing both men to a halt. Rhoco buckled to his knees and Feodras released the rudder grips to cradle his head in his arms. He continued to pedal, but much more slowly and without direction.

"Mine. Mine. Mine."

"Tasty men, I've been so starved."

"I eat first!"

"We eat together."

"Must you eat us?" Rhoco asked from his knees.

A low growl underscored the earsplitting buzz. Their pretty faces morphed with savagery at the sound of his voice. Teeth bared, they moved in with slow aggression.

"How dare he."

"We eat him first."

"He'll taste so good."

"Like a mushy dullard."

"I love a fluffy brain."

"Feodras, help!" Rhoco begged as the sylphs advanced.

"I'm trying," he insisted as he returned his hands to the rudders and once again began pedaling quickly. He grimaced at the noise, but persisted through the pain.

The sylphs fluttered inches above Rhoco, still chattering, and he prepared for impact. He could not feel them land on him, but the moment they began grazing his skin, his senses awoke. He tried to shake them off, but their incisors dug deep.

"His sins taste like candy," the sylphs murmured even while chewing.

"Must have more."

"To the bone!"

The pain was so severe he began to lose consciousness.

The heart, he thought as his mind went dizzy. He looked over at Feodras, who still pedaled fast but was now using his elbows to hold the rudders in place so that he could use his hands to protect his ears from the shrieking sylphs. Feodras wouldn't be able to hear what he was about to reveal.

"Killing me will also kill a woman," he told the sylphs.

"Kill a woman?"

"We don't kill women."

The gnawing slowed and Rhoco pulled the heart from his pocket. He lifted the pouch into the air, relishing in the momentary pause in their attack.

The sylphs lingered, halting their feast to assess this new development. They could feel the heart's presence through the satin casing.

"It's a lady."

"Belongs to a lady."

"He must have stolen it."

"Sneaky man demon."

"I did not steal it," he explained. "It washed ashore, and I am trying to return it to its owner."

"We won't eat the heart."

"Just the man."

"We can see your soul."

"We know what you've done."

"We must devour you."

"Correct your misdeeds."

"Without me, the heart is lost at sea and the woman it belongs to will perish," Rhoco argued. "She needs me. I am trying to save her."

The sylphs snarled in debate.

"But he tastes so good."

"I want more."

"We cannot break our vow."

"Why don't we deliver the heart?"

"Yes. Yes, we shall."

"You can't lift an object as heavy as this," Rhoco challenged.

"Your doubt will be your downfall," the sylphs warned.

"I only say that because you're so tiny," he stammered, but he realized it was too late. He had offended the sylphs and he'd suffer their wrath.

They sang a soprano tune in unison.

Rhoco listened, wanting to tell them that he meant the heart no harm, that he meant *them* no harm. He wanted to swear that he had never hurt a female in his life, but then he remembered Almadine. His thoughts ran deeper, retrieving memories of Grette. The scene around him faded as he remembered her face, wearing both the glittering gaze of adoration and the ravaged look of betrayal. His resolve diminished as he recalled the love he destroyed.

Maybe the world would be a safer place without him in it.

A cool, salty wind swept through, intensifying the pain of his wounds. The world filled with music and the tune of a different song entered the air, conveying that they were now somewhere new.

The sylphs detached from his flesh and scurried, screaming, as dozens of wooden vines whipped through the air over the boat.

Rhoco went blind with pain, but Feodras's joyful cries revealed that this change in fate benefited them. Knowing they were safe, Rhoco silenced his suffering by slipping into a state of unconsciousness.

Chapter 19

Their boat collided into the dirt shore and a long, lanky arm made of wood reached into the boat. It picked Rhoco up with its long, branchlike fingers and cradled his motionless body in its hand.

"Do not hurt him!" Feodras pleaded.

"Of course we won't, we do not wish him dead. I am Beaumont, a triumphant healer and bringer of hope to the woebegones of the sea."

"Woebegones? We are no such thing!" Feodras insisted. Then the knobby arm of a different Woodlin extended into the boat and snatched him by his belt.

"Put me down!" Feodras demanded. "We have not lost hope, and we most certainly have not lost our courage. Let me go!"

"You are with us now. The sea can cause no further distress if you stay here. Comply, we beg, for the ocean offers nothing but death."

"We cannot," Feodras replied, struggling in the Woodlin's grip. "We have matters to attend to."

"The wenches of the sea have followed you here, and those of the sky, well, they crave your demise. We will help you, if you allow. We wish nothing but life for our friends of Orewall."

Feodras paused to scan his surroundings from his current vantage point. He hung hundreds of feet high, trapped in the unbreakable clutches of a quiet Woodlin.

Wicker was an ocean of trees. From afar, the forest seemed still, but when Feodras concentrated, he saw that the sea of green swayed ever so slightly with vibrant life. Wicker pulsated with energy; its soul was born from the terrain and was pure in purpose.

"What's your name?" Feodras asked his captor.

"Bolivar."

"Is every tree a Woodlin?" he asked.

"Of course," Bolivar answered.

Feodras looked around. "But not every tree is animated."

"We are swimming with life," Beaumont objected.

"What about him?" Feodras asked, pointing to a statuesque Woodlin situated behind Beaumont.

Beaumont turned his entire body, bending at the waist and twisting at a painful speed, to see what Feodras referred to. The branches of his head, which were thick with broad basswood leaves, shook as he moved. Time creaked to a halt as the giant Woodlin made the simple turn. Despite the stiffness, there was a rigid fluidity in his motions.

"You mean Brynmor?" Beaumont asked, slowly placing his free hand on the side of a petrified Woodlin. "He's just napping."

"We take long naps here," Bolivar confirmed.

Brynmor's beautiful face was delicately carved into his trunk, just as the faces of Beaumont and Bolivar were. He was equally tall, slender in build, and his head was crowned in leaves, but he appeared to have taken his nap mid-motion.

"Are you sure he meant to fall asleep?" Feodras inquired. "Looks as though his nap arrived mid-step."

"We are ancient creatures, keepers of nature. It's a consuming task, so sleep comes without request."

"What about Rhoco? Can you heal him?" he asked Beaumont.

"Naturally, and with ease. I am healing him as we speak."

"How?"

"Terrestrial magic," Beaumont explained, his wooden eyes twinkled mischievously as he spoke. "This land holds all the enchantments of Gaia, and Her charms course through our forms and into whatever we desire."

"We are Her favorite child, guaranteed," Bolivar added with a wink, "but you didn't hear that from me."

Feodras's eyes narrowed, offended they would claim that title. Not everyone believed in the Mother of the Universe, but the Murks certainly did, and they went above and beyond to solidify Her favor.

Feodras changed the subject, unwilling to argue with the tree men.

"When will Rhoco be well enough to leave?"

"Watch as he mends," Beaumont said, moving his hand closer to where the Murk hung in Bolivar's grip. Feodras looked on with wonder as Rhoco's shredded stone skin melded itself back together. The process was slow, but visible. Wound by wound, the skin crawled to meet its broken half. The raw cuts fused, and as the last lesion closed, Rhoco's eyes opened.

"Where am I?" Rhoco asked, voice hoarse from the lingering pain.

"Wicker," Beaumont said, looking down on his patient. "Land of tricks by twigs with wit. Welcome, friend. Your landing in my hand wasn't random, though I suspect you've already detected that."

"I haven't," Rhoco said as he coughed. He looked beyond the Woodlin's palm to see his stone boat a hundred feet below. He patted his pants, relieved to feel the lump of the heart in his pocket. "I thought the sylphs would surely kill me."

"They almost did. We saw your ghost, rising, hovering over its ravaged host. Your body clung to strands unstrung when we stepped in and swept the sylphs to the west." Bolivar spoke with excitement as he recalled the rescue.

"Refugee, what called you to the sea? Where were you going and why did you flee? Does it revolve around the secret you keep?" Beaumont poked his long wooden finger into Rhoco's thigh.

"It's really not your concern," Rhoco replied, unnerved that the Woodlins were onto him. "Just know that we mean no harm to anyone."

"What you hide is dangerous. Its past is no stranger to us."

"Let us go," Rhoco replied with a groan. Concerned by the warning, but undeterred.

"You won't last a day if you don't remain," Beaumont warned. "Safety resides in the place you now hide, and I wouldn't recommend leaving."

"We have to. Though I appreciate you saving my life, we cannot stay."

"I already told them that," Feodras interjected. "They don't understand and I've been hanging here, helpless, since we crashed."

"Won't you let us go?" Rhoco asked Beaumont.

"It would be against our code to let you go. Creatures await, ready to seal your fate, and we'd be remiss to allow such violence."

Rhoco tried a different tactic. "Then teach us how to defend ourselves. Show us how to ward off the monsters."

Beaumont lifted his head to look at Bolivar, who also hesitated at this request.

"Our wisdom is not free. You'll forever be in our debt if we share the secrets we keep," Beaumont explained.

"What does that mean exactly?" Rhoco asked.

"Chief Goran guards our knowledge with vigorous conviction; he does not like to share, he views disclosure as a malediction."

"Relaying knowledge is a curse?" Rhoco asked in disbelief.

"If we grant your demands, we lose our upper hand, and though we believe in prosperity for all, we don't condone the loss of our own."

"Then don't tell Goran," Rhoco stated the obvious.

"He knows all," Bolivar cautioned.

"Then we will leave without your help. Put us down," Rhoco demanded. He detested feeling small and helpless.

"That too would be breaking code," Beaumont objected, but then obliged by placing Rhoco on the forest floor. Bolivar followed his lead, placing Feodras down too.

Rhoco did not care how ethereal or exquisite these creatures were, he would not let their grandiose presence snuff his nerve.

"You better figure it out," he told them, "because we aren't staying here."

Before the Woodlins could respond, a foghorn sounded in the distance. Beaumont and Bolivar tensed.

"What was that?" Rhoco asked.

"The Mudlings," Beaumont explained as the ground beneath their feet turned to muck. The soil became wet and glued them in place. The once jovial and mystic nature of Wicker suddenly grew dark, and the atmosphere filled with gloom.

"They're coming to collect."

Chapter 20

"Collect what?" Rhoco asked.

"Seedlings," Bolivar explained. "And you, if you're spotted."

"Climb and hide within my leaves," Beaumont said, placing his hand near the ground so the Bouldes could step on. "The Mudlings are greedy thieves and I will not let them steal more than seedlings."

Rhoco and Feodras obeyed with difficulty. The muddy ground sucked their feet into its depths and the sludge reached their ankles. With great effort, they pried their feet free and clambered onto Beaumont's outstretched hand. Once aboard, the Woodlin lifted his arm and rested it upon his highest branches. There, Rhoco and Feodras exited and found a safe hiding spot between two large and sturdy boughs. Up high, the Bouldes could see for miles.

The Mudlings traveled in droves, foghorn growing louder as the creatures grew nearer. The deep notes of the horn were accompanied by a chanted bass line hum. They skated atop the muddy ground, gliding with speed and agility and sniffing the air as they approached.

They arrived at Beaumont and Bolivar's section of the forest in a pack of a hundred. The Mudlings were small creatures made of soil and slick with muck. Their skin appeared alive as the wet mud dripped off their little bodies and more oozed from where the previous had dispensed. Their vile appearance mirrored their hostile energy. What they lacked in stature, they compensated with force. The Mudlings demanded respect and inspired fear.

They swarmed the trees, smelling the air as they did so. They slipped along the slick ground and formed a circle around Beaumont.

"What do we smell," the closest Mudling growled.

"I am of the male breed; I do not carry seedlings," Beaumont explained, his ethereal voice quivering as he spoke.

"It is not the aroma of seedlings we detect," the Mudling explained.

"What you conceal is not from Wicker," another added.

"Or Soylé," a third chimed in.

"Smells delicious."

"Reveal the odor to us, or suffer the pits."

"I do not know what you speak of," Beaumont insisted.

The terrain quaked and the Woodlins sank deeper into the mud pit.

"I am Valterra, princess of Soylé, do not test my mercy," the first Mudling threatened the Woodlins. Rhoco peered through the branches of Beaumont's head and noticed the creature wore a crown woven of twigs.

"I swear, we have nothing to reveal."

Valterra's burnt-orange eyes widened with rage. A guttural growl started in the pit of her stomach and rose in volume as it reached her throat. In unison, the Mudlings each stomped their left foot and leaned toward Brynmor, eyes fixated on the soil at the base of his trunk. The ground underfoot collapsed and the mud consumed the sleeping Woodlin. He sank into the pit faster than a blink, gone forever.

Beaumont trembled, forcing Rhoco and Feodras to hold on tighter.

"I won't let him go down because of us," Rhoco concluded with annoyed but determined conviction. "If I turn myself over, do you promise you'll find me in Soylé?"

"I promise," Feodras swore. Rhoco had no choice but to believe him.

"Stay here," he told Feodras, then stepped out from his hiding place.

"Do not harm this tree," he roared from the edge of Beaumont's bough. "I am what you seek."

"A Boulde?" Valterra questioned, intrigued. "How ever did you wind up here?"

"Bouldes never leave Orewall," a tinier Mudling stated in wonder.

"Shut up, Horlach," Valterra snapped. The Mudling obeyed and stepped backward into her shadow. She continued, "A Boulde is worth much. Come to me."

"Are you sure?" Beaumont murmured to Rhoco.

"Yes," Rhoco whispered. "You will not fall on my behalf. Help me down."

Beaumont raised his hand, Rhoco climbed onto it, and the Woodlin slowly lowered him to the ground. Rhoco stepped off and his foot slushed into the thick mud. He was stuck.

With long strides, Valterra skated toward him. She was hideous from afar, but up close, a majestic aura hid beneath the layers of dirt on her face.

She was no taller than his waist, but her brilliant, yellow eyes still bore into him.

"King Alun will pay nicely for a traitor," she said with such menace that Rhoco actually felt threatened. She slid around him in circles, never breaking eye contact. "And there's no doubt you're a traitor."

"What makes you say that?"

"You're here. Bouldes are like the Metellyans: labor lugs with no spines. You do what you're told, live a pitiful, uneducated existence, then die. You don't leave, you don't fight back, and you are ignorant and complacent. You being here at all reveals much."

"I haven't done anything wrong. King Alun has no reason to consider me a traitor."

"You cannot fool me. You are in alliance with the anarchists."

The what? Rhoco thought before speaking aloud. "I am in alliance with no one but myself."

With her large nostrils, Valterra sniffed the air again. She moved in closer and gave Rhoco an olfactory inspection. She used her nose to search every inch of him, flouting his personal space as she traversed his body. He tried not to gag when he noticed that she stank of rotted vegetation and moldy pond water.

"There's more," she finally said with a deep exhale. "You hold a dark secret."

"I do not," he swore.

"Lies. I can smell it."

"I live by the sea and simply had a desire to explore more of Namaté."

"You're coming with me."

She circled a finger in the air and her Mudling minions surged Rhoco. Though they were little, they were fierce, and they had him bound in seconds. It took fifty of them to pull his large body back to Soylé, but they managed with efficiency. They skated south, Valterra leading the way, dragging him through the thick sludge. Those who did not help lug his body carried satchels filled with stolen seedlings and hummed a deep, rhythmic tune in time with the foghorn.

New wounds formed atop his old ones as he was dragged through mud that concealed sharp rocks and branches. Though his wounds were closed, his nerves weren't fully healed from the sylph attack, and he felt every jab and scratch. After a particularly rough drop down a small ledge, he felt the lump of the heart against his thigh. It remained in its pouch in his pocket and he hoped this bumpy journey did not cause it harm. This was another setback, another delay in its delivery to its owner, and Rhoco prayed that his trust in Feodras wasn't misplaced.

Chapter 21

Soylé was a stark contrast from Wicker. The lands were connected by a swamp-ridden isthmus, but they were so different in nature they might as well have been located in different seas. Thick sludge covered the entire landscape of Soylé, which was a barren wasteland of dead trees and boulders. The darkness was so engraved into the atmosphere that Rhoco suspected the sun did not shine here. Though Soylé was not covered by a dome of fog, like Vapore, a dense patch of clouds hovered motionlessly overhead, unmoving despite the winds. The Mudlings lived in the shadows like true creatures of the night. The world here was soggy and dead, a true testament to its inhabitants' temperaments.

"It's daytime. Where's the sun?" Rhoco asked.

"Hidden, as we like it," Valterra scoffed. "We hate the light and Gaia gives us what we want."

"Why would she cater to you?" Rhoco asked.

"Because we follow Her rules, unlike the rest of you."

Rhoco wasn't sure what that meant. Despite all these foreigners from different lands claiming Gaia's existence was true, he was never presented with facts to prove it so.

The Mudlings tied him to a dead tree, where he sat atop a mound of loose, wet soil.

"How do you plan to contact King Alun?" he asked, curious to know their methods.

"We have our ways," the princess sneered. "Bouldes know nothing of the relationship between lands outside Orewall."

"Why don't you teach me?"

"That's not my responsibility," she snapped. "Nor is it my fault you're a heaping mass of primitive ignorance. Your lack of education is not my burden to carry, nor remedy."

She turned her back on him and skated away with grace and speed. He was left amongst her minions, who were far less refined.

"Stupid rock," Horlach remarked as he smacked the back of Rhoco's head with a small branch. The little Mudling laughed upon contact. "Does it hurt? Or is your stone skull too thick to feel pain?" He struck the side of Rhoco's head again.

Normally, Rhoco wouldn't have felt the puny assault at all, but his body was still healing and every tiny touch hurt.

"I can feel your pathetic attempts to break me, but they don't hurt," he lied. "You aren't strong enough to harm a Boulde."

Horlach flared his nostrils and furrowed his brow.

"Tell me if you still think that's true after Valterra is done with you."

Rhoco spat at the Mudling's feet.

Horlach whaled him across the face with his branch one more time before marching away.

A group of quiet Mudlings sat around a fire to Rhoco's left. They were the smallest of the troupe and did not radiate the same ruthlessness.

"Is it true?" Rhoco called out, catching their attention. Their heads turned in unison at the sound of his voice. "That she can reach King Alun?"

Without answering, they turned back toward the fire.

"Please, I need to know. I've caused you no harm, why are you doing this to me?"

The smallest of the group lifted her head and considered his question while the others ignored him.

"Pay him no mind, Dharani."

"He's not wrong, though," she replied to her cohort's warning.

"Valterra will have your head if she finds out you showed him kindness."

"Do you plan to snitch on me, Daelan?"

"Never."

"And the rest of you?"

The group of tiny Mudlings shook their heads.

She stood. "The civil war between us and the Woodlins is bad enough, and now we're dragging other cultures into it. It's not right."

"We are the pirates of the planet, the nefarious raiders of Namaté. Dharani, you know this," Daelan argued. "We take what we want, when we want, as we have for decades. It's how we survive."

"But is it necessary? Is it the *only* way to survive?" Dharani questioned. "I think not."

"I fear you'll regret any pity you show the Boulde," Daelan asserted. "One of the elders might overhear, or return and catch you in the act."

"You better act as my lookout then," she countered, then walked toward Rhoco.

Because he was sitting, Dharani stood a few inches taller than him, and she glared down at him with skeptical interest.

"The Bouldes provide us with rock dust. It keeps us alive."

"How?"

"It's a mineral fertilizer. It allows us to digest seedlings for nutrients and reproduce. Without it we'd die."

"What does King Alun receive in return for this invaluable gift?"

"Our eternal devotion. We scour the seas and obtain whatever he desires, no matter the location or cost. Same with

208

deliveries. We are the reason your people haven't been forced to leave Orewall in so long."

"I thought that was because we bowed out of the Great Fight for the scepter of alchemy."

"Yes, the Bouldes abandoned that war a long time ago, but when they did, the Voltains branded your culture with cowardice and deemed the seas unsafe for any Boulde to cross. I suspect you've already faced the cecaelia and sylphs?"

"Yes," he admitted. "They found us quickly."

"That's because they are bribed to do so. Guarding the ocean and sky borders of Orewall is part of their duty, as decreed by the Voltains—they have the scepter, so they make the rules."

"How did you become one of our allies then?"

"We were never part of the war for the scepter. Neither were the Woodlins or Bonz. When Valterra heard your people dipped out of the race, she sailed to Orewall and offered her services. We were weak back then—we were barely surviving. Deals were made and here we are."

"I still don't understand what I'm suffering for."

Dharani lowered her voice, looking back at the other Mudlings, who did not seem to be watching. "Valterra worships King Alun and Queen Gemma. The Mudlings have never been this strong before, and it's all thanks to them." Dharani grimaced. "But the princess is only interested in how it benefits her. If she senses she has something that the Royal Bouldes might value, she'll do whatever it takes to capitalize on it, even if it means sacrificing and endangering her own people."

"Help me escape," he pleaded.

"Absolutely not," she countered. "Your fate is sealed. I just thought it might give you comfort if you understood why this was happening to you. I know how ignorant the Bouldes have become since their borders closed, and while others see it as foolish and spineless, I see it as a shame. It's not your fault you're stupid."

"I'm not stupid."

"If you weren't, then you wouldn't be in this mess."

"Every single element on this planet has been working against me since I left," he growled. "Actually, it started long before I left, and not at my own fault, need I remind you. This predicament I'm in is not a result of my intelligence, it's a tragic series of ill-starred incidents I never had control over."

"Perhaps. Still, here you are."

"But you could change my luck."

"I cannot. I will not. Speaking with you was risky enough. I will not gamble more."

"Then why bother speaking to me at all?" Rhoco demanded.

"To prevent your quest from being a total waste. Now you have some answers and I hope that helps you find some peace in death."

"What I'm after is far greater than the peanuts you just gave me. There are lives on the line."

"Not my concern," Dharani said, shrugging as she returned to the fire. Her Mudling companions barely acknowledged her return and refused to look at Rhoco again. He sensed the inhabitants of Soylé had very little freedom.

Since the landscape was minimal, he could see the black ocean lapping against the distant, swampy shores. He concentrated on the horizon, willing Feodras to materialize with their ship, but the night passed with no sign of his Murk shipmate.

Valterra returned in the morning with a bounce in her glide.

"You seem chipper," Rhoco noted once she was near. "Did you contact King Alun?"

"Not yet, but I got word that your delivery will pay nicely."

"From who?"

"The Obsidians."

"You don't even know my name. How could they possibly know I'm missing?"

"They don't know that *you're* missing. *You* are unimportant, but the return of any runaway is heavily rewarded." Then, with eager greed, she speculated, "Perhaps I'll receive a payment of gems in addition to rock dust. I haven't received diamond dust since the death of the Ice Queen."

"Who?"

Valterra ignored his question and began walking in predatory circles around him.

Rhoco grimaced, unable to think of anything that might change the princess' mind. His arms and torso were tied to the dead tree with vines and he could not reach the heart. Though he could feel its weight in his pocket, accessing it was impossible.

"In the meantime," Valterra continued, "there's no reason you can't prove yourself useful."

"How so?"

"We are running low on rock dust and I can smell the nutrients in your limestone skin."

"You're going to eat me?"

"No, just shave you down. You'll be a weak and skinny Boulde when you return to Orewall," she sneered.

Rhoco squirmed beneath his restraints, alone and terrified. He should have never trusted Feodras. With his normal strength, he could have broken the vines easily, but he had not fully healed and the harsh mode of transportation in Soylé only delayed his recovery. Still, he tried.

In the distance, Dharani, Daelan, and crew helped Horlach and the elders gather the torture devices they'd use on Rhoco to grind his skin into dust. With his gaze fixed on the Mudlings, he continued to struggle beneath his restraints, hoping he'd miraculously break free before they returned.

A pair of cold hands grabbed his wrists from behind, startling him so much he almost yelped.

"It's me," Feodras whispered as he sawed at the vines with his serrated knife.

Rhoco turned his focus to the horizon.

"Where's our boat?"

"It's there. It's gray and blends in with the bleary scenery."

The knife severed the vines and Rhoco was free, but they had to be smart.

"If we start running, we'll never make it. They skate atop the mud, moving at speeds we cannot outrun," Rhoco advised. "Go back to the ship and be ready to set sail as soon as I get there."

Feodras nodded, then handed him a hollow bamboo shoot and a bag of damp seeds.

"Shoot these at them."

"What is this?"

"Lime pits. The juice hardens mud. It won't stop them completely, but it should slow them down." Rhoco stared at him in confused amazement, so Feodras explained, "I understand every chemical in each element, every weakness and strength. I was born with a Murk brain, remember?" He smirked. "And the Woodlins made me these shooters."

"Got it. You ought to go."

Feodras agreed and began the trek back to the ship.

Rhoco loaded the pipe and took aim at Valterra. With a deep breath he propelled a seed in her direction, missing and striking Daelan instead. The seed pierced the Mudling's temple and disappeared into his head. The mud around the bullet seed hardened, and in an instant, he was paralyzed.

Horlach noticed first.

"Why'd you stop?" he barked. He pushed Daelan on the shoulder and the small Mudling fell to the ground like a toppled statue. Dharani knelt by his side and pointed at the hole in his head.

Rhoco already had another seed prepped and aimed. It missed Valterra again and hit Dharani's shoulder. The damage only paralyzed the left side of her body.

"Lime seeds," Dharani declared, eyes wide with rage as she dug her fingers into the wound to retrieve the bullet. Their heads turned in unison toward Rhoco.

"He must be stopped," Valterra growled. "Charge!"

The Mudlings abandoned their work to address their unruly prisoner, but Rhoco had already loaded another shot, which he sent flying toward Horlach's head. The seed struck him between the eyes, and as it melted into his mud, he went slack.

The gummy ground made for a strenuous getaway, but Rhoco did not give up. With all his strength, he jumped and ran as fast as he could toward the shore, shooting seeds at every opportunity.

His aim improved with each shot and he managed to land a few more bullseyes into his aggressors' skulls. The ship was now in sight, but the Mudlings were on his tail.

Turning, he aimed over his shoulder and rocketed a seed into the eye socket of his closest pursuer. She tried to keep pace, but the dryness of the acidic lime juice crept through her brain and caused her to falter. A moment later, she fell to the ground. One down, but another fifty closed the gap. They skated toward him, gaining distance as Rhoco continued his ungraceful hop-run. These Mudlings were intimidating little creatures, and as they got closer, their determined gazes focused sharply on their target.

"Use me," a voice echoed inside Rhoco's head. The heart called to him.

Between leaps he reached into his pocket and lifted the satchel containing the heart. Unlaced and exposed to the world, the heart released a deafening shriek.

The preternatural sound was so shocking, it forced Rhoco to halt. He looked behind, certain that the Mudlings would now be inches away, but they weren't. The entire pack lay motionless in the mud.

"Run," the heart demanded without ceasing its screech. Rhoco obeyed and clambered through the mud toward the boat.

"What is that awful noise?" Feodras shouted from the deck of the boat, his hands covering his ears.

Rhoco pulled the strings of the pouch tight, concealing the heart again. The moment the heart was returned to the darkness of the satchel, the shrieking stopped. Before Rhoco could think of an explanation, Feodras spoke again, panicked.

"Hurry!"

Rhoco glanced behind to see that the Mudlings were back on their feet and dashing toward him. He splashed through the shallow water and then raced up the ladder Feodras lowered for him.

"Your ears are bleeding," he exclaimed as Rhoco climbed aboard.

"There's no time," Rhoco panted, touching his eardrums to find that Feodras was right. "We must go."

Feodras raced to the pedals, turned the paddle wheel, and maneuvered them away from Soylé. Rhoco manned the patchwork, squirrel-hide sail to complement the direction

Feodras had taken. Finally, when they were a safe distance from Soylé, Rhoco glanced over the side of the boat to find the Mudlings seething along the shore. Valterra doled out orders while her minions glared at the stone boat with contempt. His escape was their failure and they would suffer Valterra's wrath until their wrong was made right.

Rhoco could do no more than hope that day never came.

Chapter 22

The waves were explosive off the coast of Soylé. Feodras had no time to discuss what had happened, as they were too busy trying to stay alive. He manned the directional devices while Rhoco attempted to keep the sail intact. The winds were so strong and the waves so large that the squirrel-hide was nearly torn from the mast multiple times.

A large wave of salt water splashed overboard and smacked Rhoco in the face, stinging his never-healing wounds.

"You have to keep the sail in place," Feodras shouted over the howling wind. "We must sail to the south of Coppel."

"I'm doing my best," Rhoco insisted. Another gust swept through, ripping the ropes from his hands and spinning the sail in circles till it was wrapped tightly around the mast. Rhoco worked fast to untangle himself from the ropes and unwind the sail. He felt frail and incompetent.

They relied on their compass to guide them. The darkness of the sky and ocean blended together and they could see nothing but what was illuminated by the lanterns on their boat. The firelight reflected off the dark surface of the sea as it swayed with each passing wave, revealing little with its feeble reach. Rhoco prayed the storm passed soon. He wasn't sure how much more he could withstand.

Wicker and Soylé were to the west of Orewall, so both men stayed awake through the night, doing everything in their power to keep the boat south of their homeland and headed east toward Coppel. They feared if they slept, the currents might crash them into Orewall.

Rhoco tried to swallow his aggravation. They had made a full circle around Orewall with only near-death experiences to show for it, and an entire week later, they were back where they started. He could not blame Feodras, though he wanted to. The Murk tried to warn him about the volcanoes.

When daylight broke through the clouds the next morning, they were sailing past the southern shores of Orewall. In the distance, to the east, Rhoco could see a patch of submarine volcanoes erupting through the surface of the sea. The glowing red lava set fire to the black water, reminding Rhoco of their initial mistake that had wasted so much of their time. They redirected their ship farther south.

The windstorm broke and the sea calmed. Feodras helped Rhoco secure the sail and they retreated beneath the platform to sleep. The boat was on course, with no outside forces to redirect them, so they rested easy, knowing that when they woke, they'd be closer to their objective.

Hours passed and Rhoco awoke, startled from a nightmare.

"The cecaelia," he panted, shaking Feodras awake. "The cecaelia. The Woodlins never told us how to keep them away!"

Feodras grumbled, "Beaumont and Bolivar fixed the warding runes on the hull of our ship before I left to save you."

"So we're safe from the sea monsters?"

"Yes."

"What about the sylphs?"

Feodras hesitated. "You won't like it."

"Tell me."

"Erlea."

"The bumblebee?"

"Yes, she is on her way to us now. I summoned her. Sylphs are olfactory hunters—they target men—and Erlea's female scent will camoflauge ours. If they can't smell us, they can't find us."

Rhoco groaned. "Fine, but she reports nothing back to the bees in Orewall."

"She won't blab a word of our adventure unless we tell her to."

"You better be certain about that."

"I am," Feodras groaned.

"I'll tear your head off if this goes awry."

Feodras sighed. Nothing he could say or do would mollify Rhoco's mistrust.

"I don't like this at all," Rhoco murmured anxiously.

"Would you rather be eaten alive by ravenous fairies?"

"Of course not, which is why I'm not fighting you about this."

"Feels like fighting to me," Feodras huffed.

Rhoco glanced at his companion, unsure why he was being so tough on him.

Erlea arrived fifteen minutes later. She went to Feodras immediately and landed on the rim of his ear. He nodded, then laughed, then shook his head with a frown.

"What are you two talking about?" Rhoco demanded.

"Just catching up," Feodras replied curtly.

Rhoco marched to the back of the boat, hoping to hide his dejection from the others. He stared at the water, which was glassy and smooth for miles. Orewall was a silhouette in the distance now. They'd gone a long way, even if the route was convoluted, and Rhoco was happy to finally reach smooth sailing.

He glanced over his shoulder at the Murk, who was having a merry time in the company of his bumblebee. Rhoco had always been happy in solitude, but for the first time, he felt loneliness; he felt left out. They had each other and he had no one.

He thought of Cybelle, and though he certainly missed her, his memory of their friendship did not fill the void this new feeling created. He then pictured Almadine, whose image filled him with guilt and shame, and he opened his eyes in disgust.

He was very aware of the heart he kept protected in his pocket and tried to ignore its presence, but it grew heavier each time he thought of an old friend.

Carrick came to mind, and though Rhoco regarded him pleasantly, it was also simple and insubstantial. They never had a deep friendship until working together on the boat, but that didn't last long and Rhoco left soon after, preventing them from growing any closer.

He cursed at himself, regretting his shallow life and ashamed that he kept so many people away. It was part of his nature; he wasn't the only Boulde guilty of living in stubborn isolation, but he was the only one to take it to such extremes. It took a journey beyond Orewall and countless near-death experiences to see his behavior as foolish.

He kept this revelation in mind when he glanced back at Feodras. He could not let his old habits shape the future. He would find a way to break the cycle.

Erlea's return gave Feodras great joy. It was apparent in the sudden turn of his demeanor. He stood straight for the first time and his expression was jovial. It was the first time Rhoco saw him smile. Feodras was unable to hide his elation, nor did he try to.

There must be someone I long for, Rhoco thought. *Someone I've kept hidden in the depths of my heart.*

He closed his eyes to try again, hoping to discover another layer of himself, and it didn't take long before Grette's smile appeared behind his eyelids. Sight of her jarred him out of this moment of self-discovery and his eyes shot open in panic. He had his answer, though he refused to accept it as truth. He buried Grette long ago, though not nearly as deep as he thought.

Rhoco wallowed in self-pity—Grette could never love him again, his only option was to let her go.

The heart thumped against his thigh as he struggled to suppress his old love.

It beckoned for his attention and he obliged, hoping it might mollify his sudden bout of loneliness. He kept it in the pouch, but unlaced the strings so he could see it. It pulsated red for him, responding to his needs.

"Do you have a name?" he whispered. The heart glowed brighter in response. "If I touch you, you must tell me."

He had no indication that the heart would obey, but he tried anyway. Rhoco placed a single finger on the heart and was swept away.

He landed in the familiar, gray room, alone but eager for the lady in white to arrive. He waited, but she did not come. His nerves heightened with anticipation and fear that she would not show.

The sound of a child's laughter echoed through the room, bouncing off the walls until it tapered into silence. Then she appeared, radiant as ever, but younger than before. The weight she carried was heavy as she glided across the dark space. When she turned, he saw the small shadow of a child holding onto her waist.

The child's laughter resonated through the space again, causing the room to darken.

"You cannot stay here," she yelled at the shadow, but it did not understand. She pushed the child away, but it sprang back like elastic and clung to her side.

The room rumbled and lightning flashed, illuminating the fear in her glass eyes. Tears fell down her cheeks like shimmering diamonds.

"I am so sorry. Please forgive me."

The silhouette of the child looked up at her, confused; its utter confidence and trust in her was unwavering. Innocence poured from the naïve child and Rhoco cringed as she struck the child, knocking the shadow to its knees.

She then crouched over the heaping mass and consumed the shadow whole.

The child was gone.

Her tears fell faster now. *"Oh, I loved you so."*

Rhoco shared in her moment of grief. When the silence passed, she glared up at him from where she knelt. The bottom half of her face was smeared in shadow and her eyes were bright with contempt. She had transformed into the grown woman he was accustomed to seeing.

"Don't look so appalled," she snarled. *"I already warned you, my darkness will consume you, too."* Her eyelashes were still wet with tears, but her expression was not remorseful; it was scorned and bitter.

As her anger subdued and her face returned to that of the kind angel he thought he was saving, Rhoco was ripped from the vision. His parting impression was of a broken woman in need of love.

He removed his finger from the heart and his sights were back on the sea. The heart sat in his hand, separated by the satchel. He pulled the drawstring tight, knotted the ropes, and then returned the heart to his pocket. He could not fathom a plausible justification for the vision, but he also saw the pain in her eyes as she sent him away. She did not gloat in the kill, she grieved it, and it appeared to haunt her daily.

While he tried to make sense of what she showed him, a spectacle emerged on the horizon. A fleet of boats raced toward them, moving so fast that water propelled into the air.

"Feodras," he shouted. "Look!"

Feodras hurried to the back of the boat and assessed the massive convoy of boats speeding toward them. A foghorn blared with authority, revealing their aggressor's identity.

Chapter 23

The Mudlings steadily gained on them. They moved fast, horns blaring and water shooting into the air from the back of their boats. Once they were close enough, Rhoco could see the little menaces crouched, ready to pounce the moment their ships were in reach. They pounded their fists against their wooden decks in unison as Valterra led the pack toward their prey.

"They are gaining on us," Rhoco said, worried, as he fiddled with the sails.

Feodras pedaled madly. "If we can reach Coppel, we'll be okay."

Rhoco looked toward the horizon and saw the brass haze separating Coppel from the rest of the world. It wasn't far—but neither were the Mudlings. Unable to do much else to help, Rhoco kept his focus on their aggressors. Eight Mudlings pedaled each boat forward, leaving Feodras overwhelmingly outmanned and out-raced.

The foghorn blared, loud and menacing, and the sound of the Mudlings' chanting battle cries was audible over the pounding of their fists. Rhoco was certain they'd be caught before they crossed Coppel's border.

Ropes with stones carved into hooks began flying overboard. As soon as those ropes were taut, Mudlings braved the line and swung inch by inch toward the Boulde ship. Rhoco raced around the boat, dislodging the hooks and sending the Mudlings into the ocean below. He watched a group go down. The moment their dirt bodies hit the water, they disintegrated into nothing. The sea ate them alive.

The Mudlings continued to encircle their boat, attaching ropes from all angles, and Rhoco hurried to detach them all. The noise from the horn was deafening, which made it hard to concentrate, but he did not quit. The Mudlings were agile and swayed with speed toward him. If he let any aboard, he and Feodras would be caught.

Just as he unfastened the sixth rope, the sound of clanging metal entered the fray. The Mudlings heard it too and it caused them to pause, dangling with uncertainty.

"Fall back!" Valterra demanded, and the Mudlings began backtracking along the ropes.

"Don't stop," Feodras urged Rhoco. "They'll only come after us again."

Rhoco continued unlatching the hooks, sending the surrendered Mudlings to their demise. They screeched as they plummeted and he did his best to ignore his sudden guilt.

He sent half the Mudlings to crumble and drown in the sea, while the other half made it back to their boats. The Mudlings cut all ropes still attached and fled with haste back to Soylé.

The monotonous drone of the foghorn faded and the clamor of tin and steel took over. Rhoco looked up to see that they were now inside the brass haze. The bustling shore of Coppel grew near and the hard-working Metellyans were visible.

"Are we safe here?" he asked.

"If we act smart," Feodras replied.

Rhoco wasn't sure what that meant, but it was too late to ask questions. They were at the docks and the stevedores were already anchoring their boat.

"Never seen a boat like this before," one of them commented.

"It's made of stone. Very peculiar," another added.

"Who's up there?" the first asked in a shout.

"Bouldes," Rhoco yelled back.

"Bouldes? How did you manage to make it this far?"

"Luck," Rhoco hollered honestly.

"Luck, indeed. The Voltains rigged all of Namaté against you."

"We learned that the hard way."

"What brings you here?"

"An attempt to escape the Mudrats."

The Metellyans snickered.

"An enemy of the Muds is a friend of ours. Come down."

"Stay cautious," Feodras whispered to Rhoco before tossing their rope ladder overboard and climbing down. Rhoco followed. Though the Metellyans seemed welcoming, he previously concluded that nothing beyond Orewall was truly as it appeared.

"I'm Sovann," the first Metellyan said in greeting. He was tall and sturdy, made of gold and copper. His face was chiseled and sharp with metallic angles that shimmered in the sunlight.

"And I'm Rezar," the second Metellyan offered. This man was made of gold and silver. The hue of his skin was colder than Sovann's, but the features etched onto his metal face were just as severe.

The Metellyans moved with stiffness, joints creaking as they helped the Bouldes onto the tin dock. Feodras appeared even more radiant in the golden haze of Coppel than he did in mere sunlight, and both Metellyans eyed him with curiosity. Their gazes were critical, but they kept their thoughts to themselves.

Rhoco was offended on the Murk's behalf—watching outsiders judge him made Rhoco feel protective. So he maneuvered his large body to stand between scrawny Feodras and the broad Metellyans.

"Will this hold all of our weight?" Rhoco asked with alarm the moment he felt the flimsy metal buckle beneath his feet.

"Hasn't failed us yet," Rezar replied. He stared intently at Feodras, who remained quiet, then back at Rhoco. "Let's get you fed."

The stevedores led the Bouldes ashore. The tin dock did not bend under their weight, but both Bouldes left dented footprints in their wake.

A bustling marketplace draped the coast of Coppel. The unintentional music of the Metellyans was noisy as the merchants, peddlers, blacksmiths, and laborers went about their day, banging and clanking with each movement.

"It's loud here," Feodras noted with a furrowed brow. He spoke softly, intending only Rhoco to hear, but Rezar was tuned in.

"What's loud about it?"

"You don't hear the rhythms?" Rhoco asked, then realized both Sovann and Rezar unknowingly contributed to the sound. Their metal feet tapped along the pewter ground and their knees cracked in tempo. It was a small rhythm amidst the larger one.

"Guess we're just used to the noise," Sovann said with a shrug. "Do you fellas like swan?"

"What's swan?" Rhoco asked.

"Only the finest meat you'll ever sink your teeth into."

"Bouldes don't eat meat," Feodras contributed in a small voice. Rhoco wasn't sure why the Murk had regressed to his former shyness, but he assumed the grandiose stature of the Metellyans intimidated him.

"Since when?" Sovann asked, scowling. His razor-sharp features bent downward in murderous fashion. Rezar mirrored his perplexed expression.

"Since forever. Meat consumption is banned."

"Not true. I shared many a carnivorous meal with Boulde soldiers, back when your lot fought beside us," Rezar informed the Bouldes.

"King Alun has done you a terrible disservice," Sovann commented, shaking his head as he did so. "What was his reasoning?"

"He told us the animals were infected and that their meat would turn us into savages," Feodras answered with wide eyes.

"Lies," Sovann snorted. "Meat only makes you stronger. The protein sharpens your wits and clears your thoughts. He's got you all living on a slave's diet."

"Of course he does," Feodras mumbled in defeat.

"I like squirrel meat," Rhoco interjected, hoping to seem a little less sheltered and weak.

"A poor man's delicacy," Rezar laughed, his shiny teeth reflecting the daylight. Rhoco caught the gleam with envy. Though his dolomite teeth were quite capable, he imagined teeth made of platinum could tear through a critter's body even quicker. Rezar continued, "But I suppose it's all you could find.

Once you try swan, you'll never be able to stomach squirrel again."

"Why'd you leave Orewall in the first place?" Sovann asked as they walked through the crowded streets. He looked to Feodras for a reply.

There was a pause as neither Boulde jumped to answer.

"Hmph." Sovann's golden gaze scanned their guests with suspicion. "I suppose there will be plenty of time to talk over lunch."

"A full belly does the brain good," Rezar added.

Though they maintained jovial spirits, Rhoco sensed something was amiss. He tried to determine what possible motive the Metellyans might have, but they reached their eating place before he could define the bad feeling.

"Eldora makes the best swan pie in all of Coppel," Rezar said as they approached the tiny teashop. Kettles and teacups ornately sculpted from copper and chrome hung from the ceiling. Beautiful boteh patterns and scenes from ancient folklore were carved into their sides, and Rhoco admired the artistry as they were led to a table.

At the front of the teashop, which was covered with a mesh canopy, was a small, copper patio with four tables for customers. The teacups hung from the checkered beams supporting the awning, and at the back of the store was a tiny kitchen with minimal lighting. As he sat at a table, Rhoco stared into the shadows, but only saw darkness.

"Eldora!" Sovann hollered. "She's old and hard of hearing," he explained to the Bouldes. He then picked up a bell that sat in the middle of their table and shook it violently. The raucous chimes, which produced a high-pitched ting, summoned their host from the shadows.

She walked toward them slowly, squinting her golden eyes as she approached.

"You boys again," she scoffed. Her demeanor reminded Rhoco of Cybelle and he immediately missed his old friend. "Tea before pie," she insisted.

"White ginger and pear for me," Sovann said.

"I'll take citrus and lavender." Rezar looked to their guests. "You have to have a cup of tea if you want swan pie. That's how this works."

"Give me your favorite," Rhoco said to Eldora, then pointed to Feodras. "Same for him."

"Mix it up nice for our guests," Sovann instructed.

She nodded, examining every inch of the Bouldes before turning to fetch the tea. Her behavior was slow and calculated, her demeanor wise and worldly, and Rhoco suspected she could assess a situation before a single word was spoken.

She returned a few moments later carrying a copper tray laden with four teacups and a large kettle filled with hot water. Inside each teacup was a handcrafted teabag.

"Apple peppermint for our guests," she said before placing cups in front of Rhoco and Feodras. Neither knew the art of tea drinking, so they watched Sovann and Rezar before unlacing their own teabags and dumping the contents into their cups.

Rhoco poured hot water over the herbs and the aroma hit his nostrils with force. The smell was divine. He took a slow sip, relieved to find he enjoyed the flavor as well. Halfway through their drinks, Sovann broke the silence.

"Eldora is a concoctionist."

"What's that?"

"Potion master," he answered, then took another sip. "Or a witch. Whichever term rings true to you."

Rhoco and Feodras looked down at their cups simultaneously. Rhoco wasn't one to be superstitious, but he was suddenly unnerved. Feodras, who was a true Boulde in this sense, placed his teacup down and pushed it away.

Rezar laughed. "No need to be paranoid, it's just tea."

Still, Feodras refused to take another sip. "I do not mingle with magic I don't understand."

"Pardon his refusal," Rhoco said, embarrassed. "Bouldes are superstitious. I hope this does not offend you or our host."

"Eldora will not be pleased."

"No need to upset anyone," Rhoco insisted, pouring the remnants of Feodras's drink into his own. "I enjoy the tea. I'll drink it."

He did not want to drink any more, but he also did not want to lose the opportunity to try swan pie, so he chugged the remaining tea. The Metellyans' eyes widened as he finished what was left.

"That's the spirit," Sovann said before smacking Rhoco on the shoulder in a gesture of camaraderie. The slap elicited a strange noise upon contact, a chimed ping with a grating scratch, and Rhoco felt the momentary discomfort of the metal hand against his bare, stone shoulder.

"We appreciate your hospitality," Rhoco said.

"If the Voltains discovered we were harboring Bouldes, we'd be in big trouble."

"Then why are you sheltering us?" Rhoco asked.

"Because we hate the Voltains."

"It would be nice if you repaid the favor by divulging what you're running from," Rezar added.

"We aren't running from anything. I'm just trying to make a delivery," Rhoco answered, unsure why he revealed so much.

"To who?" Sovann pried. Although he spoke to Rhoco, he was glaring at Feodras with annoyance.

"I'm not sure," Rhoco answered honestly. A slow fog crept through his mind.

"Then to where?"

Feodras shook his head, but Rhoco was no longer in control of his wits. Words were coming out that he didn't mean to say.

"Crystet." His eyes widened in panic as he realized he would answer any question they asked.

"Land of glass? Home of the Glaziene?" Sovann pondered aloud, his expression mischievous. "How perfect."

"What have you done to me?"

"You should never drink a witch's brew," Sovann advised with a devious smirk.

"Is the Murk your prisoner? Has King Alun sent you here to disband the resistance from the inside?" Rezar asked.

"No. What are you even talking about?" His obliviousness was apparent.

"What are you delivering to Crystet?"

"Stop," Feodras exclaimed, breaking up the interrogation. The Metellyans refocused their rage.

"How dare you come here, expecting safety, without fulfilling your end of the deal," Rezar seethed.

"But I have. I brought the crystals."

"What crystals?" Rhoco asked, utterly perplexed.

"The crystals from Orewall. They negate electricity," Sovann explained in irritation.

"Where are they?" Rezar demanded.

Feodras stammered, "I built our boat with them. Black tourmaline is scattered throughout the hull."

"You rotten traitor," Rhoco exhaled as he spoke with fury. "You used me."

"I never meant to ruin your mission."

"But you have." He turned his attention back to the Metellyans. "What do you need the crystals for?"

"To fight the Voltains, of course," Rezar explained, his passion aflame.

"To fight them?"

"Oh, I see." Rezar made the connection. "You must be one of the benighted Bouldes."

"What does that mean?" Rhoco demanded, chest puffed, offended by a word he did not understand.

"The Voltains treat us as slave laborers, then herd us like animals to conduct electricity from our bodies. Hundreds of Metellyans are slaughtered each month."

"Why do they need *you* for electricity? Aren't they born from it?"

"Yes," Sovann jumped in to explain. "The Voltains *are* electric—that energy courses through their veins and gives them life. But in order to harness that energy to power their entire kingdom, they'd need to kill thousands of their own, so our deaths are the better choice."

"We just want tools to defend ourselves," Rezar added.

"Fine, but you can't have our boat. Not yet, at least," Rhoco countered. He placed his hand into his pocket and held the pouch that concealed the heart. Despite the fabric separating his skin from the glass, its magic radiated through, releasing him from the spellbinding hypnosis of the tea.

"The boat was built for us," Sovann noted, reminding Rhoco of Feodras's betrayal.

"You cannot have our boat until I complete my task." Rhoco repeated.

"What exactly are you delivering to Crystet?" Rezar inquired.

"That's none of your business."

Both Metellyans furrowed their metallic brows in confusion; the potion shouldn't have worn off so soon.

"You know," Sovann tried a new tactic. "Metellyans and Bouldes ought to be allies. We are both held captive by the Voltains. We are their workhorses and you are their silent prisoners. Together we could rise and take back the scepter."

"You should've seen the Bouldes of years past," Rezar added. "Enormous heathens, dressed in the bones of nature's most savage predators. Every being trembled with fear when the Bouldes showed up to battle."

"You can become that way again," Sovann enticed. "You have it in you to be fierce warriors."

"Even so," Rhoco shot back, "I'm a Fused and he is a Murk. We have no power back in Orewall. We cannot convince anyone to reenter the war."

"And we are only dockworkers. It doesn't take a royal to make a change; it takes hundreds of nameless warriors. A thousand soldiers will always be greater than one king."

Rhoco decided to bargain with them. "We can pledge the eventual delivery of crystals in exchange for safe passage out of Coppel, but we cannot promise more than that."

"Don't you want to set your people free?"

Rhoco remained silent. He had never thought much beyond his own emancipation.

Sovann continued, "You can be the change your people need. Pledge your allegiance, and together, we can rule Namaté."

"I'm pledging nothing to either of you," Rhoco spat. "Instead of talking to me openly and honestly, you drugged my tea so that I would spill my secrets."

"A necessary precaution. We weren't sure if Feodras kept his promise or if he was here as your prisoner. We needed to know all the details before revealing our plan in case you were against the revolution."

"Well, I am."

"You shouldn't be. We have our king, Oro, on our side," Rezar explained. "Along with the entire population of Coppel."

"Then leave the rest of us out of it."

"Our numbers aren't enough. The Voltains have grown immeasurably strong during their mostly unchallenged rule. They've had centuries to harness and perfect their defenses. No one can get close. We need more power than what we currently have."

"We need the Bouldes and Glaziene to stand by our side," Rezar declared.

"You'd have better luck recruiting the Mudlings," Rhoco argued. "They're itching for a fight."

"We might use them in the early stages of battle, but they are insignificant in the bigger picture. The Woodlins, Mudlings, and Bonz have no leg in this race. They're too fragile and easy to subdue. Nor do any of them have a desire for power beyond that which they already possess."

"The Mudlings didn't seem fragile to me," Rhoco remarked.

"They are terrors on the sea or when antagonizing one adversary at a time," Rezar agreed. "They raid our boats any chance they get, which is why they don't come near our shores.

They understand that they stand no chance against us on land. Small, fast, and agile works against our slow ocean tankers, but it does not bode well in battle. We outsize them in stature and strength."

"The Bouldes don't want the scepter," Rhoco returned to his part in their request. "King Alun enjoys reigning over a false utopia. We'll never change his mind, and neither will you."

"We already know that," Rezar sighed. "Which is why we had to take the revolution underground. We need to gather massive numbers of ordinary folks with little power. Once we have enough, the reluctant kings and queens will have no choice but to reenter the Great Fight."

Sovann stepped in. "We will let you keep your boat, for now, so long as you try to convince the Glaziene to stand beside us. You're heading there anyway, so persuade those you make contact with."

"If I promise to try, you'll let us leave without any additional tricks?"

"Yes," both Metellyans promised in unison.

"Fine," Rhoco conceded, but he couldn't shake his remaining questions. "But why doesn't King Oro just talk to King Alun and whoever rules Crystet directly?"

"For one thing," Rezar explained, "contact is forbidden. King Lucien of Elecort banned all communication between rulers of each land. It's how they maintain control."

"It hasn't stopped the kings and queens from finding other ways, though," Sovann added. "King Oro sent carrier cardinals to Orewall for a while, but Alun wouldn't listen. His fear of the Voltains was too great. So King Oro tasked us, his people, to reach the Orewall masses. Kings cannot refuse a fight if their people insist."

"You're not doing a very good job if this is the first time I'm hearing of this," Rhoco noted.

"Infiltration from the bottom up takes time and patience. It also takes great discretion and caution. More Bouldes are aware of the revolution than you realize."

"Mostly the Murks," Feodras added timidly.

Rhoco eyed him suspiciously, but was intrigued by the notion. "And the Glaziene?"

"They started the revolution but backed out after King Ignatius, Lucien's father, shattered their former queen and melted her pieces. Their next queen was a sociopath who was blinded by ruin and personal vengeance. For decades, she turned Crystet into an isolated hell for its inhabitants. We were never able to reach her," Rezar explained. "Their current king is relatively new to the throne and withdrawn. He refuses to answer King Oro's carrier notes. As for the people of Crystet, they too are hard to reach." Rezar's aggravation was apparent. "They are a vicious breed, unwelcoming and designed for destruction. Their instincts instruct them to ruin what they do not understand so that it cannot ruin them first."

"It's a sick little world in which they fester, drowning in self-pity and despair," Sovann contributed.

"They are all mentally deranged," Rezar scoffed. "A steady flow of melancholy fills their hollowness."

Rhoco removed his hand from his pocket.

"But since you're headed there anyway, you might as well give it a try. If they are anticipating your delivery, perhaps they'll also listen to your message."

"Maybe," Rhoco replied, suddenly unsure of everything he was after. He swallowed the uncertainty and lifted his chin. "I'll see what I can do."

"Very good. You will stay the night and we will show you a good time," Sovann stated.

Rhoco understood that neither he nor Feodras had a say in the matter.

Eldora returned with the swan pie. She carved out a piece for each man, but neither Boulde took a bite until they saw their Metellyan hosts eating without any side effects.

Once the food was determined to be safe, Rhoco dug in, delighted to discover that the meat was the best he'd ever eaten. The swan muscle was tender, exuding sweet juices with every chew. His dolomite teeth tore the food apart, filling his mouth with flavor.

"Just a small taste of the good life," Rezar said, his mouth full.

Rhoco tried not to let the bribe affect his outlook moving forward, but the protein filled his belly and cleared his mind, and suddenly, all they offered seemed tempting. Perhaps there was more to this adventure than just returning the heart. Maybe this was the awakening of his greater purpose.

Chapter 24

Sovann and Rezar led them farther into the crowded village until they reached a shabby hostel constructed of welded slabs of iron, each panel a different shade of gray.

"It's a bit in disrepair, but still comfortable lodging."

"You won't be sleeping much anyhow," Rezar added.

The Metellyans left them to settle into their temporary quarters, and after the door was closed, Rhoco went in on Feodras.

"You lied to me."

"Not really. I told you I didn't want to be a slave anymore, that I wanted to find a home where I was welcome. The success of this rebellion would do just that."

"Looking for a new place to live versus performing a task on behalf of a resistance are two very different things."

"I understand why you feel betrayed."

"Why didn't you tell me from the start?" Rhoco demanded.

"You wouldn't have let me on the boat."

"You could have explained."

"You were too fixated on completing your own mission. Plus, I'm not nearly as well-spoken as the Metellyans. I never would have convinced you to change your focus."

"I'm still not convinced, but I am letting the idea brew. My initial mission remains our focus, but I'm willing to return to this after."

"Will you tell me what we are going to Crystet for?"

"No."

"Secrets are dangerous," Feodras warned.

"No kidding. Are you keeping any others?"

"No, you know everything now."

"Good."

"And what about your secret?" Feodras asked.

"Don't worry about it."

"I hope it doesn't get us into more trouble."

"I said, don't worry about it." Rhoco was not in the mood to forgive. He would in time, but right now, he was too angry to let it go. He looked like a fool in front of the Metellyans and he blamed Feodras for this mishap. Rhoco retreated to the washroom to prepare for the night.

Feodras sulked in the corner, upset by the unanticipated turn of events. Though he was remorseful that Rhoco felt deceived, there was no changing that now. They were at the mercy of the ocean and Gaia was the master of their fate. She chose his mission over Rhoco's as the greater priority. He would not argue with Rhoco to convince him to see things his way, instead he'd wait for forgiveness, certain that with time it would come.

A fist pounded on the door.

"Time to carouse," Sovann declared as he barged through. Rezar followed with two Metellyan women on each arm.

"Rhoco is still washing off," Feodras stammered.

"Fantastic. He reeked."

"And you?" Rezar inquired, examining the Murk with a grimace.

"I don't like water."

"You've *never* showered?" Sovann asked in disgust.

Feodras shook his head.

Rhoco exited the washroom with a towel wrapped around his waist. His hosts' unexpected arrival and the sight of their female guests turned his lime skin pink.

"I didn't realize you all were here," he stammered, firmly gripping the towel around his waist. "Are these your friends?"

"I suppose you could call them that," Rezar replied with a devilish smirk.

"Did you know your pal here doesn't shower? Ever?" Sovann teased. He elbowed the woman on Rezar's left. "Aurelie is in for a trying night."

"Why am *I* stuck with him?" the woman groaned. The sultry smile etched onto her sterling skin creaked into a frown.

"Because *I* always get my way," Kailasa, the woman on Rezar's right, sneered at her fellow harlot, golden eyes bright with superiority. Each word she spoke reverberated with a clang, like that of a dream.

Rhoco examined the woman named Kailasa with hesitant wonder. Her golden skin smoldered in the shadows of the sunlit room, shimmering to the beat of his heart. He found his gaze fixated upon her chest and hips, which were draped with sheer fabric and jewels. Kailasa smiled at him, aware that she had seized his desire.

"You're mine tonight," she cooed as she sauntered toward him and pushed him onto the bed.

"I don't want to hurt you," Rhoco stammered, terrified that he accidentally might—he did not trust his Boulde strength.

"I am made of metal," Kailasa whispered as she straddled him, leaving his towel precariously draped over his groin. "You cannot hurt me." There was nothing beneath her sheer skirt; nothing separating them except the towel. Her warmth reached him with ease and he was entranced.

Excited by the prospect that he might be able to feel something without destroying it as well, Rhoco allowed the seduction to continue.

"Guess the party has begun?" Rezar commented with a laugh, then pushed Aurelie toward Feodras. The Murk cowered as she stumbled toward him. Her expression contorted with revulsion as his natural stench assaulted her nostrils.

"Don't worry," he whispered. "I won't touch you."

"You have to or they'll punish me."

Feodras didn't understand, but placed a hand on her shoulder anyway to appease her, planning to go no further, but she hurled him against the wall and pressed her lips to his. Her touch paralyzed Feodras, who had never felt such a sensation before.

"Wonderful," Sovann said with glee as he lined the small table near the washroom with narcotics. A choice of drugs for different ends; options for every desire. Rezar departed and returned with Fizza and Oriane—two more scanitly clad women—and Sovann broke up the Bouldes' revelry.

"Ladies, pause your seduction so we can enjoy a bit of candy together."

Kailasa and Aurelie obeyed without hesitation, leaving their prey in a stunned state of confusion.

"Join us, won't you?" Rezar asked as he, Sovann, and the four harlots gathered around the table. Feodras snapped out of his daze first, but remained in the shadows. Rhoco, still lying on the bed, breathed heavily, willing the heat in his groin to subside so he could join the group. It took a moment of focused concentration, but once he relaxed, he grabbed his pants from the washroom, put them on, and approached the table.

Atop the tin surface was a buffet of narcotics. The colors were beautiful and inviting.

"The pink darts are tranquilizers, fun if you're into submission. Paralyze your top half and let the ladies have their way with the rest of you. Or use it on them if you like to dominate. Your choice really," Rezar explained. "The green pills are sedatives. They'll relax you into pure serenity." He glanced back at Feodras, who was recoiled in a corner. "*You* need one of these." Rezar took a green pill and marched toward Feodras.

"No, I don't want any of this," Feodras insisted. "Rhoco! Don't let them," the Murk pleaded, but before Rhoco could intervene, Rezar was upon Feodras, force-feeding him the drug.

"He'll thank us later," Rezar said to Rhoco.

"Leave him be!" Rhoco insisted, stepping forward and seizing Rezar by the forearm. His stone grip dented Rezar's metal flesh.

"Have you lost your mind?" Rezar bellowed, yanking himself free from Rhoco's hold.

"He doesn't want to participate," Rhoco growled. "Leave him alone."

Rezar raised his arms in surrender, his hands empty—the drug had already dissolved on Feodras's tongue.

Feodras collapsed to the floor; a wide grin was plastered to his face.

Rhoco turned to Rezar, his fury rising. "I will carry him out of here and never return with your precious boat if you touch him again."

"Is that so?" Rezar asked, ready to challenge the stone brute.

Rhoco slammed his foot against the tin floor, which left a massive dent, and then punched his fist into the wall, causing the entire flimsy structure to shake.

"Enough," Sovann declared to diffuse the tension. "Relax. Feodras can enjoy his sedative in solitude." He looked to Rezar with concern, then back at Rhoco. "Enjoy one of our special candies. Or the pipes—those hold hallucinogens."

Rhoco took a deep breath to steady his rage. He looked over at Feodras, who was high, but safe, and decided not to make enemies out of the Metellyans.

"Hallucinogens?" Rhoco asked.

"Yes," Sovann explained. "On the blue herbs, you'll have visions and see things that aren't really there, but it rarely turns dark or dips into the subconscious. The purple herbs are a bit more dangerous and they affect everyone differently. If you smoke those, there's really no telling what you'll see, where it will take you, or what you will do, but you'll be guaranteed an experience. My recommendation," Sovann transitioned, picking up the most colorful pills on the table, "are the amphetamine mash-ups. These are called bliss pills, and they are just as wonderful as they sound. They give you energy and make every sensation feel ten times as delightful. Colors brighten, sounds enhance, every caress touches your soul." He tossed a neon orange bliss pill into his mouth, swallowing it with ease.

"I don't take drugs," Rhoco replied.

"Why not?"

"I like to be in control."

Sovann shrugged. "The choice is yours."

He fed a bliss pill to Fizza, then pressed her against the wall, ripping off the minimal clothing she wore as they kissed. Rezar did the same with Oriane, except their indiscretions were much louder. They grunted and groaned with pleasure, soiling the suede chair near the door.

Rhoco looked back to Feodras, who sat on the floor, utterly relaxed and wearing a huge grin.

Aurelie took a long drag from the pipe filled with blue herbs, then sat on the floor next to Feodras, content to sit with him in quiet.

Erlea, who had stayed hidden behind Feodras's ear, emerged to attack despite Aurelie's passive presence, but her stinger could not penetrate metal skin. Aurelie swatted the bee away, but Erlea returned with force and stung a soft spot behind the harlot's ear. Aurelie cursed and tried to smash the bug against the wall, but Erlea was too fast and managed to dip outside the open window. Aurelie slammed the window shut and the bumblebee collided with the glass pane. Erlea slammed her fuzzy body repeatedly into the window, futilely trying to stay by her friend's side, but to no avail. She was trapped outside, unable to do anything but watch helplessly. Feodras's smile remained vacant as a scene of debauchery unraveled around him.

"Which poison do you choose?" Kailasa asked Rhoco.

"You," he replied, his voice laced with lust.

She smirked, picked up a yellow bliss pill, and placed it on her tongue. With her golden finger, she caressed his lips until they parted, then transferred the pill from her tongue onto his with a sensual kiss.

Too distracted to fight it, Rhoco began to feel the high of the bliss pill. The room went fuzzy before turning exceedingly crisp.

"This will make me taste even better," she promised before taking a bliss pill for herself. She then forced him onto the bed and unbuttoned his pants, which fell in a pile around his ankles.

"Are you sure?" Rhoco asked in a slur.

"Yes," she promised in a whisper. "Trust me."

She touched him—her metal skin against his was rough, and her touch carried a slight scratch, but the discomfort was nothing compared to the pleasure she offered. Her fingers tiptoed across his manhood, followed by her tongue, and his senses exploded.

He grabbed her by the hips and she screamed with delight, caressing her breasts as their bodies swayed together in rhythm. The room disappeared; it was only them now. Her sighs and groans were the only sound he heard and all he could see was the golden glow of her beauty. He was ready to combust, ready to fill her with passion. He'd never felt such delight before.

"Yes, you have."

The voice shook him from his revelry.

"What did you say?" he asked Kailasa.

"Nothing," she moaned. "Don't stop."

He tried to continue, tried to reach the precipice of climax again, but it was too late. He was rattled to his core and Kailasa sensed it.

"What's wrong with you?" she demanded.

"I heard a voice."

"It's just the bliss pill."

But Kailasa was wrong—the voice belonged to the heart.

Kailasa leaned in to kiss him again, and though it suddenly felt wrong, he allowed her lips to touch his. The moment they did, the voice returned.

"Discard her, or I'll kill you both."

Rhoco's eyes widened, but he hesitated. He did not push Kailasa off him fast enough and the heart grew to a scalding temperature inside the pocket of his pants, which were still in a pile around his ankles.

"Stop it," Rhoco demanded.

"Have I done something wrong?" Kailasa asked, but her question was answered with flames. The fire started at her toes and crawled up her naked body. Rhoco slithered out from under her as the bed caught fire.

"Leave her alone," he ordered as he pulled up and buckled his pants. The heart burned against the side of his hip.

"You've betrayed me."

The others tuned into the scene, which was so horrific it broke the trance of their bliss pills.

Sovann pushed the women through the door and Aurelie ushered a wobbling Feodras into the hall.

"How did this happen?" Sovann questioned in outrage.

"I don't know," Rhoco lied.

"She's lost," Rezar said. "We must go."

The men exited, but Rhoco lingered in horror. Kailasa's beautiful, golden body was melting beneath the flames. In her last moments, she stared up at him, pleading for help, but there was nothing he could do to save her. Her death was on his hands, for he possessed the heart that killed her.

Sovann returned a moment after Kailasa turned into a metallic puddle amidst the inferno.

"What's wrong with you?" he asked, appalled that Rhoco hung around to watch. He grabbed Rhoco's arm and yanked him out of the burning room.

They joined the others outside the evacuated building, standing alongside the other displaced patrons. The fiery heat in Rhoco's pocket had subsided and the heart's anger was allayed. He looked up to the window of the burning room they narrowly escaped and saw that the flames were also gone. All that remained was the billow of smoke exiting the broken window.

The authorities of Coppel arrived a moment later to extinguish a fire that was already snuffed. The air reeked of sulfur and the crowd observed with their noses and mouths covered. No one wanted to breathe in the welding fumes of the deceased.

Everyone was confused, except Rhoco. He placed his hand into his pocket and wrapped his fingers around the pouch concealing his secret.

The heart always won.

Chapter 25

"Did you do this?" Sovann challenged Rhoco as the chaos around the hostel persisted. The whores had already left to inform their mistress of the tragic accident and the fire marshals now raced into the building to make sure the fire had ceased.

"Of course not. Why would I?" Rhoco spat back. The intensity of his own voice rang back as an echo inside his mind. He was still high.

"Which drug did you choose?" Rezar asked.

"Kailasa gave me a bliss pill."

Both Metellyans paused in thought.

"Purple herbs, maybe, but a bliss pill wouldn't turn a man into a monster," Sovann said to Rezar. He looked back at Rhoco. "How did this happen?"

"I have no idea. One minute, we were having fun, and the next, she was burning to death on top of me." He recoiled as he remembered her burning, gold body melting into the mattress. The stench of her blazing, metal flesh would live with him forever.

"Metellyans don't spontaneously combust into flames. *Something* must have triggered it."

"Your guess is as good as mine," Rhoco lied.

"Oh, boy," Rezar said with a groan. "Here comes Madam Zahavah."

"Who is she?"

"Head mistress of the brothel."

"Those women were prostitutes?" Rhoco asked. "You paid them to seduce us?"

"Obviously. What right-minded Metellyan woman would want to sleep with a Boulde?"

Rhoco felt dirty and used, but more so, he felt guilty for hurting yet another person. The crushing weight of his past returned as a furious woman made of titanium stormed toward them. Aurelie, Fizza, and Oriane followed close behind.

"My girls tell me my star harlot is dead," Madam Zahavah bellowed as she reached the accused.

"It's not our fault," Rezar declared. "We swear. It was some sort of freak accident."

She grabbed his face with her firm, titanium grip and pulled him in close for examination. She scanned his eyes, looking for signs of foul play.

"What are you on?" she demanded.

"Bliss pills, and nothing more."

"This type of behavior usually results after smoking purp."

"But we didn't, I promise. We had it with us, but no one smoked any."

Without loosening her grip, her eyes darted to the men standing behind him.

"Who are they?"

"Our guests from Orewall. They're only here for the night."

"You let them touch my girls?" she asked, appalled, shoving Rezar away.

"Yes," he stammered, unsure which rule he might have broken. "That's allowed, right?"

"Absolutely not," she exclaimed. "Are you dense? Don't you know that metal against stone creates sparks? And you let them transgress on a bed, I presume?"

Rezar's silence answered her question. Rhoco breathed a little easier, happy to know there was a plausible explanation and that his secret would be spared.

"Fools," she hissed. "This is your doing and you'll pay every cent Kailasa would have earned me for the remainder of the year."

"We can't afford that!" Sovann objected.

"You'll find a way, or I'll report you to the king."

"This whole ordeal was for the benefit of King Oro." He leaned in closer to Zahavah and whispered, "These men have joined the revolution. Your whores were a down payment for their allegiance."

Zahavah's brow furrowed. "I was not consulted, therefore, it was an invalid transaction. King Oro knows how I operate."

"Sure, we may have taken a few liberties and gotten ahead of ourselves, but he would've signed off on it after the fact."

"Except you incinerated my best girl before he got the chance. Your problem, not mine." She turned to her harlots. "Girls, you will never engage with these men again unless I directly tell you to."

They nodded and strutted away, leaving the men alone in their lingering highs. Rhoco glanced at Feodras, who wore the same vacant smile he acquired before the accident. Rhoco flicked the Murk's cheek with his finger, but got no reaction. Feodras was far away, in another time and space, and Rhoco wished he could join him there.

"You're guilty too," Rezar snapped at Rhoco.

"You set up the party, not me. I had no idea my stone hog would kill her."

"Well, it did, and you've got to own some of the responsibility."

"Fine." Rhoco did not wish to argue. He wanted to put this tragedy behind him. "What gems and minerals are valuable for trade in Coppel?"

"Diamonds."

Diamonds were hard to come by, even for a miner. "What else?"

"Emeralds."

Rhoco sighed. Another scarce gem. "Fine. When we return with the tourmaline, I'll bring whatever else I can find to help you pay this debt."

He wobbled in place as the drug began to wear off. Rezar and Sovann faded in and out of focus. Their shiny skin appeared to melt off their metal skulls as they became fuzzy. The vibrant colors of Coppel nightlife dulled drastically, losing all luster as his vision faded. Rhoco crouched over, afraid he might vomit.

"Is this normal?"

"You have to bump to avoid the comedown," Rezar explained, but his voice sounded miles away. "You want another?"

Rhoco shook his head, then heaved swan pie all over the pewter sidewalk.

"Pathetic," one of the Metellyans laughed as Rhoco slipped into a state of unconsciousness.

A few hours later, Rhoco awoke to the lurching sway of their boat. The stone deck scratched the back of his scalp and the slowly forming wound roused him from his slumber. He opened his eyes to a blue sky.

The world was quiet again; the unending jangle of metal clinking and clanging had ceased. The chaos of Coppel was behind them now.

Feodras sat at the pedals, rudders in hand, guiding them away from the metal city. Rhoco stood with care and hobbled to the stern. The shoreline opposite from where they arrived was in view and he saw the Kingdom of Coppel gleaming in the morning sunlight.

The castle was built at the edge of a raging waterfall. The water gushed by too fast to safely approach via boat, so the only way in and out was over the golden bridge that stretched for miles to each shoreline. The structure was made of platinum and engraved with golden details that blasted the sun's reflection from specific angles. The tips of the tall, spiked peaks were pointed like arrows, and the expansions extending from the main building were octagonal. A single glass window garlanded the entire front entrance. It was stained with colors and decorated with archaic images from the Metellyans' victorious past.

Though Rhoco was too far away to make out all of the details, the brilliant shades coloring the scepter of alchemy radiated for miles in the sun. Centuries came and went since they last ruled Namaté, but the Metellyans still clung to their glory days.

The beauty of the Coppel castle mesmerized Rhoco as they sailed away, momentarily diminishing the agony of his hangover. But once the image grew too small to appreciate, the pain recaptured the reins and he turned to face Feodras, whom he suspected felt a similar discomfort.

The Murk kept his head down, refusing to acknowledge Rhoco's stare.

Rhoco held his gaze for a moment, unsure the cause of their sudden tension, then spoke.

"You never apologized for lying to me," he began.

Feodras responded with a scornful glare, but said nothing.

"I did nothing wrong," Rhoco noted, still unsure what caused Feodras's anger.

"I wanted no part in that debauchery."

"What was I supposed to do?"

"You could've told them to leave me be."

"I did!"

"She kissed me." His head dipped and his chest filled with sorrow.

"And that was as far as it went. After Rezar shoved the drug into your mouth I threatened that we would never return if they touched you again."

Feodras paused. "The minty green powder dissolved on my tongue and I don't remember anything after that."

"I protected you, I promise."

Feodras kept his gaze lowered. "I still feel violated."

"Come on!" Rhoco proclaimed.

Feodras glared upward and he shook as he spoke. "I have been a slave all my life. Beaten down and oppressed with zero freedom since the day I was born. I finally break free, only to find myself oppressed, yet again. Their actions were unwanted and arrived disguised as revelry." His eyes were wide with angry tears. "I've saved you, so many times, and when I needed the favor returned, you let a group of strangers strip me of my dignity."

"What more was I supposed to do?"

"Stop Rezar from shoving that pill down my throat."

Rhoco felt defeated. "I'm sorry that I stepped in too late. I'm sorry that I let you down."

Feodras continued to speak, his tears spilling silently.

"That was the first time a woman ever touched me."

Rhoco's guilt doubled. "I had no idea."

Feodras glared up at him, betrayal and pain replaced the shy and stubborn wonder his eyes used to convey. And in that moment, Rhoco remembered the look of innocence lost—he remembered Grette.

He tried to swallow the memory.

"I'm sorry," Rhoco reiterated. "I tried. Please forgive me."

"I need time."

Feodras returned his gaze to the stone deck.

Rhoco exhaled deeply, aware that nothing he said would correct the situation. Grette returned to the forefront of Rhoco's thoughts. She was his first love, as well as his first heartbreak—their tragic, young romance shaped him into the broken man he was today.

Rhoco sat at the stern of their boat with eyes closed and let her memory flood his mind.

The sound of her small whimpers. The silent fear that lingered between them—hers for what she suffered and his for what he had done.

That night was the last time he saw her. The experience sliced him clear in half. On one side was the man he wished to be, on the other was the savage he could not control.

Not long after that night, Grette was officially granted her Grade V work visa and went to work in the gardens within Amesyte Valley. Rhoco heard the news through desert whispers and happily retreated into the mines—hiding in the darkness of the caves felt fitting.

The first moon began to rise.

Looking back at Feodras, Rhoco empathized for his friend, who was still sullen.

"Please forgive me," he called across the large boat as he walked toward the Murk.

Feodras nodded, accepting the apology.

"Erlea told me what you did," Feodras replied with a sad smile. "I'm sorry. I assumed the worst of you, yet you gave me your best."

"It's okay. You were drugged—you lost a large chunk of time."

"Always forgive, never forget. It's the way of the Murks. Our memories give us strength. One day, I hope they'll save us."

Rhoco exhaled with relief. He was grateful for his friend's forgiveness.

Feodras lifted a finger to his ear and let Erlea climb onto his fingernail.

"I'll be okay," he whispered, a guttural buzz underlined his words. "Let the others know we need to deliver diamonds or emeralds to the Metellyans, a cost for a mistake on our end. Don't go into details." Erlea buzzed loudly in understanding. "And check on the mining Murks."

She buzzed again and then took off, viciously circling Rhoco's head twice before heading west toward Orewall.

"I thought she could telecommunicate?"

"Her left wing and antenna broke when she slammed into the window, so her capacity for long-distance communication is now spotty. She cannot heal here; there is no pollen."

"Will she make it all that way with a broken wing?"

"A swarm from her hive will meet her halfway."

"Don't we need her to keep us safe from the sylphs?"

"Her scent will linger for a few days and we'll be far past their territory by the time her scent fades. Sylphs don't like the cold."

Rhoco accepted this answer, then continued, "Why did you ask her to check on the mining Murks?"

"Because they act as spies for King Alun."

"What do you mean?" Rhoco asked, his anxiety rising.

"They are contracted by the king to find and expose members of the resistance living in Orewall. Mining Murks work against the resistance, while the carving Murks work with it. That's why I don't trust them."

"Why didn't you tell me this sooner?" he demanded.

"I wasn't ready to reveal my role with the resistance yet. And you were so angry in Coppel after finding out, I couldn't tell you then."

"King Alun is going to think I made this boat for the resistance, that I left Orewall to join the revolution. *That* is a far worse crime than what I'm actually doing." Rhoco slammed his fist into the deck of the boat, leaving a crater in the stone surface. "Has she been receiving updates from the bees in Orewall?"

"Last time she talked to them was after we escaped the Mudlings, before entering Coppel."

"And?"

"They know you're missing. The Hematites noticed when you stopped showing up for your shifts at the mines, but the mining Murks could not prove your motives."

Rhoco punched the stone deck again, creating a new crater. Limestone-Malachite blood spilled from his knuckles.

"Stop hurting yourself, everything will be okay," Feodras pleaded.

"Will it? This could be my undoing."

"I won't let that happen."

"Will Erlea return to give us an update?"

"Yes, once she is healed."

Rhoco was too furious to continue discussing the matter. The notion of being falsely accused of treason festered, fueling his fury.

"Where are we heading now?"

"Crystet."

"Finally," Rhoco said, relieved, before departing for the front of the boat; he did not wish to subject Feodras to his rising anger. Once out of sight, he dug his fingernails into the stone railing of the bow, filing them against the hard surface until he drew blood. The wounds cut through layers of gritty flesh, shaving his fingertips to the nerves hidden under stone. The pain silenced his anger and when his fury subsided, he cursed himself for what he had done. He allowed himself to slip into his old ways, he allowed his bad habits to return to the surface, and he used destruction to soothe his temper.

I'm not that man anymore, he reminded himself.

One setback would not cause his unraveling.

He returned to Feodras. They did not speak, but the company was calming for both.

After a few hours, Feodras broke the silence.

"You realize that the friction between you and Kailasa did not create that fire."

"Why do you say that?"

"Because a normal fire, one unaltered by chemicals or magic, could never burn hot enough to melt a Metellyan."

"What are you trying to say?"

"That this secret you keep is dangerous. I'm not sure what it is, or what we are heading into, but I sense more trouble is stirring."

Rhoco paused to assess Feodras's concerns. He wasn't wrong, but Rhoco couldn't possibly turn back now. The heart had grown on him; it had not only bonded to him, but he to it as well.

He loved the heart. It was the only connection he dug back up after burying it. It was the only bond he actively pursued. All the others were left to rot in the graveyard of his mind. Perhaps the mystery of its owner was to blame, or perhaps their connection was true; in either case, he was certain he could not give up on it now.

"I won't say you are wrong," Rhoco began. "I, too, am unsure what we're sailing toward. What I *am* prepared to tell you is that I will not drag you farther than you're willing to go. I will cross the shores of Crystet alone to spare you whatever tragedy the delivery of my secret might cause."

"I wish you'd just tell me what you're delivering, and to who."

"I don't know who it belongs to, that's the truth. And I'll tell you what it is once we part. I'm afraid your thoughts on the issue might sully everything I've grown to hold dear."

"You don't want me to ruin the illusion."

"I'd prefer to hold onto the hope that it *isn't* an illusion."

"I understand."

The men fell silent, aware of the bond they inadvertently created over time. The danger, the mistakes, the survival; it solidified a friendship that neither wanted, but both were grateful to have.

Rhoco was a better man, thanks both to the Murk, who pried compassion from the depths of his stony being, and to the heart, which inspired their shared adventure.

It became clear that this was why he loved the heart. The heart made him feel something for the first time in years, both physically and mentally. It gave life to the man he never knew he could be, a good man who valued those around him and took an interest in learning about the world beyond his home.

Rhoco wasn't exactly sure who he was becoming, or who he would be when the adventure ended, but the outlook was promising. A man with feeling would always outshine one made of stone.

Chapter 26

The ocean was vast and the horizon unending. They had not seen land in two days and Rhoco was beginning to wonder if they were heading in the right direction. He grabbed the map and compass from Feodras to determine their whereabouts. They were sailing southeast when they should be sailing northeast.

"I think we are off course," Rhoco said to Feodras, who sat at the pedals in a trance.

"We are headed northeast, just as you requested."

"No, we're not. We're heading southeast. When was the last time you checked the compass? It's been two full days, we might be long past Crystet by now."

Feodras looked up, his sorrowful stupor fading momentarily. After a quick look around with clear vision, he confirmed Rhoco's fears.

"Yes. We are long past Crystet."

Rhoco growled, "What's wrong with you?"

"I do not feel like myself today, for I am still lost in yesterday."

The sound of fluttering wings swooped in overhead. Rhoco looked up, horrified to see that the sylphs had returned.

"I thought you said Erlea's scent would keep them away?" he demanded, panicked.

"It faded before we reached cold air."

"We have no protection."

Feodras looked lost and confused, alarmingly apathetic about the razor-toothed fairies swarming toward them. He pedaled their boat forward with no urgency.

Rhoco turned his attention to the map and saw that their current heading took them toward Fibril, home to the Bonz. He lifted his head and saw a coastline far in the distance.

"Would we be safe with the Bonz?"

Feodras lifted his head, his eyes wide with curiosity.

"With the spider men? Their reputation is a mix of horror stories and heroic tales."

"Let's hope for the latter." He pushed Feodras off his chair and took over the pedals. "Refuge with them has to be better than a date with the sylphs."

He moved his legs as fast as they allowed, recalling the pain he suffered the last time the sylphs feasted on him. The memory served as great motivation to pedal faster.

As Rhoco steered toward Fibril, Feodras walked to the middle of the deck and opened his arms wide.

"What are you doing?"

"Sparing you."

"No!"

"You saved me. I save you."

Feodras invited the sylphs in, beckoning them to graze on his skin. Rhoco pedaled faster in protest; he would not let Feodras suffer any more.

The sylphs chattered incessantly as they circled Feodras's head. Rhoco couldn't make out their words, as it was pure noise from where he sat, but he imagined they were taunting and teasing, just as they had done to him before tearing into his flesh.

Large boulders jutted out of the black water and Rhoco glanced up, eager to see salvation within reach, but what he saw only caused him distress. They were still a great distance from the shore of Fibril.

It didn't make sense. They were so close moments ago, and though he pedaled furiously, it was for nothing. They were stuck in a time trap, in some illusion that kept them sailing in place.

The first batch of sylphs nose-dived and latched onto Feodras's skin. Their little bodies clung to him by their teeth, ripping him apart as the next group dove to gorge. Feodras screamed in agony.

Rhoco could not bear to watch. He abandoned his post, certain that the current and wind would continue carrying them to the shore, and charged toward the slaughter. Grabbing the closest sylph by its nose and mouth, he pried it off of Feodras. Its elongated teeth came out slowly, covered in Feodras's russet blood.

It squealed in shrill objection.

Rhoco crushed its skull in the palm of his hand to stop the jarring sound. He then continued to pluck the sylphs off of his friend, snapping their skulls in half and tossing their tiny bodies overboard. Though he made swift progress, he was radically outnumbered and Feodras's body remained buried beneath their wrath.

Rhoco was beginning to lose hope when the cluster of hovering sylphs waiting for their turn to feast vanished. Rhoco did a double take—the winged-monsters hit an invisible wall. Glancing backward, he saw that the sylphs dangled, paralyzed, in mid-air.

A few feet overhead hung an intricate maze of silk thread woven into a marvelous design. The web was massive, with crisscrossing orbs that formed a tangled maze of threads. Silk towers stemmed from the various rocks protruding from the ocean and connected above into a more spacious labyrinth. Archways were formed beneath the web for boats to pass through.

They sailed through the funnel web, away from the ensnared sylphs, and though Rhoco could no longer see the tiny, captured creatures, he couldn't miss the shadow of the predator who scuttled toward them.

It was skinny and tall, with four legs that allowed it to move at unnatural speeds. The distant silhouette was harrowing. Rhoco shuddered at the sight. He wanted to turn their boat around to dodge the looming nightmare, but knew a worse fate waited behind them.

With no danger of another sylph attack, he returned to Feodras's side, tearing the lingering sylphs from him and lodging them into the web overhead. A trail of screeching sylphs littered the sky in their wake. When the noise lessened, Rhoco turned to face his newfound fear.

A Bonz skulked toward them, eating each sylph Rhoco tossed into its web as it approached. It was a giant, four-legged skeleton with sharp teeth and a pointed spine. Horns protruded from the top of its head, spiraling with grandiose majesticism. The eye sockets in its skull appeared empty, yet it managed to stare right through him as it ate the sylphs he provided. Rhoco winced. He was feeding the beast and leading it directly to them. It followed, maintaining its distance, surely aware that they could never escape now.

All the sylphs were detached from Feodras's body. Rhoco tried to shake him awake, hoping for some wisdom regarding the Bonz, but Feodras was knocked out from the pain.

Rhoco was on his own.

The web grew more complex the deeper into it they sailed and he could no longer see the opening archway behind them. The Fibril shore still appeared to be miles away, though he knew it must be near.

The Bonz who followed their progression scaled the fine threads with ease, observing the Bouldes while eating the last sylph. Rhoco could not bring himself to look at it again, could not stomach a closer observation of the grotesque being.

"You ought to anchor," the monster shouted, though its voice caressed his ear like a whisper. Rhoco quivered at the sound, too distracted by fear to heed the warning, and their boat crashed into land.

"Why didn't you listen?" the Bonz hissed.

Rhoco stood with his back to the beast, paralyzed with dread and unable to turn.

"Look at me," it demanded. Its voice was soft and carried with it a hiss-like echo.

Rhoco turned slowly, eyes glued to the ground. He took a deep breath before looking up.

The Bonz hovered over him with unintentional menace. Sensing his fear, it backed away.

"You shouldn't be frightened of me."

"I'm not usually frightened of anything."

"My name is Chesulloth," the female Bonz said.

"Thank you for saving us from the sylphs," Rhoco managed. His eyes returned to the ground.

"I did nothing, that was all you. You simply provided me with lunch." She inched closer, dropping below the webbed ceiling of the archway and hanging upside down over Rhoco. He tried not to tremble and offend her further, but he was certain he flinched and certain she noticed.

"Am I so ugly you cannot bear to look at me?" she went on.

"Of course not," Rhoco replied, gaze fastened downwards.

"Then why don't you?"

"I've never seen a being like you before."

"If it's any comfort, I find you to be odd-looking too."

Rhoco looked up, amused that something so repulsive found him equally off-putting.

Chesulloth's demeanor was calm and Rhoco suspected she meant him no harm.

"Do you eat cecaelia too?" he asked.

"Nope, just the lady-bugs. They're rotten monsters." She turned her head to examine Feodras, who lay motionless. "We ought to tend to your friend's wounds. Sylph bites infect if they aren't promptly cleansed."

She sank lower and the thread exiting her spigot extended as she dropped. With unexpected grace, she cartwheeled her body upright and released the thread from her spinneret.

Rhoco held his breath as she skittered toward Feodras. Each of her four legs stepped at different times, perfectly syncopated and powered by hydraulics hidden beneath the gossamer wrapping her bones. Her spine was located in the middle of her four-pronged hipbone and could rotate so that any side of her became the front. She twisted, then lifted the portion of her body that Rhoco had initially deemed as her posterior and balanced on what were previously her front legs. She lifted Feodras with her back legs and raised him to her spigot. Then, she turned him slowly, encasing him in gossamer, silk threads.

"What are you doing?" Rhoco asked hesitantly, fascinated by the procedure.

"Healing him."

He let her continue without further interruption. When she finished, Feodras was mummified in her web. Rhoco wasn't sure *how* this would heal him, but he anticipated the outcome. He was mostly recovered from his sylph bites, only scabs and scars remained, and he was interested to learn if Chesulloth's remedy was better than that of the Woodlins.

Chesulloth placed Feodras's swathed body on the deck of the boat, returned to all four legs, and twisted her spine back to its original position. Her empty eye sockets focused intently on the healing Murk.

Rhoco's curiosity overtook his apprehension. "How do you see without eyeballs?"

"I have six eyes," she informed, but her answer helped him none. Rhoco took a deep breath, unwilling to ask the obvious and appear even more uneducated. He was prepared to abandon further questioning when she continued, "They are hidden beneath my armor."

She removed the horned skull from her spine to reveal a second head beneath. This head, with its fine outer layer of gossamer, matched the rest of her body. Beneath the silky coating was a fleshy skull with eyebrows, eyeballs, and enough substance to produce expressions. Though the head looked more real, more alive, than the skull helmet, it was still made of bone.

Etched along her cheekbones were zigzags and triangles, markings he imagined held great meaning. Each of her six eyes was orange with green accents and they managed to catch the light from the sun through the intricate netting above. She even had hair, which came as a shock to Rhoco. It was thin and blonde and tied in knots that cascaded from the top of her skull to the top of her spine.

Even more shocking was that he suddenly viewed her as beautiful.

Chesulloth had little interest in his roundabout epiphany regarding her appearance. Looks mattered little, and she was capable of stunning him with any of her countless different faces and bodies. What mattered now was that Feodras survived.

"Your friend stirs," she noted, pointing at the Murk with her skinny, bone finger.

Rhoco turned back to Feodras. Beneath his crushing confinements, he fidgeted. A moment later, his eyes shot open. The light within the webbed nest mirrored like fire in his brown eyes.

Feodras was panicked, unable to break free.

"Stay still, small Boulde," Chesulloth advised, but the moment her echoed hiss caught his ear, he turned his head to find the source. Seeing her for the first time, his will to escape tripled. Fear spiked his adrenaline and he wriggled futilely beneath his restraints.

"She isn't here to harm us," Rhoco tried to explain. "She saved us. She saved you."

But Feodras could not understand reason. The healing process stripped him of his wits, of all the wisdom he learned throughout his life, and temporarily left his brain as blank as a newborn's.

"Give it time. He'll come around," Chesulloth promised, unconcerned by the Murk's hysterical reaction to his recovery.

"He's in bad shape," Rhoco said, concerned.

"This happens sometimes when foreigners are healed by our fibers. It usually passes, though."

"Usually?"

"Stop worrying. Your energy could alter the return of his memory."

"I don't understand."

"Our webs strip the mind of the suffering so that the healing can occur uninterrupted. Right now, Feodras is as innocent as a freshly born infant. He knows next to nothing and likely feels very overwhelmed."

"He doesn't remember me?"

"I'm sure he recognizes your face, but I doubt he can remember why."

Rhoco exhaled slowly. This was much worse than suffering a few days of pain.

"Thank you for helping him."

"It was my duty."

Rhoco sensed there was more to that statement than Chesulloth revealed.

"It's your duty to save distressed sailors?"

"No, just you two. The command was carried to me through the wind."

"By who?"

"The Mother."

Rhoco rolled his eyes. "Gaia?"

"Of course."

"Why would She instruct you to save us? We are nobodies; we aren't important."

"You must be, otherwise She'd have let you die."

Rhoco recalled the beginning of their journey and how many close calls they narrowly survived. Perhaps this imaginary force was watching over them from the start.

He shook his head, still unable to believe that gods orchestrated their fate. If anything was their savior in those moments, it was the heart.

"What did She say?" His tone reeked of skepticism.

"That there was a great love to protect. That I had to scale to the edge of our territory and save said love from peril. I obeyed and found your ship under the assault of the sylphs." Her pretty eyes glanced down at Feodras, whose cheeks were streaked with tears, then back at Rhoco. "Are you two in love?"

"Absolutely not," he scoffed.

"Then what love am I saving?"

"There's no love here. While I appreciate you saving Feodras from death, the voices you heard were mistaken, or maybe they weren't really there at all."

"The Bonz are divinely connected to Gaia. She speaks to us through nature and your retrieval was a direct command."

"Fine, if you insist. But no one here is in love."

Chesulloth scrutinized him with narrowed eyes. "You're foolishly ungrateful."

"I'm eternally grateful to *you*, but that's where my gratitude ends."

"It's unwise to shun the heart that gave you life."

Rhoco was taken aback by her statement. She referred to Gaia, but Rhoco's thoughts immediately returned to the glass heart in his pocket. It gave him life, a renewed, more meaningful life, and he realized this was the love Chesulloth was directed to preserve.

The enormous spider woman closed her eyes to focus. She channeled the energy of her surroundings until she found what she was looking for. When she opened them, she wore a grave scowl.

"I do not understand," she said to herself, then looked toward the sky. "Why?"

"Why what?" Rhoco asked.

Chesulloth shook her head. "I should not question Her."

285

"I don't understand."

"I sense your secret," she said, eyeing Rhoco with intense concern. "Be careful."

"Did Gaia tell you that?"

"Her mercy and patience won't last forever. For whatever reason, what you hold is of great value to Her, and if you forsake it, or misplace it, I suspect She'll forsake you, too."

"Come what may."

He could sense Chesulloth's rising anger. She did not appreciate his dismissal of the deity she adored.

"I've done my part. You're okay, and your friend will be okay. I must go." She placed her horned helmet onto her head, bent the multiple joints in her legs, then rocketed into the netting above.

"Thanks again," he shouted up to her.

She replied with advice.

"There is more to our world than you know. Open your heart and perhaps She'll show you Her true beauty."

With that, she departed, her giant spider-like silhouette scaling the web with nimble elegance.

Rhoco was perplexed; he had no idea what her departing words meant, but as he tried to ponder the message, Feodras screamed to be released.

"I'm not cutting you free until you relax."

He let Feodras scream until his lungs were raw as he turned the boat around. They sailed away beneath the cobweb archways and away from Fibril without any trouble. When he looked up, that particular swarm of sylphs was gone, but the netting where Chesulloth devoured them remained stained with their pale, glittering blood.

He looked in the direction of the shore they just left, realizing that he never actually saw any of the land. From his current vantage point, the entire landscape was covered in Bonz webs. Far in the distance he saw a cluster of Bonz gathered, observing their departure.

Though they meant no harm and seemed relatively docile, he could feel them radiating strange energy. Was it curiosity? Judgment? Disapproval?

He let it go. He never planned to return to Fibril anyway.

The stone boat exited the cobwebbed archway and reentered the world. Erlea was waiting for them a few miles from the start of the web. Wise, Rhoco noted, as she was easy prey to such a trap.

"I'm happy you are healed and have returned," he shouted to the bee overhead.

She did not acknowledge him and instead, buzzed around the boat to assess their current state before landing on Feodras's forehead. She walked the perimeter of his face, calming him as she tightened her trajectory with each lap. Her final circle ended on his glabella. Feodras was still as a statue as she rested between his eyebrows.

For the first time, Feodras relaxed, his hysterics ceased.

There was no telling the full extent of Feodras's fate, not yet, at least. But he was safe and Rhoco had to continue his mission. Compass and map in hand, he steered their boat back on course to Crystet.

Chapter 27

Feodras's calm only lasted an hour. The moment Erlea left his brow, he erupted into a fit. All that soothed him was the bumblebee's direct contact, but the only way he would heal was if she let him go. Her magic needed to run its course, without interference. So they stomached the noise the best they could and soldiered on.

Erlea left the proximity of the stone boat to hover overhead. When the bawling was particularly dreadful, she hung back and flew over the ocean in the boat's wake. Rhoco, however, could not escape the horror of Feodras's recovery. He was forced to watch the Murk bellow in agony, bound and trapped in his misery. His eyes swelled with glimmering tears of desperation as he pleaded to be set free.

It was an awful sight, one Rhoco would never forget. He felt responsible for the pain, and the longer it dragged on, the guiltier he felt.

He reached into his pocket, hoping the heart might grant him solace, but the fabric separating him from the glass blocked any temporary relief. He hesitated, unsure what the heart might do if he touched it, but then Feodras released an exceptional shriek and Rhoco plunged his hand into the pouch.

Upon contact with the heart, his mind was torn away from his disturbing reality aboard the stone boat and sent to a place that was quiet.

The room was empty and endless. There were no walls, just perpetual darkness. Only an approaching silhouette provided light. The silhouette, which could only be that of the woman in white, stopped at arms' length, and though her glow illuminated the area around them, it was too bright to see past.

"You've come back," she said, her expression pained.

"I never left."

"You haven't visited in a while."

"A lot has been going on, but we are nearing Crystet."

"I missed you."

"There's no need for that. You've been by my side the whole time."

"I've never kept someone for so long."

"What do you mean?"

"Everyone leaves. I thought you would too."

"I see the good in you," Rhoco explained.

"Even after I showed you my deepest horror?"

"Even so."

Her eyes narrowed. *"Give it time. You'll run from me too."*

"Do you want me to?" Rhoco asked, confused.

"Of course not."

"Then why are you pushing me away?"

"I'm not, I just know how these things go."

"I bet you pushed all the others away too."

"Don't assume to know me."

"Don't assume I'll run."

They were at a standstill, so he decided to confirm his loyalty with a kiss. With a tender touch, he placed his stone hands over her glass cheeks and pulled her in.

When their lips touched, every doubt was erased. Their love was pure and untarnished, never touched by betrayal or lies. Formed slowly with caution and care, and only accepted after proven genuine. And now, Rhoco could be certain that his love was returned. She felt for him, just as he felt for her, and all that he'd gone through to get here was validated.

He released her from his kiss and stared deeply into her eyes.

"Won't you please tell me your name?"

She hesitated. Each blink held centuries of consideration. Finally, her eyes sparkled and the corners of her crystal mouth turned upward.

"Gwyn."

"Gwyn," he repeated, smiling. "A beautiful name for a beautiful woman."

She blushed.

"I must return. We should be reaching Crystet soon."

"Thank you."

Rhoco nodded. *"I am happy to help."*

She released him from her magic and Feodras's screams of anguish welcomed him back to reality.

Another full day passed before Feodras stopped screaming. When he finally calmed, both Rhoco and Erlea were mentally spent. Between their lack of sleep and concern for his well-being, his awakening was welcomed with tired enthusiasm.

"How do you feel?" Rhoco asked from his seat at the pedals. He hadn't moved from that spot since they left Fibril and he kept the compass on his thigh to ensure they did not veer off course again.

Feodras groaned and looked around, though his ability to move was minimized by the web he remained wrapped in. He peered at his confinements, then up at Rhoco.

"You were safer like this," Rhoco explained as he walked over and cut Feodras free with the serrated knife.

"I thought the sylphs killed me."

"So did I."

"They were feeding on me, then I went to a dark place. I was there for months. I thought my soul floated out to space."

"You were only gone for two days."

"It felt like forever."

"You *let* the sylphs feast on you," Rhoco explained with disapproval, "and we were lucky enough to reach Fibril in time for a Bonz to help you."

Erlea buzzed into Feodras's ear.

"It wasn't luck, it was Gaia. She pushed our boat into their web," he explained.

Rhoco sighed. "Regardless, Chesulloth of the Bonz saved our lives. She ate the sylphs and then healed you. The web she wrapped you in fixed your wounds but sent you into a state of prolonged dissociation, hence your mental absence and constraints."

"I see."

"What do you remember?"

"The sylphs eating my flesh," Feodras recalled with a shudder.

"And before that?"

Feodras paused, struggling to recall the order of events. "The Mudlings, I think, chasing us toward Coppel." He looked around, suddenly afraid. "We lost them, right?"

"Yes. They're long gone."

"Right," he nodded, remembering they had just left Fibril, which was hundreds of miles from Coppel. He glared up at Rhoco as the memories came back. "Were you hoping I'd forget?"

"Of course not."

"Well, I remember everything."

"How do you feel?"

Feodras paused, assessing his own transformation before responding. "I feel whole again."

"Good."

"Better than ever, I think. Surviving the sorrow has made me stronger."

Rhoco nodded with a smile, glad that the Murk was in better sorts. The blanket of sorrow that covered him previously had lifted and he was back to his old self.

Erlea buzzed into Feodras's ear again. He listened intently for a while before looking up at Rhoco with dread.

"We've got a problem."

"What now?"

"There is a bounty on your head."

"A bounty? What for?"

"Treason."

"It's happening," Rhoco said, dismayed that his greatest fear was materializing.

"The Mudlings reported their sighting and near-capture of us on the Coppel Sea, which confirmed that you were alive and well, and left King Alun to conclude that you were acting on behalf of the resistance."

"This is wildly unfair. The bounty is only on me?"

"No one cares about the Murks. They likely don't even realize I'm gone."

"This is terrible. Now I can't return to Orewall."

Erlea spoke again, and Feodras repeated.

"You have to. Cybelle needs you."

"What does *that* mean?"

Feodras listened to Erlea's explanation, then translated.

"She went to the king to explain your innocence. She insisted you knew nothing of any revolution and simply had an itch to explore. The king did not believe her and took her prisoner. She's being held captive until you return." Erlea buzzed loudly, and Feodras continued, "She's been hung by her wrists in the middle of Amesyte Valley and is covered in a slow-moving, ore-eating lichen. She'll die if you don't turn yourself in."

Rhoco's chest caved and it became hard to breathe. He could not escape his innate ability to cause harm. Even from a distance, he managed to hurt those closest to him.

"I'm so sorry," Feodras sympathized.

"How far along is the lichen?"

"She's paralyzed. Fingers to elbows, toes to knees. It's a slow moving, reversible strain of yekî mirî, so she might have another month or two before it reaches her heart."

"We are so close to Crystet. If I can just get there to make my delivery, I should have time to get back to Orewall before the lichen reaches her heart. Then I can save two lives."

"Two lives?" Feodras inquired.

"Cybelle's," he paused, "and the one in Crystet." Though difficult to reveal, he could no longer hide the truth from Feodras. They were in this together and it was time to come clean. He pulled the pouch from his pocket and loosened the strings so Feodras could see the glass heart inside.

Feodras's jaw dropped and his eyes darted back and forth from the heart to Rhoco.

"I didn't tell you because I was afraid you'd have the same reaction as Cybelle," he explained apologetically, "and I would've thrown you overboard if you spent the entire journey trying to talk me out of my mission."

"Who does it belong to?"

"I'm not sure. I'm hoping that will become clear once I'm there."

"Hearts are powerful relics—"

"I know," Rhoco cut him off. "Cybelle already gave me the doom-and-gloom breakdown."

"Why didn't you just throw it into the ocean?"

"I guess I'm not the coldblooded bastard I always thought I was," Rhoco admitted. "This heart belongs to someone. I read how the Glaziene work and I bet the owner is desperately looking for her missing piece. I have to return it to her before she shatters."

"You've fallen in love with it, haven't you?"

"Excuse me?"

"You ought to tread lightly if I'm correct. A heart removed from its cage often has minimal ties back to its owner."

"You don't know what I know."

"That statement goes both ways."

"I haven't fallen in love," Rhoco declared, choosing to hold on to some of his secrets.

"So you can return the heart and be done with it forever?"

"I can," Rhoco agreed, hoping that if the heart could hear him, it would understand.

Feodras eyed him suspiciously. "I don't believe you."

"I don't care what you believe," he scoffed. "I shouldn't have told you."

"I'm not going to try to stop you, I just worry that you still don't understand the true nature of the Glaziene. I think you're in so deep you don't want to see the way out."

"You know nothing of what I've gone through to get to this point. You know nothing of what goes on in my mind. Do not place your assumptions on me."

"Fine. I won't say another word about it."

"And you and your bee cannot tell a soul."

"We won't. We promise."

After another night sailing north, the weather began to change. Unlike their detours, which kept them in warm water with a similar climate to Orewall, the men now entered into a glacial freeze. The air was frigid and Rhoco could feel the cold despite his stone-senses. He shivered so severely he had to wrap a spare blanket around his bare torso.

"Why is it so cold?" he asked Feodras, who also hid beneath a wool blanket.

"We are entering the Arctic. Here, the sun only graces the sky for eight hours each day."

"Why?"

"It's just the way the world spins."

Rhoco picked up his map of Namaté, concerned that they were off-course again, but the compass pointed in the right direction and they were still on their way to Crystet.

"The Glaziene live in these conditions?"

"They *thrive* in these conditions," Feodras clarified.

"How? We are made of stone and we shouldn't be able to feel a thing, yet we're both crippled by this cold."

"I guess glass and ice go well together. Sharp, razor edges. Deadly. Perfect pairing, really."

Rhoco walked to the edge of the boat to scan the horizon for any sign of land. The white sky was blanketed with snow-swollen clouds, and against the black ocean, the view was monochrome. The pure and pristine sight mesmerized Rhoco. When he realized the monotony of the view had sent him into a stupor, he glanced down at his skin to remind himself there was still color in the world.

He wasn't sure how long he had been staring into the distance when the sight of land arrived, but it came into view with elegant authority. Rolling hills covered in untouched snow and dressed with crystalized evergreens greeted them. Beyond the picturesque scenery stood a castle. Rhoco could tell it was crafted with precious diamonds by the way the sun reflected off the corners. The light echoed off its walls and illuminated the surrounding area with patches of rainbows. As the sun moved, so did the only colors Rhoco saw on the landscape.

"We're here," he exclaimed, but when he turned to celebrate with Feodras, he was horrified to find that an ocean tanker dressed in neon lights approached from the stern.

Feodras whipped his head and waved Rhoco away.

"You need to hide," he demanded.

"No."

"This is my fault, my burden to carry, not yours."

"We are in this together," Rhoco insisted.

"You never agreed to be part of a resistance mission. Let me take the fall."

"It doesn't feel right."

"If you want to save the owner of that heart, then you have to let me do this."

Rhoco grimaced, aware that Feodras was right.

"I'll be fine," Feodras continued. "They won't realize who I really am until we're back at Orewall."

"And then what?"

"I'm a Murk. They think little of me and will likely send me back to my cave."

"This is wrong," Rhoco stammered, unable to shake the guilt he felt for allowing Feodras to sacrifice himself.

"They'll turn me back into a slave, sure, but you, they'll execute. Do what you have to do. We've come too far to let this mission be a waste."

"What about this boat and the Metellyans?"

"That cause is lost for now."

"I'm sorry."

"This is Gaia's will. Succeed in your task, then all of this won't be for nothing."

Rhoco nodded, reenergized by Feodras's certainty. "Thank you for being a friend."

Feodras smiled, a shape his mouth rarely formed. "Thank you for the adventure."

Rhoco placed his right hand on Feodras's left shoulder. Feodras looked up at him, happily shocked by the gesture. He mirrored Rhoco's stance, eyes welling with tears of validation. No matter what happened in the future, they had shattered expectations by becoming friends.

Rhoco departed for the front of the boat, thankful to finally make peace with the vexing Murk. He managed to reverse the years of hateful conditioning and learn to view Feodras as his equal. He smiled back at the Murk, who stood tall and bravely faced the incoming ship. Again, Rhoco found that who he used to be was amended by this journey, and if death greeted him, at least he'd die proud of the man he had become.

Rhoco threw a rope ladder overboard and descended halfway. The glacial, black sea lapped against the boat, splashing his ankles and wetting the legs of his pants. The chill was so severe it broke through his stone senses. Rhoco eavesdropped over the loud grumble of the sea as his friend took the fall for him.

"Are you Rhoco Leath?"

"I am," Feodras lied.

"We are the guardsmen of Elecort, protectors of King Lucien's kingdom, and you are under arrest for being a traitor to the scepter."

"How am I a traitor?" Feodras argued.

"King Alun told King Lucien of your treachery. When you disobey the king of your own land, you disobey the king of all the lands."

"I've done nothing treacherous," Feodras insisted. Rhoco was impressed by his gusto. The Murk who left Orewall with him would have never spoken out with such conviction. Rhoco grinned. It appeared this journey changed Feodras for the better, too. "I simply craved an adventure."

"Lies. We can feel what your boat is made of. You *and* your boat are coming with us."

Two large, electrified hooks latched onto the side of their stone boat. The moment they made contact, their buzzing ceased.

"Proof that you're a traitor," one of the Voltain guardsmen scolded before seizing Feodras and constraining him in high-voltage chains. The vibration made Feodras shake with vigor, but it wasn't enough to knock the stone man out.

The boat began speeding away from Crystet and Rhoco panicked. After all he endured to get here, he was being effortlessly towed away from his destination. Beneath him was the deep, dark ocean, and ahead was the snowy coast of Crystet. He looked down and saw his reflection on the surface of the sea. He had no other option.

Rhoco held his breath and jumped.

The moment his body hit the water, he sank. With speed, he plummeted thirty feet and his bare stone feet hit the ocean floor with a silent thud. Sand sprayed in all directions, blocking his view momentarily. The intense, icy temperature of the water sent his body into shock and all his senses numbed — a survival tactic he never realized he was capable of.

He didn't bother trying to swim. Instead, he began marching toward the shore. He moved as fast as he could, but the dense water impaired his speed, and though he tried to push through with force, he still felt as if he were moving in slow motion.

The world beneath the ocean was shaded by the black hue of the water, and though the visibility was clear, everything appeared as a shadow. Every fish that swam by, all the ocean flora and frozen coral, appeared ghost-like in this light. He felt as if he were walking through a daydream that would quickly shift into a nightmare if he didn't reach the shore in time. His lungs expanded, reflexively understanding the gravity of his predicament. He'd die here if he didn't conserve his oxygen.

Time stood still as he fought to survive. The pain of each step resonated through his stone bones, intensifying the longer he remained submerged. It was too dark to determine the distance he covered, or how close he was to reaching land, but he held onto hope.

Another minute passed and a searing pain shot through his chest. He opened his mouth in shock and icy water poured in; this was a setback he could not afford. His body trembled as his progression slowed. The lack of oxygen made him weak and he could no longer fight the faintness that clouded his brain. Everything turned blurry. Still, he soldiered forward, up the sandy incline toward the shore.

The shadows of the ocean grew darker and he could barely see, but he stayed true to his course and pushed forward.

Another flare of searing pain. Rhoco fell to his knees. His chest was on fire as his lungs fought to hold on to their last pocket of air. Death hovered over him and there was nothing he could do to send it away.

He reached into his pocket and removed the glass heart from its satchel.

I did my best, he thought as he examined it in his hand. It glowed bright red in a sea of black.

"I can feel my body," it replied. *"Take me to it."*

Rhoco's eye widened as a jolt reenergized his body. The place where the heart sat on his palm tingled as it radiated its magic into him. It coursed up his arm, into his spine, and bolted into the back of his brain. The pain in his chest vanished, his vision cleared, his stone flesh warmed, and his lungs filled with air.

The magic of the heart saved him again. Invigorated with renewed life, Rhoco returned to his feet and resumed his march toward Crystet. Nothing could stop him now.

Chapter 28

The water began to brighten. Dark gray turned to light gray, and soon the crown of Rhoco's head crested the water. Once his head emerged, the heart's magic retracted, allowing him to breathe on his own again. He returned it to his pocket as he continued forward, shivering as he pushed through the water. The warmth the heart provided was gone and he was on his own to fight the cold.

Step by step, he moved closer to the shore. When the water was shallow enough that only his ankles were covered, he noticed how strange the sand ahead appeared. The beach was made of large pieces that shimmered and gleamed in the sunlight. Upon closer inspection, he realized that the entire beach was covered in shards of glass. He paused on the wet sand, which contained the type of granular pieces he was used to. The waves broke and kissed his feet as they charged the shoreline. He wrung the water from his pants as best he could but accepted that he'd be walking around in damp clothing until he found new items to wear.

Rhoco marched forward, breaking the glass underfoot.

"Stop!" a small voice shouted after he'd taken a few steps. He paused, unsure who spoke to him or why.

"Who are you?" it asked in a voice as delicate as chimes in the dying winds of a storm.

Rhoco squinted, attempting to find the source, but the light reflecting off the glass beach was too bright.

"My name is Rhoco," he replied.

"Why doesn't the glass hurt you?"

"Because I am made of stone."

He heard the fragile tinkling of glass against glass, and a moment later the source of the voice emerged a few feet in front of him.

It was a small Glaziene girl. She wore a white, woolly dress with a large fur hood covering her head. The skirt was short, revealing her skinny glass legs and bare feet. The only color in her entire appearance derived from the blood-red veins visible through the translucent, blushed skin covering her glass legs and face, as well as the bright blue gaze with which she stared at him.

A gust of wind blew past, displacing the long, blonde curls that spilled out of her hood. She stepped closer and he noticed that her glass skin was smooth and pristine. Not a single crack in sight.

"What's your name?" he asked.

"What are you doing here?" she countered, ignoring his inquiry. Her subtle trepidation was mitigated by curiosity.

307

"I'm here on an errand. Something that belongs to a Glaziene washed up on my shore and I've come to return it to its owner."

"Do you know much about Crystet?"

"No."

She smirked, delighted by her newfound power.

"I'm Kirsi."

"Nice to meet you, Kirsi. How old are you?"

"Twelve," she answered. "What item are you returning?"

"A heart."

Her eyebrows raised and her delicate expression of shifty intrigue morphed into shock. Rhoco watched in awe, amazed by how calculated every small movement was, though he suspected if he were made of glass, he'd move with great care too.

"Who does it belong to?"

"A woman named Gwyn."

Kirsi's gaze shifted downward as she tried to recall a woman named Gwyn.

"There are numerous women with that name *within* their full name," she finally surrendered. "How do you know *this* Gwyn wants it back?"

"I could sense her desire to return home."

"You ought to be careful with matters you don't fully understand," Kirsi advised. "You might be subjecting yourself to a world of trouble by bringing that back here."

"Or maybe I'm saving someone's life."

"You don't know why that heart was discarded, or by whom," the young girl warned.

"That's what I'm here to find out. I will gladly leave if I am no longer welcome after I've returned the heart to Gwyn."

"I'm not sure how you'll find this person."

"Can you take me to someone who might know how to help?"

"I suppose," she replied with a sigh, angry to transfer control of the newcomer to someone else. "Follow me."

She led him up the snowy, glass beach to a tall, glass gate coated in ice. The world on the other side appeared blurry through the thick door, but once she opened it, a frozen wonderland greeted Rhoco. Everything was made of glass and was draped in a layer of snow and ice. The ground was pure crystal, with jagged edges buried beneath its smooth finish. Kirsi walked ahead, gliding with delicate steps on the immaculate ground. But as soon as Rhoco took one step past the gate, he felt the ground crack beneath his weight.

He cursed at himself, angry that he was already causing damage. The fissure spread quickly, traveling with speed toward the little girl. When it crossed under her, she caught sight of the damage and snapped her head back.

"Our land is broken enough," she scolded. "Be more careful."

"I'm sorry."

"Wait here," she huffed, then glided out of sight.

Rhoco swallowed his nerves, ignoring the little girl's instruction to stay put, and took another step with greater care. This time, after placing his foot down as gently as possible, he managed a step forward without breaking the ground.

He felt relief and dismay simultaneously. If he had to move this slow at all times, he'd never get anywhere. As he began to take another slow and meticulous step, Kirsi returned with a strange-looking pair of cotton slippers.

"I told you to stay still."

"I didn't break anything."

"Put these on," she ordered as she thrust them into his hands. "You're slowing me down."

Rhoco examined the shoes, which were bolstered by eight-inch soles of sturdy foam. The shoes were too small, so he wrapped the ribbons into knots around his large, stone feet until the foam slippers were securely attached.

"Those slippers are usually used for the Voltains. They're the only outsiders who visit Crystet. Well, until you showed up."

Kirsi glared back at Rhoco, still suspicious of his presence, but she said no more. Instead, she skated forward, leading them past what appeared to be a giant bottomless pit in the middle of the market square. Rhoco proceeded with caution, but Kirsi appeared unafraid, darting along the edge with speed.

When they exited the main strip lined with shoddily repaired shops and eateries, they crossed through another gate, which led them into a Glaziene housing metropolis. Rows of connected glass homes lined the entrance and deviated in all directions as the streets diverged. The streets formed an intricate labyrinth encased by tall, glass dwellings, and the farther they walked, the more the streets bent and turned. The buildings were cracked, many left in a state of disrepair, but Rhoco saw past the damage and recognized the beauty beyond the breaks. From above, he imagined that the patterns formed by these sprawling complexes were lovely and ornate, but from the ground, the maze was rather overwhelming.

Kirsi had no trouble finding her way, though. She led him down multiple streets, taking so many turns Rhoco lost track of the path back to the entrance gate.

The young girl stopped at the stoop of a glass row home that looked just like every other one they had passed. The only defining feature on the house was its unique identifier: next to the door, etched into the glass, was the letter T and a seven-pointed star.

"We're here," Kirsi informed.

"What's that?" he asked, pointing at the star.

"That's a stjörnu, one of Devotene's symbols for protection."

"Who is Devotene?"

"The Vorso goddess of loyalty and guardianship," Kirsi replied, appalled that Rhoco still evinced confusion. "Daughter of Gaia."

"Gaia is the only god I've ever heard of."

"You have a lot to learn," Kirsi reprimanded before returning her attention to the locked door.

Rhoco looked up and down the row. Though the homes were made of glass, he could not see through the frost-tinted walls. Kirsi pulled a key from her pocket and unlocked the door. A shrill scrape assaulted Rhoco's ears as the door scratched the threshold. Though the sound was horrible, Kirsi traipsed inside, unaffected.

Rhoco shook off the chills inflicted by the noise, then followed her inside. The home was created entirely of glass, just like the majority of Crystet, and while the sight was stunning, Rhoco couldn't help but view it as a personal hell. More things to break, more damage to cause. He crossed his arms and locked his hands inside his armpits before following the girl up the stairs.

"Kirsi, is that you?" a nasally voice called from another room.

"Who else would it be, Mamma?"

Kirsi was answered with silence, and when she turned the corner, she was greeted by the scornful expression of her mother. Rhoco hung behind and peeked out from behind the wall. Their looming family tension made him uncomfortable.

Her mother absentmindedly traced her fingers along the large crack that ran from her forehead, down her neck, and over her heart. Beneath her glass skin, the red glow of her heart pulsed.

"Stop looking so sad," Kirsi demanded.

"Did you see him in the market?"

"No."

"I'm certain he misses me," her mother said, more to herself than to her daughter.

"Perce isn't coming back," Kirsi said with a huff. "You made certain of that."

"Have you been eavesdropping again?"

"You talk loud enough for the entire row to hear."

"You're too young to know about such heartache. I am buying you earmuffs." Her mother snagged a glass tablet from the table and began etching a note below the long list of items she wished not to forget.

At that moment, Rhoco stepped out from behind the wall. Kirsi's mother yelped, "A man has followed you into our home!"

"He needs our help," Kirsi tried to explain. "Rhoco, this is Trista, my mother. She is a Valið of Gaia and a former andlega ráðgjafi to Queen Dalila. Mamma, meet Rhoco."

"He's not Glaziene," her mother exclaimed with a gasp.

"Obviously," the young girl stated.

"We aren't in armor, he could shatter us with a sneeze."

"He means us no harm."

Rhoco stepped in. "Truly, I mean you no harm."

Though his voice was gentle, all Trista registered was his menacing figure moving closer.

"Stay away," she demanded, slamming her fist against a weak spot in the wall and wielding the shard that broke off as a weapon. Rhoco raised his hands in surrender.

Trista capitalized on his submissive reaction and leaned in till the tip of her glass rapier touched his chest.

"Tell me your darkest secrets," she sneered.

"Excuse me?" Rhoco stuttered, confused.

"All of them."

"Mamma, stop," Kirsi protested.

"He's entered my home, uninvited, so I can take from him what I like."

"*I* invited him here."

"Without my permission."

Kirsi pursed her lips and pushed herself between the adults. With a single swat, she batted the weapon away, causing it to shatter on the floor.

"You are a pestilent brat," Trista spat. "It's a miracle you've survived twelve years without a single crack. If I didn't love you so much, I'd have littered you with them by now."

"Lucky me."

"So, what am I supposed to do? Offer tea to the talking stone? Do rocks even drink tea?"

"Stop being rude," Kirsi pleaded, exasperated by her mother's maddening personality. "He's here to find a woman named Gwyn. Something of hers washed up on his beach and he traveled all this way to return it."

"And what exactly is this precious item you've journeyed oh so far to return?" she asked, mocking Rhoco.

"A heart," Rhoco answered.

"A heart?" Trista repeated, dropping her sardonic tone as morbid fascination took over.

"Yes."

Her eyes widened with excitement, then returned to normal as she tried to appear casual.

"Gwyn is a common name. I'll need to hold the heart to determine who it belongs to."

"No," he replied with stern authority.

"Don't you want my help?"

"Yes, but I don't know if I can trust you yet."

"At the very least, you need to show it to me. I cannot help you if I cannot get a sense of the heart."

Begrudgingly, Rhoco obliged, pulling the heart from its wrapping and revealing it to Trista. It was black, with a faint glow of red at the center.

"Gwynessa," Trista gasped before averting her gaze to the ground.

Rhoco had no idea who she spoke of, but when she flinched at the sight, retreating internally in its presence, Rhoco was forced to acknowledge that there was more to the heart's story than it let on.

Chapter 29

"Who is Gwynessa?" Rhoco asked.

"I hope you haven't fallen in love with it," Trista warned, still avoiding eye contact.

"Who is Gwynessa?" Rhoco demanded again.

"Put that thing away," she said, shuddering. "Please."

Rhoco obeyed and concealed the heart in his pocket. Once it was out of sight, Trista lifted her gaze.

"You can identify the heart just by looking at it?" he asked.

"My daughter already told you," Trista fumed. "I am chosen by Gaia, which gives me the gift of sight and touch. In my youth, I was the spiritual adviser to Queen Dalila; therefore I know the heart you conceal far too well."

"Are we in danger, Mamma?" Kirsi asked, sounding her age for the first time since Rhoco met her.

"No, darling, so long as he keeps that relic hidden away."

"Who is Gwynessa?" Rhoco asked again.

"You don't know about Queen Nessa?" Kirsi asked, bewildered.

"Do they teach you nothing in Orewall?" Trista jeered.

"If she is a queen, then returning her heart is even more imperative. Where will I find her?"

Trista's mischievous demeanor returned.

"Jökull Cliff."

"Where is that?"

"You must leave. I do not wish to be associated with this inevitable disaster any longer." She went to shove Rhoco, but her skin splintered upon contact.

"You've cracked my fingertip!"

"I did no such thing," he said in defense.

"Get out!" she screamed, unable to contain her fury. "Get out!"

Rhoco obliged, uninterested in intensifying her anger.

As he departed, Trista cursed him in her native tongue. "Vorso Vindicene, bölva þennan mann!"

He did not know what she said, nor did he care. She gave him the information he needed and he was happy to leave her hostile home. For a supposedly religious woman, she was rather vile. Her brash and dithering personality was unbecoming, and it left Rhoco with a foul opinion of the priesthood to whom the Glaziene bestowed ultimate authority.

As he left, he wondered how the Glaziene ever participated in the war for the scepter. They were so fragile and potential peril existed with every move they made. Surely a single battle would have obliterated the entire population.

He had no answer for this thought, only more questions.

The moment he stepped outside into the frigid air of Crystet, he remembered how inappropriately he was dressed. He had no shirt and his pants were still damp. He shivered and hoped the act of walking would warm his bones.

It took some time to navigate the intricate maze of fissured row homes, but after finding the main road, he continued onward, away from the market and the shore. There was nothing back there for him; his boat was long gone and the heart needed him to keep moving forward.

After a few miles of walking, Rhoco came upon another gate, which led him out of the close quarters of the metropolis and into a shopping village. The buildings were spaced out here and far more humble than those lining the shore.

"Are you a madman?" a raspy voice bellowed. Rhoco snapped around and saw an old fellow sitting in a crystal rocking chair outside an armor shop across the street. He twirled a glass figurine of a fox between his fingers. "Your skin wasn't designed for these conditions."

"I know, but this is all I have," Rhoco explained, pointing to his wet pants as he walked over.

"Come inside my shop, ya loon."

The old, glass man stood slowly and then moseyed inside at the same sluggish speed. Rhoco made it into the store before the old man and he waited by a table covered in diamond-crested breastplates.

With gentle but intense focus, the old man carefully placed the glass fox down on the counter before addressing Rhoco.

"My name is Jahdo Uveges, son of Spiegel Uveges, the originator of Uveges Armor and Shields. We design and manufacture Glaziene battle attire. Our panoply is aplenty, as you'll see if you turn your head and look."

Rhoco obliged. He sensed the old man hadn't sold an item in a while, so he waited patiently as Jahdo proudly regurgitated a well-practiced spiel.

"Every item is top-notch quality with a twenty-year guarantee upon purchase. My father and I perfected the glass-and-diamond-welding technique and have run a booming business ever since. No one competes with Uveges. We own the armor market and you won't find a better shield in all of Crystet. When there is a battle to be fought, Uveges is the brand Glaziene soldiers trust. Impenetrable, indestructible, a promise from my family to yours that in our gear, you'll become invincible." Jahdo paused, his previously animated gaze softened as he recalled an old emotion. "My family," he said, the volume of his voice decreasing, but he slayed the moment of weakness before it lingered too long. "My family vows longevity and durability."

"It's an excellent collection," Rhoco agreed.

"That it is," the shopkeeper sighed, aware that the strange man exercised great patience as he spoke words that hadn't left his mouth in years. Though nostalgia plagued him, Jahdo kept his vulnerability suppressed.

"Unfortunately," Rhoco went on, "I am not in the market to buy diamond breastplates, helmets, or shin guards."

"I'm not blind. What you need is a shirt and dry pants."

Rhoco smiled as Jahdo hobbled toward the back wall.

"I've got sweaters made from the fur of boreal bears and gelid foxes," Jahdo explained, pointing at two stacks of sweaters. He then motioned to the shelf beneath and Rhoco noticed that the entire garment selection was colored white. "Pants lined with hyperborean moose pelt and meridional wolf fuzz. Even socks made from austral sheep fleece. What do you have to barter?"

Rhoco's gaze transitioned from the racks of warm clothes to the old Glaziene man.

"I've got nothing."

Jahdo grunted, "Sure you do." He grabbed a pair of hyperborean moose pants from the middle of the stack. "You'll take these in exchange for the brown pair you're currently wearing."

"Why would you want the ones I have on?"

"I've never made pants with cotton of that color before. Once your pants are cleaned and altered, they'll sell for a great price."

Rhoco shrugged and agreed to the trade. He went into the curtain-drawn changing room to switch pants. The pants lined with moose pelt were soft and incredibly warm. The outer layer was made of silvery silk, while the inside of each pant leg was thick with moose pelt. He carefully removed the pouch containing the heart from his old, damp pants and transferred it into the new.

"Where did you find such fine fabric?" Rhoco asked as he exited the changing room.

"Fibril, of course. The Bonz deliver silk and other fine fibers in exchange for glass and crystals."

"Don't you get crystals from the Bouldes?"

"Only the colored ones, which we rarely desire. We have a plethora of our own, neutral-colored crystals provided by the underground volcanoes."

"I see. So you don't need us."

"Not for crystals," Jahdo confirmed. "Let's discuss a sweater." He retrieved one made from the fur of a boreal bear. "This is the warmest. What can you give me in exchange?"

"I already told you, I have nothing."

"It would be irresponsible for me to let you leave this store without a shirt. Despite your stone genetics, you'll eventually freeze to death. But I also cannot justify giving it to you for free. There must be *something* you can barter."

But all Rhoco had was the heart, and that wasn't for sale.

Then an idea struck.

"How about a secret?" Rhoco suggested.

Jahdo's eyes narrowed, enhancing the fissures encasing them, then gleamed with sinister intrigue.

"Go on."

"The Voltains tried to arrest me on my way here."

"I hate the Voltains."

"As do I. But instead of capturing me, they took my boatmate and I escaped."

"So they are in possession of the wrong person?"

"Correct."

"How wonderful," Jahdo said with genuine delight. "I love a good trick."

"But you can't tell anyone. If they find out, they'll come here to retrieve me and I'll be in far worse trouble."

"I don't snitch, I stitch." The old man snickered at his joke. "I'm so good with secrets, you might say my mouth is sewn shut." He chuckled again before handing the sweater to Rhoco. "A fantastic secret indeed."

"Thank you," Rhoco said as he pulled the sweater over his head. Its warmth would do him wonders once he left the shop.

"A pair of socks and boots to replace your foam slippers if you tell me *why* they were trying to arrest you," Jahdo said, dangling a pair of sheep fleece socks as a bribe.

"I cannot tell you that. All I can say is that I was wrongfully accused and that I bring no harm to you or your land."

"Interesting," Jahdo mused. "Still, no socks for you."

Rhoco regretted losing his chance to warm his bare stone feet, but revealing too much was unwise. Though Jahdo seemed harmless, there was no guarantee. The world already proved itself to be far more devious than he ever dreamed possible, and doling out trust too easily now would be foolish. His guard was up; he had a mission to complete.

"Will you tell me how to get to Jökull Cliff?" Rhoco asked.

"The graveyard?"

"No, the cliff."

"You shouldn't go there. It's cursed."

"I have no choice."

"I suspect you won't tell me *why* you need to go to such a wicked location." He raised the socks as a bribe again.

"It's better if I don't."

"Fine," Jahdo yielded and lowered the socks into his pocket. "I'll take you there, but I will not accompany you to the top."

"Any help is appreciated."

Jahdo put on his fur-lined wool jacket and shoved the crystal fox into his large pocket. Then, still barefoot, proceeded to walk outside. He waved for Rhoco to follow.

"Don't you need socks or anything for *your* feet?"

"Haven't you noticed? No one here wears shoes. I don't even need this jacket, but it feels better with it on."

"The temperature doesn't affect you?"

"No, we thrive in the cold."

"Then why bother with coats at all?"

"I mostly wear the jacket for my cracks. Those are the only parts of me that ever catch a chill. When the wind blows just right, it pushes its way through the breaks and will nip a Glaziene to the core. Most of my cracks mended nicely, but some will never fully heal," Jahdo explained.

Rhoco pondered this while Jahdo led the way forward. He didn't have actual cracks like the Glaziene, but he did have a few breaks, both in his heart and spirit, which he suspected had not fully healed. If something as simple as a gust of cold air could bring his old pains back to life, he'd wear protective gear too.

Now that he wore dry clothes and had found a more amenable guide, Rhoco noticed the countless scrutinizing eyes staring at him through the windows of stores and homes as Jahdo paraded him down the middle of the boulevard. Rhoco glanced around to find that their expressions were just as harsh as the energy they radiated. Though their behavior was unwelcoming, they did not pose an immediate threat. He was safe with Jahdo and he hoped they'd all forget about him once he was out of sight.

The boulevard stretched on for miles, as did the silent speculation. He thought he'd never escape the unkind observers when Jahdo led him past the last glass building on the road.

"We're entering the Wildlands now," Jahdo explained as they approached an untouched field of snow. The woods were thick and blanketed in ice. "You're gonna wish you had those socks and boots."

"Lead the way," Rhoco encouraged, too stubborn to admit that the old Glaziene was probably right.

"Try not to make any noise. The animals hate us."

"They hate you?"

"That's what I said."

"Why?"

"The Glaziene children maim and torture the creatures of the wild so that they leave us alone. We are, after all, made of glass, and without armor we can break from the slightest mishap. Since this is our reality, we've allowed generation after generation to tame the wild animals with violence. It helps us all in the long run. If the animals did not fear us, they would surely destroy us."

"So you hunt in order to maintain control?"

"Correct. But as an old man reflecting back on my life, I've come to recognize that we do not need to terrorize the animals to earn their respect." He paused in thought. "A young girl once taught me that—she showed me the gentle nature of the monsters." His energy tensed. "But, alas, kindness rarely wins. The Glaziene children resumed their hunting parties decades ago."

"Seems unwise to anger packs of bears and wolves."

"It's the foxes you need to look out for. They tend to get the brunt of the abuse because they're small. Worst part is that the children don't usually don't kill the creatures, they merely maim them, and the animals live on with a seed of hatred ingrained in their hearts. It's a contrived and manipulative way to take control over another living creature."

"Why not eat them? Seems like a waste of good meat."

"It's tactical. They need to live, ravaged and mutilated, in order for the fear to thrive."

Rhoco shook his head, understanding the rationale, but flabbergasted that such behavior was commonplace. He could justify killing for food, but killing for fun felt sinful. He tried not to judge, but each time he heard a distant rustle in the trees, he cursed the Glaziene for creating the dangerous path he now walked.

"Look over there," Jahdo whispered after pausing abruptly. "A boreal bear." He sniffed the air. "It's a female."

"How do you know?"

"They smell better than the males. A hint of honey and flowers accompany the usual stink of feces and wet fur. The lady bears are ferocious, much worse than the fellows. It's best we move on."

Rhoco happily obliged.

The trek was lined with dense, snow-draped forestry. The slippers he wore were soaked and the foam was pressed flat. They no longer cushioned his weight and he wondered what damage he was causing to the glass ground hidden underneath all the snow. His feet were freezing and felt as if they had morphed into two large icebergs. Still, he walked on them, even though each step sent sharp pains into his ankles and knees. The shadows grew taller, and as the sun set, the darkness swallowed them whole.

"Are we almost there?" Rhoco asked, shivering.

"Not even close. We will return here tomorrow, but tonight, we need to stay in Quarzelle."

"What's that?"

"The royal village."

"We aren't royals. Will we be welcome?"

"Don't let the name fool you. It's the most run-down village in all of Crystet. The closer you are to the castle, the worse off you are."

"Is that where Jökull Cliff is?"

"No. That's on the other side of the Wildlands."

Torches illuminated the town of Quarzelle from a distance. As they approached, Jahdo's description of the village was proven accurate. Shards of glass littered the streets, at least one window on every building was broken, and the air smelt of decay. He could not determine what was rotting, but the aroma was sharp and offensive.

"What's that smell?" he finally asked.

"Smell?" Jahdo asked, unsure what he referred to.

"That rotten stench," Rhoco elaborated, covering his nose.

"Oh, that's kolkrabba. A fine delicacy in Crystet."

"Delicacy?" Rhoco asked, disgusted by the thought of eating anything that smelled so putrid.

"Fermented cecaelia meat cured for two weeks and enjoyed with a sprinkling of salt."

Rhoco gagged, but said no more. He did not wish to offend his guide.

"Where will we sleep?" Rhoco asked, still holding a hand over his nose.

"Bicchieri Lodge. I used to be pals with Keane."

Jahdo led the way into town, stopping at a six-story glass inn. It was the tallest, most rickety building in Quarzelle. The entire structure leaned to the left and had shoddy welding connecting each story.

"That thing will collapse the moment I step foot inside," Rhoco warned.

"Glass is stronger than you think."

"Look at it. It isn't safe."

"Would you rather sleep outside?"

"I would."

"Well, I don't feel like waking up next to a dead Boulde in the morning. I'd never be able to explain *that* to the king."

Jahdo grabbed the sleeve of Rhoco's sweater and yanked him through the front door of Bicchieri Lodge. The moment Rhoco stepped into the entrance foyer, his weight created a crack that splintered all the way to the front desk and up the podium the concierge stood behind. The man was looking down, reading an itinerary, when the crack reached the spot just beneath his gaze. His eyes shifted up toward the new arrivals with contempt.

"Sorry, Keane," Jahdo apologized. "Big fellow here wore out his foam slippers in the snow. Do you have any extra he can wear while we're here?"

"What makes you think you're welcome to stay at my lodge?" Keane growled as he glided toward them.

"Why wouldn't we be welcome?"

"I haven't seen you since your son shattered an entire floor of my lodge. He destroyed it so thoroughly, I have yet to piece it back together."

"That was over sixty years ago."

"That's my point."

"I lost a lot that day too," Jahdo retorted, his tone lethal. The men shared a tense moment of silence before Jahdo spoke again. "I can guarantee we will not ruin anything in your establishment."

"You already have," Keane exclaimed, pointing at the crack in the floor.

"To be fair, the entire entranceway is littered with fissures."

"That's *not* the point."

"Okay, fine," Jahdo huffed. "Get him slippers and there won't be another break in your building."

"You're mighty presumptuous."

"Keane," Jahdo pleaded. "We were long-time friends. Please let us take shelter in your establishment."

"Five diamonds."

"For one night?" Jahdo protested loudly.

"Shh," Keane demanded. "You'll wake my paying guests."

"Five diamonds for one night is preposterous."

Keane narrowed his glare in angry contemplation.

"Three diamonds," Keane bartered.

"I can't believe you're trying to charge me at all."

"You never sent me anything to help fix the damage your son caused years ago. You ignored all my letters, all my attempts to resolve the mishap. You avoided me like a plague."

"I was in a dark place." Jahdo hung his head. "I lost everything. I should've answered your attempts to connect, but I wanted to be alone."

"Ario got what he deserved."

Jahdo's expression tightened. "How dare you."

"Harsh, but true."

"Can we stay here, or no?"

Keane hesitated, but relented reluctantly.

"Stay where you are," he directed Rhoco, then returned a moment later with new foam slippers. He turned to Jahdo. "You both can stay so long as you leave before sunrise. I detect troublesome energy from your friend and I don't want to be associated with any bad business."

"I understand," Jahdo said.

Keane left to retrieve a set of keys. When he returned, he carefully removed a long, ornate key from a ring carrying hundreds.

"This opens room 333 on the third floor." He handed the key to Jahdo. "Be so stealthy in your departure that I don't even notice you've left."

"We will."

"It wasn't good to see you again," Keane remarked.

"You either," Jahdo agreed.

Rhoco's brows furrowed at the peculiar exchange, but decided it was best not to ask questions. Their friendship, or the loss of it, ran deep, and the complexities were likely too convoluted for even Jahdo to explain. In this instance, Rhoco was acutely grateful for his Boulde tendencies. He was able to drop all meddlesome interest and mind his own business.

He put on the foam slippers and they walked through the foyer. Four fireplaces, constructed of fire-rated glass, roared with tall flames in each corner of the room. When they reached the grand staircase and ascended, Rhoco took delicate steps and was able to follow Jahdo to the third floor without any incidents. Upon entering their room, Jahdo brought the awkward altercation with Keane back to life.

"I suppose you want to know who Ario is."

"I don't."

"He's my son."

Rhoco sighed.

"He wrecked an entire floor in this lodge many moons ago," Jahdo continued. "Smashed it to pieces."

"You don't have to explain anything to me," Rhoco assured the conflicted old man. "You're helping with something that's very important to me and your past is of no concern."

"You have no questions at all?"

"Your secrets are yours to keep."

"Hmph." Jahdo was at a loss.

"It's the Boulde way."

"I like it," Jahdo confessed. He reached into his pocket and tossed the pair of socks to Rhoco.

Rhoco caught the gift and smiled. "Thank you."

Jahdo nodded and Rhoco sat on the bed nearest the door.

A thick down comforter filled with feathers separated him from the glass frame. With great care, he reclined until his large, heavy body rested comfortably on the fragile bed. Jahdo followed his lead after blowing out the candles. The old man fell asleep fast, and with the glass fox figurine clasped tightly over his heart, he snored loudly as he dreamt.

But Rhoco was not granted the same easy slumber. He found himself dreadfully awake, staring at the black nothingness above him, wondering about the fate of his friends.

Feodras was in the clutches of the Voltain guardsmen. When they returned him to Orewall, King Alun would curse at the sight of the Murk and they'd be onto Rhoco's escape. Even though Feodras was the true traitor, they'd never believe that a Murk was capable of organized crime and would see him as Rhoco's henchman. Rhoco worried they might kill Feodras for acting as an accomplice, but then reminded himself that they'd be too focused on catching *him* to worry about planning an elaborate, public execution for a Murk. Their focus would remain on Rhoco and Feodras would return to the carving fields and be forgotten.

He worried more for Cybelle. She was King Alun's prisoner because of him. They arrested her in an attempt to lure Rhoco home. She was his closest friend and ally, and they were trying to use that against him. He wasn't sure how to help her from the other side of the world, but he would find a way. And if it meant returning home to exchange his life for hers, he would, he just needed to return the heart to Gwyn first.

Chapter 30

The night was windy and Bicchieri Lodge creaked with every blow. Rhoco found it hard to sleep for fear that each howling gust would be the one that knocked the establishment down. But the hours passed and the building never fell.

Without any alarm, Jahdo rustled awake as the first sign of daylight touched the sky.

"We have to leave," he advised Rhoco, who was already aware that it was time for them to go. He sat up, exhausted, and then stood to stretch. As he spread his arms wide, the sound of a tinkling crack filled the quiet room.

Both men looked down and saw that Rhoco had pressed his feet onto the floor wearing only the socks Jahdo had given him. Rhoco quickly grabbed the foam slippers from where they sat on his bed and put them back on, but it was too late. The fissure ran deep, slicing the room in half.

Jahdo tiptoed carefully to Rhoco's side of the room, which was next to the door.

"We must go," he insisted, pushing Rhoco out of the room. They heard the room creak as the fissure continued to spread, but they did not stick around to see the damage.

They raced down the stairs and out the front door, and as they hurried out of town, the explosive clamor of shattering glass forced them to pause. They turned to see that half of Bicchieri lodge had disintegrated into tiny pieces and now rained onto the street below.

"Sweet Rebelene," Jahdo swore. "Do you think that woke up Keane?"

Rhoco stared blankly in response.

"So much for my promise to leave quietly," Jahdo continued. "Karmandel is a cruel trickster."

"Keane is going to be furious."

"Right, he will. We need to hurry before he storms into the forest to find us."

The sound of Keane's angry hollering in the distance inspired them to run. When they were deep in the forest and far from Quarzelle, they slowed to catch their breath.

"Will you pay for the damage?" Rhoco asked.

"I can't afford that," Jahdo panted. "I haven't sold a piece of armor in months."

"I thought you said Uveges was the best in all of Crystet?"

"It is, but no one needs the protection anymore. We are out of the resistance, out of the race for the scepter. We lost everything shortly after the throne switched hands; the sea took it all away."

"I'm sorry," Rhoco tried to sympathize.

"Don't be sorry. It's for the greater good that I suffer. A long time ago, I would have cursed at this development, I would have been angry to lose my fortune, no matter the trade-off, but I am old now and I can see reason. Though we all have less now, we are safer than ever. In any case, I have no one to pass the Uveges legacy on to. It would've died with me anyway." Jahdo paused, then continued. "Let's go back to that whole privacy thing you taught me. I find I don't like talking about this much."

"Sure," Rhoco agreed, and they continued in shared silence. Though they didn't know each other well, the quiet was comfortable and appreciated. Jahdo didn't want to dwell on the painful past that landed him in the lonely predicament he faced today, and Rhoco preferred no questions about why he was traveling to Jökull Cliff.

The forest was dense, and when they reached a clearing, Jahdo halted their progress.

"Jökull Cliff is up that hill," he stated. "My journey ends here."

Rhoco nodded. "Thank you for your help."

"I'm surprised to say this and mean it, but it was my pleasure. You taught an old man new tricks." He pretended to lock his lips with a key, then tossed the imaginary key to the ground.

Rhoco smiled.

"I hope you find what you're looking for," Jahdo expressed with sincerity before walking away. Without Rhoco to slow him down, Jahdo glided away and out of sight in mere seconds.

Rhoco took a deep breath.

"This is it," he said to the wind before starting his hike toward Jökull Cliff.

Chapter 31

The hill was covered in snow and ice. Rhoco's feet were drenched again and his foam slippers had gone flat.

His aggravation multiplied when he felt the ground crack under his next step. He froze where he stood and cursed under his breath.

He hated breaking things.

Rhoco couldn't see the crack beneath the snow, but he felt its creation and heard it expand. Once the creaking fissure ceased its spread, he continued forward, taking slower and softer steps.

When he crested the hill he expected solitude, but instead, was greeted by the sight of an old man tossing white flower petals over the cliff's edge. The old Glaziene did not see him, nor sense his arrival. He was dressed in a long, pale blue robe made of dyed rabbit fur and wore a platinum brooch that was covered in sapphires and emeralds. A diamond sword crossed the pin diagonally, separating letters that Rhoco did not know the significance of.

The well-dressed Glaziene continued to pick the petals off the bouquet he held, one by one, releasing them into the air and watching them flutter as they fell onto the jagged rocks below. He hummed a melodic tune whilst throwing the pieces off the cliff. Rhoco took a single step closer, sending a loud crack into their quiet surroundings.

The man turned to locate the source of the noise. When he saw Rhoco, a heaping man made of stone, he scrunched his nose in disgust before turning back to his mindless destruction of the flowers.

"Go away," he announced. "I am mourning."

Rhoco felt bad to interrupt such a personal moment, but he had come too far to turn back now.

"I said, go away," the man growled, turning to face Rhoco again.

"I can't."

"Don't you know who I am?" the man roared.

"No."

"Hmph." Rhoco's answer amused the regal Glaziene and softened his assault. "Clearly, you are lost. Very lost, by the looks of you. A man made of stone shouldn't be anywhere near Crystet."

"I'm sorry to interrupt your solitude."

"Who are you?"

"Rhoco Leath," he answered.

"That means nothing to me," the incredibly fissured Glaziene spat back. "I am Lorcan," he explained, choosing his words with care. "Brother to the late Queen Dalila."

"Is that who you mourn today?"

Lorcan laughed. "I cannot possibly recount every life I grieve. There are too many."

"I'm sorry to hear that."

"Why are you here?"

"I am looking for someone," Rhoco revealed.

"You'll find nothing but ghosts here."

Rhoco was not deterred. "I am looking for Nessa. Gwynessa. The queen," he stammered. "I was told she'd be here."

Lorcan's eyes flickered with malice as he mumbled to himself, "My niece."

"I have something that belongs to her."

"Someone played a cruel joke on you."

"What do you mean?" Rhoco asked, but Lorcan ignored his question.

"What item of hers do you possess?" The cracks on his face furrowed with concern, but there was a malevolent glow in the old man's stare.

"Her heart," Rhoco answered.

The moment he said the words, his pocket grew so heavy he thought he might fall to his knees. He casually placed a hand inside and touched the heart.

"*Tell him nothing more,*" the heart insisted. He wanted to ask why, but could not say the words out loud, not with Lorcan there.

"Let me see," Lorcan continued, hand outstretched, beckoning for Rhoco to hand the heart over.

"Tell me where she is first."

Lorcan played along, taking a step closer to the cliff's edge and pointing downward.

"She shattered decades ago."

Rhoco joined him at the edge and peered over.

Scattered amongst the jagged rocks was glass sand — the same glass sand he trampled upon when he arrived. The beach was a graveyard, littered with the shattered pieces of the deceased.

"She's one of many down there," Lorcan explained.

"I don't understand," Rhoco stammered. "This isn't possible." His chest grew heavy with uncertainty and the rock that sat safely inside his ribcage, pumping blood, threatened to break.

"Reality is a devil."

"But it felt so alive."

"Didn't anyone tell you that outside the body, a heart turns into a relic with great power?"

Many people had warned him.

"You've been chasing a ghost," Lorcan added. His tone was harsh and unforgiving.

Rhoco's eyes filled with tears as he lost something he never truly had.

"Give the heart to me. I am her family and you have no rights to it," Lorcan said, moving closer, hand outstretched.

"No," Rhoco stated firmly. "She is mine."

"Her heart does not belong to you."

"Nor does it belong to you," he spat back. His unexpected grief was full of rage.

"Interesting, that a foreigner with no ties to this land thinks he has more ownership over my niece's heart than her own family." Lorcan's tone was laced with danger. Rhoco sensed he might be overstepping his bounds, but he did not care. He loved the heart more than Lorcan; that truth was apparent in the space they shared.

"I cannot hand her over."

"But you will," Lorcan seethed. "For now, I will leave you to release your grief and compose yourself, but you *will* deliver that heart to me before you depart. And if you refuse, I will return with an army. My advice? Your death will not bring her back to life and there will be no meeting of souls in the afterlife. Do not sacrifice yourself for someone who cannot be saved."

344

Rhoco wanted to argue, but the words did not form in time. Lorcan tossed his bouquet of white flowers at Rhoco's feet and stormed down the hill.

Alone, Rhoco knelt at the side of the cliff. He removed the heart from his pocket, then placed it in the snow by his knees. He looked over the edge and spoke to the wind.

"I do not know who killed you, but I will avenge you."

The heart simmered red, pulsating with color in response to his words. He lifted a finger and touched the heart where the color glowed brightest.

"I can avenge myself."

"But you're dead," Rhoco replied, feeling hopelessly confused.

"You have my missing piece," she said. *"Bring me back to life."*

Thank you for reading *Orewall*—I hope you enjoyed the story! If you have a moment, please consider leaving a review on Amazon. All feedback is very helpful and greatly appreciated!

Amazon Author Account:

www.amazon.com/author/nicolineevans

Facebook:

www.facebook.com/nicoline.eva

Twitter:

www.twitter.com/nicolineevans

Goodreads:

www.goodreads.com/author/show/7814308.Nicoline_Evans

Instagram:

www.instagram.com/nicolinenovels

To learn more about my other novels, please visit my official author website:

www.nicolineevans.com

Made in the USA
Columbia, SC
28 September 2021